The Wisdom of Bug

Alyson Root

J&M Books

For permission requests, write to a.rootauthor@alysonroot.com

Published by J&M Books

483 Green Lanes, London, N13 4BS

Print ISBN: 978-1-917785-57-0

Ebook ISBN: 978-1-917785-56-3

Cover design by:

Tara Sullivan, The Write Gal Co.

www.thewritegal.com

Proofread by:

Morgan Bonito

The Wisdom of Bug is written in British English.

Deck the Halls with Blurry Budgets

EVELYN

Evelyn sat forward in her chair, staring at her laptop. Squinting, she closed her left eye and tried to concentrate on the screen. Still blurry.

Closing her right eye and focusing with her left eye yielded the same result.

"I'm not wearing those bloody glasses," she mumbled to herself.

"Can I ask why you're winking at your laptop?" Maggie asked as she walked into Evelyn's office, sitting herself ungracefully into the chair opposite her boss. "I hope you're not having video sex," she added with a smirk.

"The chance would be a fine thing," Evelyn answered, still trying her hardest to get her uncooperating eyes to focus on the number in front of her. "Anyway, I'm not sure what kind of video sex you're used to, but I can't say winking would really get the job done."

"How should I know what you're into?"

Evelyn pushed back from her desk and rested her head on the back of her ergonomic chair. "When would I find the time to have video sex? I'm here all the time."

Evelyn Crawford had been thrust into the CEO spot two months ago when her father, Richard Crawford, CEO and founder of Crawford's Pet Supplies, announced he was off on a world tour with his new floozy, Lyla, and shouldn't be expected to return anytime soon.

"You don't have to be here all the time, Evie," Maggie stated.

It wasn't the first time Evelyn had heard those words from her assistant, and it wouldn't be the last. Truth be told, Evelyn *did* need to be there twenty-four seven. Her father had buggered off at the busiest time of year, dumping Evelyn in the deep end.

Now, Evelyn loved her dad dearly, but sometimes his laid-back attitude really clawed at her nerves. How he'd built a multi-million pound pet supply empire was anyone's guess. Evelyn always thought it had been her mother who was the real brains behind the operation.

Roslyn Crawford was a magnificent woman. The world was a much darker place without her, especially for Evelyn, who had always been close to her mum. It was nearly three years since Roslyn passed away from cancer. Richard had grieved, Evelyn knew that, but she found it in poor taste that he seemed to replace her mum so easily. Lyla—the floozy—was half his age and clearly in it for the money.

Evelyn shook her head, dislodging Lyla and her dad from her mind. There wasn't enough space for them to take up residence, not when she had a company to run. With Christmas around the corner, there was a mountain of work to get done.

"There's a lot to get done, so lay off, Mags," Evelyn grumbled.

Maggie Peach was one of Evelyn's closest friends. As soon as Evelyn had taken up the mantle as CEO, she'd contacted Maggie and begged her to work as Evelyn's personal assistant. Maggie had been a receptionist for five years in a small law firm and Evelyn knew she was ready for something different. Maggie jumped at the job offer, and, as they say, the rest is history.

"Yes, there is a lot to do, but overworking yourself isn't going to get anything done faster. In fact, you'll do a terrible job and I know that's not what you want."

"I'll finish by ten tonight, I promise. I need to complete some things for the Christmas line." Evelyn was coming to hate the festive season. All it did was put her under more pressure.

As well as the work she had to wade through, Evelyn knew she had to keep the board happy. Her father hadn't consulted them *at all* about her appointment as the new CEO. Evelyn wasn't stupid. She knew there were a couple of board members who were pissed she'd got the job. Her job security would never be in question, not when her dad owned fifty-one percent of the company, but that wouldn't stop the board causing problems for Evelyn if they so wanted.

Christmas was the company's golden goose. Every pet owner in the UK went bonkers for cute sweaters, new toys, and treats. Crawford's had a stellar reputation for quality products at reasonable prices—no wonder they were the number one pet supply store in the entire country.

This would be Evelyn's first Christmas in the big chair, and she didn't want it to be her last. Even though she hadn't asked for the job, she wasn't about to mess it up. Evelyn took pride in her family's hard work and the company they had built. Evelyn herself had started at the company straight out of university, officially. Unofficially, she'd been coming to the office since she could walk with her mum and dad.

So, as much as she was irritated at her dad, she wanted to make him proud. Her mum, too.

"Okay, tonight it's ten. Tomorrow, you're clocking out with me and we're hitting the pub," Maggie stated.

"Mags, come on," Evelyn whined.

"Nope, it's non-negotiable. Tomorrow is Friday, it's the law."

Evelyn chuckled, "It is not the law, you idiot."

"I'm pretty sure it is. Anyway, stop arguing. Tomorrow, you and me and a few pints or several glasses of wine. Whatever, I'm not fussy. Oh, and one last thing—" Maggie stood and made her way to the door "—put your bloody glasses on."

As soon as Maggie was gone, Evelyn let her head thump to the desk. How was she going to get through the Christmas season in one piece? The trill of her phone echoed through her office.

"I have to change that ringtone," she grumbled. Without moving her head, Evelyn removed her phone from her blazer jacket and sighed. "Hey, babe," she said, trying as hard as possible to sound upbeat.

"Where are you?" Mindy huffed. These calls were becoming a frequent occurrence. Evelyn had told her girlfriend the next few months were going to be tough, and at the time Mindy had said she understood.

Apparently not.

"I'm in the office, Min, you know that."

"It's nearly nine o'clock. Are you coming home tonight at all?"

"Yes, of course. I'll be out of here by ten at the latest."

"Ten?" Mindy screeched. Evelyn pulled the phone away from her ear. Her head was still firmly planted on her desk.

"Yes, ten. I have a budget to approve and it can't wait."

"Fine, but this needs to change, Ev. Seriously, when was the last time we had an evening to ourselves?"

"Last Saturday," Evelyn answered.

"Oh, you mean the hour I got between you working on your laptop and your phone?"

Evelyn hated fighting with Mindy, but what was she supposed to say? The company had to come first for a little while.

"Min, I swear, as soon as this god-awful season is over, I'm all yours. We'll take a trip, somewhere tropical. I just need you to support me, just for a bit longer."

Silence filtered down the phone. Evelyn was far too tired for this, but she didn't want to lose her girlfriend. They'd been together eighteen months and mostly it was good. This was just a blip.

"I support you, Ev, I do. I just want a little more time with you. Is that so bad?"

Evelyn's stomach dropped. Of course it wasn't a bad thing. They should spend time together, but it just wasn't possible at this exact moment in time.

"Just a few more weeks, okay? That's all I ask."

"Fine, I'll see you later." Mindy didn't wait for Evelyn to reply before ending the call.

"Great," she huffed to no one.

It was almost eleven thirty by the time Evelyn crawled into bed. Mindy wasn't waiting for her. Hours later, Evelyn was jolted awake by a very drunk Mindy stumbling in the door.

"Baby, you're home," Mindy crowed far too loudly. Evelyn flipped over her phone, noting the time.

"Jesus, Min, it's half three. What the hell?"

"Oh, hush. I just went out with a few friends. It's not like I had anything else to do."

Evelyn was not about to get into it again with her drunk girlfriend. "Can you just come to bed? I'm wiped and I still have a full day's work tomorrow. Sorry, scratch that: in three hours."

Mindy didn't seem to be paying attention...or she was ignoring Evelyn. Ten loud minutes later, Mindy finally crawled into bed and promptly started snoring. Evelyn lay on her back, staring at the ceiling. There was not a cat in hell's chance she was getting back to sleep now.

Turning her head, Evelyn studied Mindy. The light from the bathroom, which Mindy had left on, illuminated the room. Her short black hair was sticking out in all directions. Her lips were slightly swollen. Screwing her eyes shut, Evelyn tried not to think about the reason her girlfriend had swollen lips.

Not for the first time, Evelyn questioned their relationship. Mindy was eight years younger than her. They'd met in a bar, and Evelyn had been swept away by Mindy's energy. They'd dated for a few weeks before making it official. A year later, Mindy moved into Evelyn's penthouse.

Their lives were good. Not great. Evelyn struggled with Mindy's need to go out all the time, but they got by. Getting by wasn't the standard a relationship should be based on, but Evelyn hated being alone. At thirty-five, she thought she would be married, possibly with a dog of her own. Evelyn didn't want children, but a house full of pets would be perfect.

Finally, Mindy's snoring became so loud Evelyn had to leave. Grabbing a quick shower, she made herself a coffee, snatched up a protein bar, dressed in her usual pantsuit, and called a car to take her back to the office. If she wasn't going to sleep, she might as well get some work done.

Coffee should be listed as an essential food group on medical websites or something, in Evelyn's humble opinion. Without it, she would crumble into a useless heap within minutes of waking up. The thing is, though, Evelyn liked good coffee. The machine in the office kitchen produced black sludge. It was only just turning six a.m. though, so unless she wanted to leave the office and trek to the nearest coffee shop herself, Evelyn was stuck.

After forcing said sludge down her throat, Evelyn cracked her neck and readied herself to tackle the bloody Christmas decoration budget. It was fast becoming the bane of her life.

As the hours slipped by, her mood grew dark. All this extra work for one goddamn holiday. Why did they need to spend all this money? New decorations for each store? No way. Evelyn put a strike through that. Real trees? Nope, plastic would do fine. And who the hell thought to ask for an extra *five hundred pounds* for staff Christmas parties?

The board was going to pitch a fit if she signed off on any of that. On the other hand, if she looked to be cutting back on the company's most important quarter, the board would also find fault. The working day hadn't even officially begun yet, but it already felt like she'd done a full day's grind.

"What time did you get here?" Maggie asked, standing in Evelyn's doorway holding two cups of take-away coffee.

"Around four." Evelyn didn't need to look up to see Maggie shaking her head in disapproval.

"I'm sure Mindy was thrilled with that."

"Mindy rolled in at half three and woke the whole building up with her snoring."

"She went out until that time? On a Thursday?"

"Yep." Evelyn didn't want to have this conversation, not again.

"And you're okay with that?"

Throwing her glasses—that she had reluctantly put on this morning—onto her desk, Evelyn massaged her temples. How she wished she had a bottle of Baileys in her desk drawer. Today was definitely an Irish coffee kind of day.

"I'm not her mother. She's her own woman. It's not for me to tell her what she can and can't do, Mags."

"I get that, but come on, Evie. What's this, the fourth night in a row she's been out?"

It was the fourth night in a row, but Evelyn didn't have the right to moan. Not when she'd been burning the midnight oil for the past two months. It was hardly fair to ask Mindy to wait around the penthouse all night for her.

"Mindy likes to party. It's just who she is."

Maggie scoffed. "Whatever, Evie, but you don't fool me."

What did she mean by that?

"Maggie, can we leave it, please?" Evelyn looked at her best friend, her eyes pleading for her to let it go.

"Fine." Sliding a coffee over to Evelyn, Maggie waltzed to the door. That woman really liked to make an entrance—and exit. "Don't think I have forgotten about tonight. It's you and me, and a slew of alcoholic drinks."

There was no way Evelyn was going to piss off Maggie anymore, so she nodded and gave a tight smile. Getting blasted wasn't the best idea, but hell, if she had to choose between a raging hangover or Maggie's ire, she'd choose the former every time.

Five o'clock rolled around and Evelyn felt as if she'd been run over by a truck. Her mind and body were tired, and now she had to go to a pub and pretend to enjoy herself. Evelyn hadn't always been like this. In fact, she was often the life and soul of the party. That's why Mindy had been so attractive to her. They shared an enjoyment of socialising, dancing, and drinking. Obviously, things had changed rapidly for Evelyn when she became the boss. Now all she wanted to do after work was don her fuzzy slipper socks and fleece hoody, grab a glass of wine, and watch mind-numbing TV.

Maggie swept in, closing Evelyn's laptop. "Let's go, missy."

After being swivelled around by her overzealous friend, she found herself being yanked out of her chair.

"Coat on." Maggie ordered.

Laughing at how ridiculous Maggie was behaving, Evelyn did as she was told. "You're buying," she commented, walking out of her office and towards the lift.

"Not likely. You're loaded," Maggie shouted after her.

The office was almost empty. Richard Crawford had implemented an early finish time of four p.m. for all HQ employees every Friday nearly ten years ago. The board—which was full of old white guys—had been super pissed, but Richard stuck to his guns and proved the board wrong. In the first year of the initiative, productivity had shot through the roof. Evelyn wasn't going to mess with that. The more productive the office, the less ammo the snooty board members had to use against her.

Fifteen minutes later, the duo swung open the door to Penny's Pub and Grill. The smell of fruity cocktails slapped them in the tastebuds. Penny Porter, owner of said pub and grill, was a genius mixologist. The pub still sold beer and bags of Scampi Fries, but it was famous for the cocktail menu. It was also a lesbian bar, which, let's be honest, meant it should be put on an endangered species list.

"Evelyn? Jesus, you're alive," Penny boomed from across the room. The music wasn't that loud, certainly not at the level where Penny needed to shout.

Evelyn gave a wave. She hated that every eye in the place was on her now.

"Hey, Pen, good to see you too," she replied when they reached the bar. Penny was already mixing something up for the two women. There wasn't a single time Evelyn had ordered a specific drink. Penny knew what her customers wanted before they did.

"Feels like a Sidecar kind of day to me," Penny said, sliding the drinks toward Evelyn and Maggie. "So, Evie, what's kept you away for so long?"

"Work." Evelyn was too busy guzzling her drink to elaborate. Penny nodded and moved to serve a couple of women further down the bar.

"So," Maggie began. "I should say sorry for this morning. Talking about Mindy like that."

"Should?"

"Okay, I want to. It's none of my business. But—"

"Apologies with a 'but' in them aren't really apologies, Maggie."

"You're right. I was just going to say that I want you to be happy, that's all. I know things are hard at work right now. I just don't want you settling for someone because it's easier than being alone."

Oof, that was a sucker punch to Evelyn's heart.

"I'm not settling," she argued, albeit weakly.

"Really?" Maggie's soft, understanding voice almost unravelled her.

Throwing the rest of her drink down her throat, Evelyn sighed. She'd never kept things from Maggie, and she wasn't going to start now.

"I think Mindy cheated on me last night." The more Evelyn thought about last night, the more obvious it became. Mindy's lips were swollen, the kind of swollen that only happened after a hot make-out session.

"Why do you think that?"

"When she came to bed last night, I could see her lips were red and swollen. Like she'd been kissing."

"Did you ask her?"

"Nope, she passed out and imitated a freight train. I haven't heard from her today either."

"That little hussy!" Maggie frowned, slamming her hand on the bar.

"Calm down," Evelyn laughed.

"Calm down? Seriously?"

"Mags, I don't know for sure."

"Um…" Evelyn watched Maggie's face pale, and her eyes grow wide. Turning to follow Maggie's gaze—which was lasered on something over Evelyn's shoulder—Evelyn watched as her girlfriend leaned in and kissed a very busty redhead. Mindy's hand was caressing the woman's hip, while the other grabbed her arse.

"Well, at least I know now," Evelyn muttered.

"I'll kill her," Maggie hissed. Evelyn reached out to stop Maggie from marching over to Mindy, but she was too late. "Oi," Maggie shouted.

Well, so much for a night out. They'd be spending their evening in the local police station if Evelyn didn't get Maggie out of there. Disregarding the mortified face plastered on Mindy, Evelyn grabbed Maggie by the arm and dragged her out of the pub.

"She's not worth it, Mags." Sure, Evelyn was pissed, but she wasn't exactly devastated.

"Evie!" Maggie protested, straining to turn back.

"No, Maggie. Enough. Come on, I want to go to Bargain Booze, grab a bottle or two of wine and drown my sorrows. It's my prerogative and, as my best friend, you have to support that."

"Fine, but I'm cutting all her thongs in half," Maggie stated.

Evelyn laughed. "Deal."

Okay, so Evelyn's love life had just gone up in flames, but at least she had a great friend to fall back on. Oh, and a couple of bottles of vino.

Life could be worse. Right?

2

Wine, Thongs, and Reorganization Therapy

EVELYN

Back at Evelyn's penthouse, the first thing she did was go to the wine fridge, deposit the bottle of white she'd picked up at Bargain Booze, and grab an already chilled

Pinot Noir she'd been saving for an occasion that never arrived. Well, if not now, when? She popped the cork with a vengeance usually reserved for opening board meetings.

Maggie planted herself on a kitchen stool, surveying the enormous, chrome-and-glass open-plan kitchen like she was trying to find a reason to hate it. She landed on the barstool's faux leather, gave it a suspicious poke, and then spun herself with a gentle push. "This place is disgustingly clean," she said, "even for you."

"I like things tidy," Evelyn replied, filling two stemless glasses with more wine than the NHS recommended as a weekly allowance. "Besides, Mindy has a cleaner."

"No, Mindy hired *you* a cleaner. This isn't her house anymore," Maggie corrected.

Evelyn set Maggie's glass in front of her and drained half of her own in a single, practiced tilt. She set it down so hard a droplet leapt out and ran down the glass, a wine tear. "Had," she agreed.

For a moment, the only sound was the light hum of the fridge and the occasional clink of glass as Maggie swirled her wine, eyes narrowed. Then, without any buildup: "Do you want to throw her things off the balcony? We could film it. I'll add slow motion."

"Too melodramatic," Evelyn said, already reaching for the bottle to refill her glass. "I'm not giving her the satisfaction."

"What about a bonfire? The Christmas market opens tomorrow. We could stage an effigy and toast marshmallows over it."

"Indoor bonfire," Evelyn deadpanned. "Very on-brand for a lesbian breakup, but I just had the upholstery cleaned. Smoke smell lingers, you know."

Maggie saluted the logic with her wine glass, eyes still sharp. "Well, what do you want to do then? We need a ritual. Otherwise, you'll just be haunted by the scent of her shampoo and the sound of her clomping about in those hideous mules."

"They're not even real leather," Evelyn muttered.

"Even worse! My God. She's an abomination." Maggie topped off both their glasses. "So, what's our move?"

Evelyn considered the question, her gaze settling on the bedroom. "I suppose I should pack her things."

Maggie made a scoffing noise. "Oh, come on. At least stick to your word and let me cut some of her thongs in half first."

"Only the ones she left on the bathroom floor. If they're in a drawer, they're safe."

Maggie grinned, wide and sharp, the sort of grin that once got them both thrown out of a Wetherspoons for "antisocial behaviour" during fresher's week. "I'll need scissors."

"Top drawer in the office."

Maggie jumped off her stool and went on the hunt, leaving Evelyn alone with the Pinot and a growing sense of anticlimax. She should feel something—anger, grief, even relief. Instead, she felt only the cloying, familiar numbness she got after marathon budget sessions.

She tried to summon anger, to feel the betrayal properly, but all she could muster was a vague disappointment. Not in Mindy—she'd never expected much there—but in herself. She'd known, hadn't she? Known that Mindy was wrong for her from the start. Known that the late nights at work were as much about avoiding home as they were about the business. The numbness wasn't shock. It was relief dressed up as indifference.

There had been a moment, early on, when Mindy had asked her what she wanted from the relationship. Evelyn had said something vague about companionship, about not wanting to be alone. Mindy had laughed and said, "That's the saddest thing I've ever heard." She'd been right. Evelyn had settled for a warm body in her cold penthouse, and now she didn't even have that.

But the apartment didn't feel colder. If anything, it felt lighter.

She finished her glass, poured another, and drifted to the living room. The city lights glared through the penthouse windows, garish and cold. Evelyn's mother had always decorated with soft lamplight and lush houseplants. Evelyn preferred the clean lines and hard edges. It made it easier to breathe, somehow.

Roslyn would have hated this flat. "Too cold, darling," she'd have said, running her hand along the chrome countertops. "Where's the life?" Evelyn had chosen every fixture, every piece of furniture, with surgical precision after her mother died. Clean. Minimal. Nothing that required care or attention. Nothing that could wilt or fade or remind her of loss.

Mindy had tried, once, to bring in a potted fern. "It'll brighten the place up," she'd said, setting it on the kitchen windowsill with the confidence of someone who'd never been told no. Evelyn had it removed within a week, citing allergies she didn't have. The truth was simpler: she didn't want anything in this space that could die.

Her mother's house had been full of life—orchids on every surface, trailing ivy in the bathroom, a fiddle-leaf fig in the hallway that Roslyn talked to like a pet. "Plants need love, Evie," she'd say. "Just like people." Evelyn had rolled her eyes then, but now, standing in her sterile penthouse, she wondered if her mother had been trying to tell her something.

The city lights reflected off the glass, cold and impersonal. Evelyn turned away.

Maggie returned with scissors and a carrier bag. "To collect the scraps," she explained.

Together, they stalked into the bedroom Mindy had claimed as her "dressing room." Evelyn opened the door and winced. "God, it's like a Hollister exploded in here."

Clothes everywhere. Mindy had never met a surface she didn't want to drape something over. She also had a preference for statement pieces, the kind of clothes that said, "Look at me!" and then screamed about it for another hour.

Evelyn started methodically pulling items off hangers and folding them into neat, soulless rectangles. Maggie immediately began rooting through drawers, making gleeful commentary about Mindy's taste in underwear. Every so often, she'd let out a feral whoop, snip a thong in half, and fling the remains into the air. She started a running tally on a notepad.

"Thongs: seven," Maggie reported, snipping one with tiger stripes. "Ew, eight. I hope she wasn't saving this one for you."

Evelyn just kept packing, not trusting herself to speak. The repetitive motion was soothing. She was in her element: disaster, meet process. She packed two large carrier bags before Maggie lost steam.

"You're so calm about this," Maggie said, collapsing onto the unmade bed and watching Evelyn box up another pair of Mindy's platform heels. "I'd be smashing every bottle in sight and cursing her ancestors."

Maggie had seen this before. After Roslyn died, Evelyn had cleaned out her mother's office in a single weekend, methodically cataloguing every file, every photo, every Post-it note. She'd worked through the night, refusing help, refusing to stop. Maggie had found her at dawn, surrounded by labelled boxes, eyes dry and distant. This was the same. Evelyn didn't break down—she broke things into manageable pieces.

"You know," Maggie said carefully, "it's okay to be upset. You don't have to be efficient about everything."

Evelyn didn't look up from the shoes she was packing. "If I stop, I'll think about it. If I think about it, I'll realize I wasted eighteen months on a relationship that was wrong from the start. So, no. I'd rather be efficient."

Maggie opened her mouth, then closed it. There was no arguing with that logic, even if it was heartbreaking.

"You're not me."

"No, you're the Ice Queen." Maggie pronounced it with mock grandeur, then softened. "But, seriously, Evie. You don't have to be okay with this."

Evelyn paused, a pair of garish metallic trainers in her hand. "What else am I supposed to be?"

"Livid. Heartbroken. Something."

"I'll get there," Evelyn said, more to herself than to Maggie. "For now, I'd rather be finished."

"Fair." Maggie sat up and patted the bed. "Come here."

Evelyn finished the last pair of shoes, tied off the bag, and perched beside Maggie. There was an awkward moment where Maggie clearly wanted to give her a hug but hesitated, probably fearing Evelyn would squirm away or bite.

Evelyn set her jaw. "It's fine, Mags. I don't need a hug."

"You do, but I'll allow it to be a virtual one." Maggie raised her wine glass, and Evelyn clinked it.

"I do appreciate you," Evelyn said, letting a little of the mask slip.

"Of course you do. I'm the best friend you'll ever have, unless you develop a sudden fondness for schnauzers."

"Schnauzers are noble dogs," Evelyn said, warming to the topic. "Unlike your last three exes."

"That's why I like you. You insult with such sincerity." Maggie cackled, then stood up, her hands on her hips as she surveyed the remains of the dressing room. "Right. What's next?"

Evelyn considered the closet, now half-empty. There was a void, a blank stretch of rail and shelf. "Now I have to reorganise," she said. "It's going to drive me mad otherwise."

Evelyn pulled each blazer from its hanger, checking for lint, loose threads, anything out of place. Navy, charcoal, black, grey—a gradient of corporate armour. She'd bought most of them after becoming CEO, each one a small act of defiance against the board members who thought she was too young, too female, too much her mother's daughter to lead.

Mindy had mocked her once for the uniformity. "You dress like a sexy undertaker," she'd said, sprawled across the bed in one of her neon crop tops. Evelyn had taken it as a compliment. The board took her seriously in these suits. They didn't see a grieving daughter playing dress-up in her mother's company, they saw a CEO.

She ran her hand along the empty rail where Mindy's clothes had hung. Sequins and leather and ridiculous statement pieces that screamed for attention. Evelyn's wardrobe whispered. It was better that way.

"You know," Maggie called from the ottoman, "you could buy something fun. A little colour. Maybe a floral print."

"I'm not a floral print person, Mags."

"You used to be. I've seen the photos. University Evelyn wore tie-dye."

"University Evelyn also thought Jägerbombs were a food group. We don't talk about her."

Maggie laughed, but there was sadness in it. Evelyn pretended not to notice.

Maggie rolled her eyes. "You're a cliché, Evie."

"Only if I alphabetise the shoe boxes."

"You do that already."

"Point stands," Evelyn said, marching into the walk-in. She pulled the first of the empty boxes down and started rearranging, her movements brisk and businesslike. Maggie followed, sat herself on the vanity chair, and provided colour commentary.

"Are you ever going to get another girlfriend, or just fill the spare room with more suits?"

"I don't date for at least three months after a breakup," Evelyn said, stacking her blazers by colour.

"You have a spreadsheet for your romantic life?"

"It's on the cloud," Evelyn said, straight-faced.

Maggie snorted. "You're a psycho."

"I'm organised," Evelyn replied.

They worked through the closet, Evelyn's focus unwavering, Maggie's banter getting looser as the Pinot took hold. By the time they'd filled four bags and a small bin with the detritus of Mindy, both women were tipsy and a little slaphappy.

"I dare you to wear one of her dresses to work on Monday," Maggie said, holding up a sequined cocktail number that looked like it had been designed by someone with a glitter fetish.

"I'm the CEO of a family company, Mags. I can't show up looking like a Christmas ornament."

"Pity. It'd shake the board up."

"They're shaken enough by my existence."

Maggie grinned, clearly picturing it. "I think you could pull it off."

"I'd rather not."

When the last box was organised and every hanger aligned, Evelyn stood back and let herself breathe for the first time in hours. The closet looked empty, but also full of possibility.

Maggie plopped down on the ottoman, kicking off her boots. "I take it you'll be sleeping alone tonight?"

"Alone is good."

"If you need me, I'm a WhatsApp away. Or, you know, I'll just show up unannounced like I always do."

"I'd expect nothing less," Evelyn said, allowing herself a small smile. "You're a pain in the arse, but you're my pain in the arse."

"Damn right." Maggie stood, wobbled a little, then steadied herself. "I should go before I start making calls to my own exes."

"Do you want a cab?"

"I want more wine, but yes, a cab would be great."

Evelyn made the call, then walked Maggie to the lift. They stood in silence for a moment.

"It gets easier," Maggie said, tone unusually gentle.

Evelyn nodded. "I know."

"Goodnight, Evie."

"Goodnight, Mags."

When Maggie left, Evelyn went back to the dressing room and stared at the new order she'd created. The closet was just hers now. Her suits, her shoes, her space.

She finished the last of the Pinot Noir standing in the doorway, let the city lights glare through the window, and imagined what it would be like not to have to make space for someone else.

It wasn't as lonely as she'd thought it would be. Evelyn caught her reflection in the darkened window—hair still perfect, makeup barely smudged despite the wine and the tears she hadn't let fall. The Ice Queen, Maggie had called her. Evelyn wondered when that had become her default setting. When had she decided that being untouchable was the same as being strong?

Her mother had never been cold. Roslyn had loved loudly, messily, with her whole heart. She'd cried at commercials and laughed at her own jokes and hugged strangers at the supermarket. She'd built an empire, yes, but she'd done it with warmth. Evelyn had inherited her mother's business sense, but somewhere along the way, she'd forgotten how to inherit her zest for life.

Maybe that's why Mindy had cheated. Not because Evelyn worked too much—though she did—but because Evelyn had never really let her in. She'd kept Mindy at arm's length, the same way she kept everyone. Safe. Controlled. Lonely.

Evelyn pressed her forehead against the cold glass and made herself a promise: the next person she let into her life, she'd let in properly. No walls. No spreadsheets. No three-month waiting periods.

She'd try to be braver, the way her mother had been brave. But not tonight.

Tonight, she'd finish the wine and go to bed and wake up tomorrow and deal with it then.

One day at a time. That was manageable.

She went to bed, the sound of snoring absent for once. It took a long time to fall asleep, but she didn't mind the silence.

In the morning, she'd wake up and start over. Maybe she'd even have time for a proper coffee.

And that, Evelyn decided as she drifted off, was reason enough to be okay.

3

Paws, Claus, and Boundary Issues

ALYSSA

A lyssa had to stop running her hand through her hair. The more she did it, the bigger her mane got. Unfortunately, it was her way of coping with stress, and, boy, was she feeling stressed.

Deciding to close her dog rescue sanctuary Four Paws over the Christmas period, starting the first of November, was causing her all sorts of bother. Mainly from irritated parents who wanted to get their kid a puppy from Santa.

That was the reason Alyssa decided to shut the sanctuary in the first place. Alyssa was sick and tired of these poor dogs being carted back to the centre because the shine of owning a cute dog had worn off as soon as the calendar flipped over to January. Even though Alyssa and her team did the best they could to warn prospective adopters that dogs were a lifelong commitment, and that they needed love and time, it still didn't stop the poor buggers from being returned.

Everything came to a head eleven months ago. January had just started and, sure as eggs are eggs, in waltzed a man who had adopted a beautiful collie mix called Benson. Alyssa had personally seen to the adoption—which had happened just before Christmas. The process was long and detailed, with Alyssa reiterating several times about Benson's needs. The time and monetary considerations the family would have to give. How he and his wife would need to make sure their son understood Benson was still a young dog and therefore needed a careful hand. The training it would require for Benson to become a well-rounded pooch.

The guy—Harry—had reassured her repeatedly that they were ready and that their son was more than capable of handling a new puppy. So, Alyssa had allowed him to take Benson home after a house check had been completed. Imagine her shock and anger when Harry came back with Benson a few weeks later, stating that his son couldn't handle the pup. That they didn't have the time to get the dog into behavioural classes.

Alyssa had seen red. It was the straw that broke the camel's back. Out of fifteen dogs adopted during the run up to Christmas, two-thirds had been returned. That's when Alyssa knew she had to do something drastic. If she couldn't talk sense into people, couldn't get them to see the damage they caused to the animal when they so carelessly returned them, then she'd simply take the option away all together.

For weeks after her blow up, Alyssa brainstormed ideas. Even though she planned to keep the sanctuary closed, she still needed to give the dogs daily stimulation, preferably the kind that involved socialising with people. That's when Lil, her co-manager and friend, had come up with a brilliant idea. Her dad was chummy with the CEO of Crawford's Pet Supplies, Richard Crawford. Lil suggested contacting him to see if they could arrange some sort of partnership over the Christmas period. What that partnership would look like was a mystery, but at least it was a step in the right direction.

The phone call with Richard Crawford had not gone how Alyssa imagined it would *at all*. Richard was friendly, down-to-earth, and a really nice guy. Not that Alyssa thought he wouldn't be any of those things, but when she imagined the CEO of a multi-million pound empire, she automatically thought of an uptight powerhouse that wouldn't give her the time of day.

On the contrary, though, Richard had been so enthusiastic about working with the sanctuary, he made Alyssa laugh. He was like a school kid hopped up on sugar at the idea of it. It was Richard who suggested the dogs be partnered up with workers in the company's HQ building in London. In fact, Richard threw himself into the organisation of it, leaving Alyssa with very little to do.

Now here she sat on the eve of November the first, arguing with another irate person who couldn't understand why she wouldn't let them come to the sanctuary and pick out a dog. Even though Alyssa had put up posters and social media blasts warning the public that the Four Paws Dog Sanctuary would be closed for two months, it still didn't stop her from getting daily emails and calls.

Instead of arguing, Alyssa should have been going over the schedule for the morning. The team had to transport twenty-six dogs to Crawford's by eight a.m.

"As I said, Ms Brown, the sanctuary is closed until the beginning of January." How many bloody times did the woman need to hear it?

"It's just ridiculous. My grandson is expecting a dog on Christmas Day! What will I tell him when he's crying because Santa didn't bring him what he wanted?"

As if that was any business of Alyssa's.

"I'm sure you'll figure it out. Now, if you don't mind, I do have to go. Take care, Ms Brown, and Merry Christmas." Alyssa slumped in her chair, dropping the phone back in its cradle.

"How many times have you run your hand through your hair, Al? It's bloody massive!" Lil laughed, sitting on the edge of Alyssa's desk.

"How big are we talking?" Alyssa mumbled.

"Big, big. Here, tie it up. You can't go outside looking like you've just been freshly..."

"Freshly what?"

"Well, you look like you have sex hair."

"Ha, I wish. No, this is my freshly stressed hair. Nothing amorous about it at all."

Lil grinned. "Either way, you need to tame the beast. You'll scare the dogs."

Alyssa took the proffered hair tie and wrangled her mane into something more manageable. Maybe she should finally get it chopped off. Could she get away with a pixie cut?

"Did you brief everyone about tomorrow?" Alyssa studied the list of jobs she needed to complete before they set off tomorrow morning.

"All briefed and ready. Don't worry, Al. We're only sticking the dogs in a van for twenty minutes."

"It's not the van that's making me anxious. It's the bit after. We must make sure all the employees that are signed on to take a dog know what's expected of them."

"Richard assures me everything is ready, and everyone at Crawford's is well aware of their duties. Alyssa, just relax. It's all going to be great."

Alyssa nodded, calming herself down. Lil was right, everything was in hand. Richard had made everything so easy, and for once Alyssa could go into the festive period happy her dogs would have a good time.

"Alright, I'm chill. Let's wrap up and get out of here. We have an early start."

"That we do, my friend. Sure you don't want to nip to the pub for a quick pint before calling it a night?"

"Nah, Hannah's staying over tonight." Hannah was a friend who occasionally shared Alyssa's bed. They had good chemistry, but Alyssa couldn't see herself committing to Hannah—or anyone else, for that matter. Not anytime soon, at least. Four Paws took up all of her time, and unless the person she got with could fully embrace that, then there just wasn't much point. Sex with no strings was much easier.

"You need to move on from that girl, Al," Lil huffed. "She's completely besotted and you are playing with fire, leading her on."

"Hey, I'm not leading anyone on. Hannah has always known it's a bit of fun."

Lil shook her head. "Not anymore she doesn't, and her 'sleep overs' are becoming more frequent. You've been so busy here you haven't noticed."

"Noticed what?"

"That Hannah is getting comfortable. This is more than just friends with benefits to her, Al. Just saying."

Alyssa rolled her eyes. Lil always liked to make a mountain out of a molehill where her love life was concerned. Lil Barnes was a one man kind of lady, which Alyssa fully respected. Lil wanted to find "the one" and settle down, which was great. What was *not* so great was how Lil couldn't—or refused to—understand why Alyssa didn't want the same thing.

"Stop fretting. It's fine." Alyssa closed her laptop and stowed it away in her messenger bag. "Let's go."

With all the dogs settled for the night, Alyssa and Lil bid Gary the night worker adieu. The carpark was empty save Lil's little hatchback and Alyssa's push bike.

"See you in the morning," Lil sang, climbing into her car. Alyssa wasted no time slinging her leg over her bike and pushing off. The commute home would take her roughly three minutes. The air was frigid as she cycled down the lane. It was times like this Alyssa was glad she'd bought a small plot of land near the sanctuary.

The light in her mobile home was already on and there was a car parked out front. Lil's voice echoed through Alyssa's head as she pulled up, resting her bike against the side door. *Was* Hannah getting a little too comfortable? Sure, she'd been around a little more than usual lately, and yeah, she kept a few items of clothing in the wardrobe.

Goddamn it! Lil was totally right. How had Alyssa not seen it? Oh, that's right, because as usual she'd been focussing all her efforts on the sanctuary.

The smell of roast chicken assaulted Alyssa's senses as soon as she stepped inside. Her mobile home wasn't exactly palatial, so it took little for the entire space to absorb smells from the kitchen.

"Hey," she called, dumping her bag on the sofa. The style of mobile home Alyssa had chosen was an open plan unit. She watched Hannah pull out the chicken from the oven and set it down.

"Hi, glad you're home," Hannah called. An uneasy feeling was swimming around Alyssa's stomach. The more she thought about it and the more she observed, the clearer it became. Hannah was acting like her girlfriend.

"I thought I was going to call you later?" Alyssa said, scratching the back of her head. This was so uncomfortable.

"Well, I was coming over anyway, right? Thought a nice cooked meal would be welcomed."

"Yeah, yeah, sure. Um, I'm just super tired. Had a really long day and tomorrow is going to be crazy."

Alyssa could see the disappointment wash over Hannah's face. "Oh, of course, I'm sorry. I should have called and let you know I was planning to come over early.

My bad. I'll just grab my stuff." Hannah made her way towards the front door, where her coat and handbag were stowed.

Feeling like an arse, Alyssa bolted over and took Hannah's hand in hers. It was out of order to behave like that to her friend. They might sleep together now and then, but Hannah was and would always be her mate, not just some random hook-up.

"Sorry, Han, sorry. Don't go, the chicken smells awesome."

Hannah hesitated for a few seconds. "Are you sure?"

"Yes, completely. Although..." Alyssa trailed off. No, she didn't want Hannah to feel bad, but they had to clear a few things up. Obviously, they weren't on the same page anymore.

"Although?" Hannah parroted.

"I think we need to talk, Hannah. About us." The glint of hope in Hannah's eyes made Alyssa want to slap herself. Surely she could've found a better way to have phrased that sentence. One that didn't give Hannah false hope. "Come on, sit down for a minute."

They made the two-step journey to the settee. Alyssa took a breath. It had been a while since she'd had to let someone down. The last person was Paul. Alyssa had only been out with him a handful of times before she realised he was way more invested than she was.

"Hannah," she began, not sure how to continue.

"I want you to be my girlfriend, Al," Hannah blurted.

Oh God.

"Hannah, are you still planning on moving to Scotland?"

"Well, yeah, but that's a long-term plan. I'm not going anywhere for a while."

"See, that's the thing. My long-term plan is to stay right here and run the sanctuary."

"I know, but that's something we can talk about in the future, right?"

"There's nothing to talk about, Han. The sanctuary is my life's work. I love it. It's my passion. There's no scenario I can see where I would pack it up, even to relocate. This is my home, and I don't want to move."

"But—"

"Hannah, there's a reason I don't commit. You know that. I thought we were on the same page."

"I can't help developing feelings, Alyssa."

"And I can't fake what I don't feel." Oops, that was a bit too blunt. Alyssa could see the tears building in Hannah's eyes. "Shit, I didn't mean it like that. You are one of my closest friends. I love you, but not in the way you want or deserve.”

“You won’t even try?” Hannah let out a sob as the first tear slipped down her cheek.

“It would be cruel of me to do that to you, Han. Knowing that we wouldn’t work but still leading you on.” Alyssa shook her head. “I won’t hurt you that way.”

“I’m hurting now,” Hannah hiccuped.

“And I hate it. I’m so angry with myself for not noticing you were feeling more than me, but don’t you see? That’s how it is with me. Unless you are the sanctuary, I’m not going to notice. You don’t want someone like me to be your girlfriend, Hannah. You want someone who treats you like the Queen you are. Someone who only wants your attention and who wants to give you all of theirs.”

Hannah brushed the tears away and took a long, deep breath. “I’m sorry, Al, you’re right. I knew you didn’t want more. I should have told you earlier, or just stopped sleeping with you. This is on me.”

“No way, it’s not on you. I don’t want to lose you, Hannah. Our friendship means the world to me. You know that, right?”

“I know, I think…I think I might just need a little time, though.”

"Whatever you need. I'm a phone call away, okay?"

"Okay." Hannah gave Alyssa a tight smile. "I'm gonna go home now," she said, heading to the door.

Alyssa helped her with her coat and gave her a brief hug. When the door closed and Alyssa was alone, she knocked her head against the wall several times in frustration. What a mess!

"Morning everyone," Lil called, trying to quiet the rabble. "Oi, shut it," she shouted after losing patience. "Now, you all have your assigned dogs ready?" There was a collective murmur. "Is that a yes or no, people?"

Alyssa laughed to herself as the team suddenly became a lot more animated. Lil was excellent at coordinating. Her take-no-shit attitude meant she got things done.

"It's only a short drive to the Crawford building, but the dogs are going to be excited. You need to be vigilant. Even the calmest of the lot might be a little hard to handle. Once the van is parked, we will take them out to the grassy area around the side of the building. Richard has had it fenced off, so I think it's a good idea to let them loose for ten minutes."

The team didn't wait to respond this time with an enthusiastic response.

"Okay, people, let's get this show on the road!" Alyssa shouted.

Following the rest of the team to the kennels, Alyssa found her allotted dog.

Like a well-oiled machine, each team member slipped on their dog's harness and collar and filed out to the van. The cacophony of noise was overwhelming as the dogs got more and more excited. It was unusual for them to go out of their kennels at the same time, but Alyssa had organised it so that any nervous dogs made it to the van first. Once the pack was settled and securely locked in their travel boxes, Alyssa jumped behind the wheel.

"Ready, Al?" Lil asked from the passenger seat.

"Let's do it!"

The drive to Crawford's was loud. Even with the radio blaring out songs, it was hard to hear what Lil was saying. The rest of the team were following behind in a convoy of personal vehicles.

As they'd discussed, the team unloaded their dogs upon arrival and walked them around to the grassy, fenced off area at the side of the building. With fifteen minutes of excited barking and playing, the pups finally calmed.

"Lil, can you fetch Joy?"

"On it."

Joy Hubbard was the woman who was supposed to help get everything organised. Richard had left the job to Joy due to his absence, something that Alyssa had only been told about recently and wished he'd mentioned before skipping out of the country. After all, it was him who set all this up, and now he was off somewhere on holiday, leaving Alyssa and someone she'd never spoken to before to get everything set up.

Lil returned with a woman Alyssa presumed was Joy. In her late fifties, Joy radiated warmth, her eyes lighting up when she spotted the dogs. "Oh my goodness, look at them," she cooed.

Alyssa smiled. Joy was going to be just fine to work with.

"Is everyone ready?" she asked.

"Oh yes, I've never seen so many happy people," Joy laughed.

"That's what I like to hear." Alyssa signalled for her team to follow. In a single line, they walked into Crawford's

HQ Tower. Twenty-five people stood lined up, ready to get their dog.

"Hello, everyone," Alyssa shouted over woofs and chatter. Several people replied, but most of them were too enamoured with the four-legged friends to pay attention to her. For once, she was more than happy to be ignored.

"To your stations," Lil called, laughing. Each team member hustled over to their respective "buddy" and began introducing their dogs.

Alyssa couldn't hide the smile that blossomed on her face. Today was going to be a good day.

4

Furry Chaos and Corporate Coffee

ALYSSA

The first hour at Crawford's headquarters felt like being on one of those game shows where you have to herd small children through an obstacle course, except the children weighed forty kilos and had fur and some of them needed to pee every three minutes.

Alyssa had never seen so many navy and grey pantsuits in one place. If you dropped her here with no warning, she'd think it was a mass wedding for accountants. But instead of confetti, there was dog hair.

At the front reception, Alyssa juggled a dog leash in each hand, a third looped around her thigh like a bandolier. The team had fanned out to distribute the remaining dogs, and the lobby—which looked like the waiting room for a Silicon Valley jury duty—was already filling with the sound of claws on tile and high-pitched "oh my God, look at his ears" commentary. It was absolute chaos, and Alyssa had organised it.

Technically, this was a success.

Three months of planning had led to this moment. Three months of spreadsheets, risk assessments, and late-night calls with Lil asking if Alyssa was absolutely certain about this partnership. "What if it goes wrong?" Lil had worried. "What if the dogs freak out? What if Crawford's sues us?"

But Alyssa had pushed through the doubts. These dogs needed this—needed people, needed purpose, needed to remember the world wasn't just kennels and concrete. And if Alyssa was honest with herself, the sanctuary needed it too. Needed to prove Four Paws was more than a holding pen for unwanted animals. It was a bridge. A second chance.

Looking at the chaos now—the laughter, the tail wags, the woman in legal cooing at a schnauzer—Alyssa felt something rare: pride.

Alyssa caught Joy, the Crawford's staff liaison, hovering nearby with a clipboard. In the way of all good middle managers, Joy looked simultaneously busy and like she might cry at any second.

"Joy, hey," Alyssa called out. "You got a minute?"

Joy beamed, which, given the state of her morning, was an act of raw optimism. "Always for you, Alyssa! How's the intake going?"

"Pretty smooth," Alyssa said. A golden retriever tried to jump on a glass coffee table behind her; the table, at least, survived. "Couple of teething issues, no pun intended, but the teams are adjusting."

Joy's eyebrows did a wave. "Do we need to add more signage about the potty area? The sign we put up says 'Paws for a Break'—I thought it was clever, but maybe it's not clear enough."

"I think it's great," Alyssa said, because Joy looked like a woman who'd fought for that pun in a thirty-person committee meeting. "Give it a day and everyone will have the routine down."

They walked together down a hall, past the security desk and through a row of glass-walled meeting rooms, each with a small pack of dogs and humans doing icebreakers. The idea was to pair each dog from Four Paws with a Crawford's staff "buddy" for the day—socialisation for the dogs, and, if the internal memo was to be believed, "stress relief and improved productivity" for the humans.

Alyssa wasn't sure about the productivity part. Every third person they passed was taking a selfie with their assigned mutt.

At the next junction, a woman in a smart pinstripe suit knelt beside a shivering whippet. "Don't worry, Beryl, you'll get the hang of these weirdos," she cooed.

Alyssa stopped. "How's Beryl settling in?"

The woman straightened up and shook Alyssa's hand. "Oh, thank you for checking—she's a little skittish, but she's got a home office buddy already. We're working up to the open-plan floor. I'm Claudia, by the way, legal team."

"Glad to hear it. Whippets need a slow ramp up." Alyssa squatted and offered Beryl a treat from the never-ending supply in her jacket pockets. "Take it slow, and if she looks overwhelmed, take her outside. Fresh air's the best therapy."

Claudia looked genuinely grateful, like someone had just paid off her mortgage. Alyssa left her with a packet of mini biscuits and a warning about the building's glass doors—"more whippet injuries than you'd believe"—and moved on.

Making a slow circuit, Alyssa checked on each dog and human team. One by one, they fell into familiar categories: the lifers who'd had dogs growing up and immediately bonded, and the softies who were already plotting to smuggle their assigned rescue home, and the few who'd clearly signed up because they were thinking about getting a pet but were still nervous. They watched their dogs like they expected them to explode, and mostly, the dogs responded by laying directly across their shoes.

Alyssa loved this phase of the job. Even though it was temporary, even though most of these dogs would be heading back to the sanctuary in a few weeks, the impact was immediate. The animals relaxed. The people relaxed. The tension in her shoulders eased—almost.

The staff kitchen beckoned, and Alyssa slipped inside for coffee, only to discover she'd beaten the first wave of office workers by about fifteen seconds. The only other person there was a heavyset security guard in a black polo, dunking a tea bag in a mug the size of his head. His name tag said 'Colin,' and he gave Alyssa a curt nod as she poured herself a coffee.

"Didn't expect to see so many dogs, ma'am," Colin said.

The coffee was, against all odds, decent.

"Are they causing problems for your team?" Alyssa asked between small sips.

"Nah, not really. They're better than the delivery guys." Colin sipped his tea. "My little girl's been bugging me to get a dog. I keep telling her, I sometimes work nights, nobody's home for it, but she won't let up."

"How old is she?" Alyssa asked, leaning against the counter.

"Seven. Going on forty." Colin's smile carried the weight of single parenthood. "Her mum left when she was three. It's just us now. I keep thinking a dog would be good for her, you know? Company when I'm at work. But I can't afford doggy daycare, and I can't leave an animal alone for twelve hours."

The math was familiar. Good people, impossible circumstances, dogs that never found homes because life was too complicated.

"What's her name?"

"Rosie."

"Tell Rosie I'll keep an eye out for the right dog. One that's okay with alone time. They exist."

Colin's expression shifted—hope mixed with disbelief. "You'd do that?"

"It's my job," Alyssa said, though both of them knew it was more than that.

He looked at Alyssa, hesitant. "How'd you end up running a whole dog rescue?"

A question Alyssa had fielded a thousand times, but still not one she'd practiced an easy answer for. "Lucky timing," Alyssa said. "I had money, a patch of land, and nowhere better to be."

He nodded, as if that was the kind of answer he respected. "You like dogs more than people?"

Alyssa smiled wide. "Depends on the people. And the dogs."

Colin laughed. "Fair. If you ever get a Rottweiler, let me know. She's obsessed."

Alyssa finished her coffee and made a note to check if they had any Rotties coming in from the next intake. As she left, Colin held up his mug in a mock salute. "Good luck out there."

She headed back to the main atrium to supervise the first "Paws for a Break" event. The room was already buzzing. Employees stood in a semi-circle, each with a rescue at their feet, except one lone man in IT who sat cross-legged and let a French bulldog walk in slow, determined circles across his lap.

Alyssa watched as Joy kicked off the session with a speech about "Crawford's tradition" and "the unique joys of canine companionship." She didn't tune out the way she did with most corporate platitudes; instead, she watched the faces in the room. Some looked sceptical. Some glowed.

Joy wrapped up and gestured for Alyssa to say a few words. It was the kind of thing she usually hated, but she'd gotten good at it—another quirk of running a rescue, the constant need to justify your existence to donors and sponsors and irate pensioners who just wanted "a proper dog."

She kept it simple. "Thanks for inviting us and our mutts. You already know most of what you need to know, but if you have questions, just ask. Or better yet, ask your dog. They're the experts."

It landed, just enough, and there was a round of light applause.

Afterward, as the employees dispersed to their stations, Alyssa caught sight of a young woman lingering by the snacks table. She had the stiff posture of a person who'd been promoted into a job they didn't actually want, and a border collie attached to her wrist via a thick leash. The collie was doing its best to look regal but kept sneaking glances at a plate of mini croissants.

"You're Gemma?" Alyssa asked, recalling the name from the roster.

The woman startled, nearly dropping the leash. "Yeah! Gemma Ng. HR."

"How's Skye doing?"

Gemma gave a shaky laugh. "She's smarter than me, I think. I already feel like I'm disappointing her."

Alyssa recognised that expression. New volunteers wore it, first-time foster parents wore it—people who desperately wanted to do right by an animal but didn't trust themselves. The look of someone told too many times they weren't good enough.

"Can I tell you a secret?" Alyssa sat cross-legged on the floor. Skye immediately investigated her pockets. "Dogs don't care if you're brilliant. They just want to know you'll be there tomorrow. That's it."

Gemma's shoulders dropped an inch before sitting next to Skye, mirroring Alyssa. "That's it?"

"That's it. Skye doesn't care if you're the best handler in the world. She just wants to know you'll be there tomorrow."

Gemma looked at Skye, who sat politely, tail sweeping the floor. "I can do that."

"I know you can."

Alyssa held out her hand to greet the collie, who promptly shoved a cold nose into her palm. "She just needs a job to do. Collies hate sitting still. Give her a task—carry your files, fetch your phone, something with purpose."

Gemma's eyes widened. "She can do that?"

"She could probably run payroll for you, if you teach her the login," Alyssa deadpanned.

Gemma grinned. "If you see me throwing a tennis ball in the main office, just mind your own business."

Alyssa liked her instantly. She left Gemma with a few more tips and drifted down the row of open offices.

The rest of the morning blurred by in a series of small crises: a pug with a sensitive stomach made an unholy mess in the elevator; a pair of interns accidentally let a shih tzu into the building's gym; one of Alyssa's own staffers got lost trying to find the toilets and ended up in a board meeting with a terrier. Alyssa triaged, reassigned, wiped, consoled. By eleven, she'd managed to catch her breath.

Midday approached, and a mass migration headed toward the cafeteria. The dogs followed, some out of hunger, some out of sheer loyalty. Alyssa took a seat by the window, her plate loaded with the kind of food she only ate at conferences. She toyed with the fries and looked out over the city.

Joy slid into the seat beside her. "So far, so good?"

Alyssa nodded. "No emergencies yet. I might actually get to eat lunch for once."

Joy smiled, then hesitated. "Can I ask something? Not about the program, just...I noticed your address on the forms is the same as the sanctuary's. Do you actually live on site?"

Alyssa shrugged. "Cheapest rent in the county."

"Doesn't that get—well, lonely?"

"Sometimes," Alyssa admitted. "But I'm not really alone. Twenty-six dogs, a team of volunteers, and Lil showing up uninvited at least three times a week with takeaway."

Joy laughed. "Still. No partner? No...human companionship?"

The question came up regularly, usually from well-meaning relatives at Christmas. "I don't really do relationships. The sanctuary takes all my time. Wouldn't be fair to someone."

"Or maybe you haven't met the right someone," Joy said gently.

"Maybe," Alyssa said, unconvinced.

Joy sensed the door closing and changed the subject. Alyssa was grateful.

"The thing is the living in town and commuting forty minutes every day, which would make me homicidal, isn't really an option." Alyssa supplied.

Joy nodded, satisfied. "I get it. My husband's a long-haul pilot. I got used to being on my own. That's probably why I like having all this—" she gestured at the room "—to manage. Better than an empty house."

The two women sat in companionable silence. Alyssa watched a schnauzer curl up at a finance manager's feet, the manager oblivious as she typed one-handed on her laptop. A few years ago, Alyssa would have considered this kind of partnership a sell out—a way for corporations to look charitable while doing very little. But it was clear, even in the first day, that the dogs were making a difference. A small one, but a difference nonetheless.

She finished her lunch and made another round of the offices. The dogs were happier than she'd expected. The humans, too.

By the time the clock hit four, the novelty had faded just enough that the building felt normal again. Alyssa gathered her team in the conference room for a debrief.

"Anyone lose a dog?" she joked as the group sat down.

"Only my dignity," said Lil, who looked slightly frazzled but pleased. "You see that spaniel in IT? Ate a whole box of jellybeans."

"He's going to have rainbow vomit tomorrow," another staffer chimed in.

They ran through the feedback, most of which was positive. The main complaint was the lack of outdoor play space, but Joy had already solved that by negotiating with the company next door to use their empty lot in the afternoons.

"Alright," Alyssa said at last. "Everyone did good today. Let's try not to burn the place down tomorrow."

They broke up, most of the team heading home, a few staying to prep the dogs for the night. Alyssa slipped out to the lobby to catch the end of the workday exodus. The lobby was a mess—paw prints, abandoned tennis balls, a chewed-up umbrella—but it felt like victory.

She grabbed her bag and made her way outside, passing the security desk. Colin waved.

"See you tomorrow, dog lady," he called.

Alyssa grinned. She liked the sound of that.

After the dogs had settled into their kennels, and Alyssa was satisfied she'd gotten everything done, she hopped on her bike and rode down the lane. The ride home was quiet. Alyssa pedalled slowly, savouring the chill and the hush that followed a day of noise and motion. Her phone buzzed with a text from Joy. "You did great, thank you again!!" along with a photo of Gemma's collie sprawled across a pile of HR files.

She replied: "No problem. I'll tell the collie to shred only the unnecessary paperwork tomorrow."

As she reached home, the familiar barks and howls from the sanctuary echoed through the night. She thought about the next few weeks—how many dogs might get adopted, how many would come home, what would happen to the humans after the novelty wore off.

She went inside, poured herself a whiskey, and drafted her next day's to-do list on the back of a pizza flyer. Her handwriting was awful, but she didn't care. It was just for her.

She'd think about tomorrow, tomorrow.

5

Uninvited Guests (Four-Legged and Otherwise)

EVELYN

Today was not going to be a good day. Nope, not at all. Not only did Evelyn have a board meeting to get through, she also had two disciplinary hearings and a budget meeting that was sure to get heated once she informed the relevant managers they would *not* be getting all the money they'd applied for.

The flip calendar on Evelyn's desk tormented her. November was the official start of Crawford's Christmas season. Ugh. Worst of all, every member of the HQ tower would decorate their offices with gaudy tinsel and plastic ornaments. Even worse than *that*, Evelyn would be expected to decorate and join in the festive cheer with the rest of her colleagues.

"Morning, sunshine," Maggie sang. "How are you this fine day?"

"Well, you're chipper," Evelyn mumbled, her face buried in her hands.

"You know, Evie, every time I come in here, you're looking more and more distressed."

"That's because the longer I sit here, the worse my day gets!"

"What's happened now?"

Evelyn sighed. Nothing had happened—well, nothing out of the ordinary. As per usual, she'd turned up at the office before the sun was awake. Her in-box was overflowing and no matter how many of those little bastards she replied to, ten more took their place. It was a never-ending cycle of electronic torture.

"Nothing, ignore me. It's just been a day."

"Evelyn, it's nine in the morning. The day hasn't even begun. What time did you get here?" Maggie's tone oozed exasperation.

"A little after three-thirty. I couldn't sleep, and honestly, I didn't want to chance Mindy showing up piss drunk again."

For the past three weeks since Evelyn had caught Mindy red-handed, she'd had to deal with Mindy rocking up to her door in the early hours of the morning, drunk as a skunk, begging for forgiveness.

"Dear Lord. Did you call the hunky security man?"

"Yes, and his name is Harvy."

"Oh, hunky Harvy, that just rolls right off the tongue, doesn't it?"

"Do you need to take a cold shower, Mags." Evelyn laughed at Maggie, who was fanning herself, clearly worked up. "You should just ask him out. He's single, you know."

"How the hell do you know that?"

"I talk to him, you goose! Something you should try." Evelyn had watched Maggie swoon over Harvy for over a year now. Maggie, a woman whose confidence melted into a puddle whenever she came within ten feet of the man. It was laughable and a little cute.

"I'll make you a deal." Maggie smiled, raising her eyebrow. "You make it out of the office by seven every night for a week and I'll talk to Hunky Harvy."

"How does that in any way benefit me?" Evelyn laughed.

"Trust me, it will do you a world of good to remember there is a world outside these four walls."

Evelyn scoffed.

"Don't scoff at me, lady. You know I'm right. Evie, honey, you shouldn't be looking this stressed, not at your age. You didn't leave your office all day yesterday! Plus, you're starting to get a bit of a reputation with the staff."

Evelyn snapped her eyes to Maggie. "What do you mean? What kind of reputation?"

"The Ice Queen kind. Evelyn, you hardly talk to anyone. Your face is permanently scowling and you keep such unreasonable hours. It's making everyone feel on edge, like they shouldn't be going home at five o'clock."

Evelyn sat back in her chair and swung it around so she was facing the floor-to-ceiling window at the back of her. She and Maggie always made a bit of a joke about Evelyn being the "Ice Queen." She'd read enough sapphic romances to know her clothes and job fit her nicely into the category, but in all honesty, Evelyn never thought herself moody enough. When had that changed? And when had she missed her colleagues regarding her as such? Tears suddenly sprung to her eyes. She didn't want Maggie to see how affected she was by what her friend had just said. The last thing Evelyn wanted was to be seen as some sort of tyrant.

Yes, she was stressed, but that had nothing to do with her colleagues. They all worked hard. The proof was in the numbers. Crawford's was a raging success. It was on Evelyn to make sure nothing changed. That's why she'd been killing herself lately, because she didn't want to let anyone down. But she was letting people down anyway.

Her father would have never made anyone feel on edge. Richard Crawford was the epitome of a perfect boss. It was heartbreaking that Evelyn was failing so badly.

"Hey, hey, hey. What's all this?" Maggie rounded the desk and knelt in front of Evelyn.

"I'm trying so hard, Mags, and I'm still letting people down."

"Sweetie, you're not letting them down. You're hurting yourself, that's for sure, but people don't need you to be perfect, Evie. You know how to run this company with your eyes closed. You don't have to burn yourself out to do it."

"But I do, Mags. Dad left me in charge. Crawford's Pet Supplies is a successful business thanks to him and now he's gone and I have to make sure it stays that way. Half the board members want me gone, so I can't put a foot wrong. I can't…" Evelyn's sentence was cut off as she sobbed. Weeks of pent-up anxiety, stress, and frustration broke free. Maggie pulled Evelyn into a hug, rocking her back and forth.

"Evelyn, honey. You have to slow down. You're doing a fantastic job. Everyone who works here supports you. Fuck the board. Your dad wouldn't have left if he thought you couldn't handle it."

Evelyn let herself cry for a few more minutes. Wiping her eyes and clearing her throat, she sat up straight. This wasn't the time to be breaking down. There was too much to do.

"I'm fine, Maggie, sorry about that."

"Don't say sorry. You clearly needed it." Maggie sat back on her heels, looking at Evelyn with concern.

"Seriously, Maggie, I'm good. I need to get back to it. I'll take onboard what you said about the staff. I don't want them to be on edge."

Maggie didn't look convinced, but she rose to her feet and headed to the door anyway. Maggie had known Evelyn long enough to discern there was no point in pushing the conversation further.

Evelyn blew out a breath, retrieved her compact mirror from her top drawer and surveyed the damage. Drunk panda was a good look, right?

After wiping away the smeared mascara from under her eyes, Evelyn got back to work. She didn't have time for breakdowns.

The morning passed like any other. Emails, phone calls…more emails. The dreaded board meeting, which turned out not to be as horrific as Evelyn first thought.

By the time lunch rolled around, Evelyn was ready for a shot of whiskey and a massage. A Caesar salad would have to suffice. The budget meeting weighed heavily on her mind as she summoned the energy to get lunch. Maggie was right, she needed to break out of her office, even if it was just for half an hour.

Shutting down her laptop and grabbing her jacket, Evelyn slipped out of her chair and began towards her office door. Her journey was cut short though when she nearly tripped over…why the hell was there a dog sitting in the middle of her office?

Minutes passed as Evelyn stood frozen to the floor in some kind of weird stare-off with the little black and white pooch. Blinking rapidly, Evelyn rubbed her eyes.

"Oh, Jesus. I *have* got a brain tumour! I knew I didn't need glasses," she mumbled to herself.

Pulling herself from the dog's gaze, Evelyn crept around the animal, who didn't move a muscle. As soon as she reached her door, she called for Maggie. Evelyn watched the dog whilst she waited...and waited. Where the hell is everyone? The staff probably had the same idea as Evelyn and were out enjoying lunch. What was she supposed to do? She needed confirmation that she was definitely hallucinating before she really started to panic and called for the family physician.

With no hope of finding Maggie, or anyone else for that matter, Evelyn slid the door shut, pivoting on her heel. It was still there, just sitting in the middle of her floor, looking serenely at her desk. Walking back to where she first clapped eyes on the little beast, Evelyn stood with her hands on her hips.

"So...who are you then, and why are you here?"

The dog—or hallucination—didn't answer with any kind of recognition apart from a blank stare.

"You're a Cocker Spaniel, I think," Evelyn continued. "Why would I hallucinate a bloody Cocker Spaniel?"

Of all the things Evelyn's fatigued and overworked brain could conjure, why a dog?

"This is stupid," she grumbled, fetching her phone from her purse. "You better bloody pick up, Maggie." Evelyn really needed to stop talking to herself. Three rings and Maggie's cheerful voice rang through the office.

"Evie, you alright, chuck?"

"I'm dying," Evelyn whined dramatically.

"Are you really?"

"Maybe...probably."

"How about you tell me what's going on and then we'll have a discussion about calling up friends and declaring you're dying, and the effects that can have on a person!"

"I'm being serious, Mags—"

"As am I."

"Look, I think I'm hallucinating. I'm going to send you a picture and you tell me what you see, okay?"

"Alright, I'll bite. Why do you think you are hallucinating?"

"Just look at the damn picture," Evelyn snapped. Bringing up her camera app, Evelyn took several photos of the little dog. "Did you get the pictures?"

After a few beeps and some curse words, Maggie finally replied.

"Why do you have a dog in your office, Evelyn?"

"You can see it?"

"Yes, it's a black and white...Cocker Spaniel."

"Oh, thank God," Evelyn sighed. Dropping her head to her chest, Evelyn started to laugh. Maybe she was going a little bonkers after all.

"I'm coming back to the office. Do you want anything?"

"A Caesar salad and some Valium."

"Okay on the salad, no on the pills. See you soon."

Okay great, Evelyn more than likely did *not* have a brain tumour. But that led to the oh-so-important question: why was there a dog in her office? Hell, why was there a dog in the building?

Sitting back at her desk, Evelyn and the unnamed pup continued to stare at each other. Their stalemate was broken when the dog stood up and wandered over to the window. Evelyn waited for his next move, but nothing happened. The dog parked his bum on the floor and sat looking out over London.

Try as she might, Evelyn couldn't ignore the creature. What the hell was he looking at? With Maggie still MIA, Evelyn gave in to her curiosity and walked over to stand by the dog.

"What are you looking at?" Evelyn scanned the horizon, then the street below. There was nothing of significance—in her mind anyway—that she thought could capture the dog's attention so avidly.

"Hey," Maggie called as she rushed through the door. Dropping Evelyn's salad on her desk, Maggie marched over to Evelyn and the mystery canine. "What's this?" she asked, waving her hand at the dog.

"I wouldn't have called you in a panic if I knew why he was in here, would I?" Evelyn shot back.

"Well, did you call someone?"

"Yes, you!"

"I meant a security guard or something."

Evelyn shook her head. "Nope, just you."

"Well?"

"Well, what?"

Maggie scrubbed her hands over her head in frustration. "Evelyn, you are vexing at times, woman. Are you going to call security?"

"Right, yes, of course." Honestly, Evelyn had been so intrigued by the little guy she hadn't thought about calling anyone after Maggie.

After a quick conversation with Terry, the building security manager, Evelyn dropped down to the settee, which sat across from her desk and inhaled her food.

"Ms Crawford?" Terry's deep voice boomed.

"Come in, Terry." Evelyn stood back up, brushing down her pencil skirt, hoping she hadn't spilt any dressing on herself.

"Sorry about the break-in," Terry laughed. "I'll get this little fella back downstairs where he belongs."

Evelyn didn't understand *any* of that sentence. Why would he belong downstairs? "Sorry, I'm confused. You know this dog?"

"Not personally, but I know he is with the others."

"The others?" Evelyn looked at Maggie, who was equally perplexed.

"Yeah. There's like twenty-six dogs all in all."

"Twenty-six?" Maggie screeched. "Why in God's name are there twenty-six dogs in the building?"

"What do you mean?" Terry asked, his eyebrows drawing in.

"Terry, why is there a pack of bloody dogs in my building?" Evelyn was tired of running round in circles.

"Well, they're part of the partnership. Over Christmas." Terry was looking at Evelyn and Maggie like they were idiots.

"Knock, knock," another voice singsonged.

"Jesus Christ," Evelyn moaned. Could this day get any worse?

"Mindy, what are you doing here?" Maggie growled.

"I'm here to talk, Evie. You owe me that." She replied, staring pointedly at Evelyn.

Was this woman for real?

"She owes you nothing, you harlot," Maggie shot back. Evelyn had to bite her lip to stop herself from laughing.

"This has nothing to do with you, Margaret," Mindy seethed.

"Alright, alright. That's enough." Evelyn was over this conversation already. "Mags, give me a minute, please. Terry, don't go far. We still need to discuss this," she said, pointing to the dog, who hadn't moved an inch, seemingly unperturbed by everyone in the room. Maggie shot Mindy an icy glare before leaving, pulling Terry out the door by his elbow.

"Thanks, Evie," Mindy cooed.

"Don't thank me. I just want this over and done with. What do you want?"

"Evelyn, do you have to be so mean?" Mindy sauntered over to where Evelyn was perched against her desk. There was a time that Evelyn would have found her sultry walk sexy. Now it just pissed her off.

"I'm not being anything, Mindy. We've already talked. It's done, we're over, and I'd just like to get on with it now. I'm busy, and you dropping by the house and the office isn't appropriate."

"It's the only way I can get you to talk to me, Evie," Mindy whined. "What do I need to do to get you to forgive me?"

"I forgive you. There. Are we done?"

"Only if that means I get a second chance."

Evelyn rubbed her forehead. A migraine was building rapidly. "Mindy, no. No second chance. You clearly weren't happy if you had to find intimacy with another woman. Nothing has changed on my end. I'm still busy, still have a company to run."

Mindy took Evelyn's hands in her own. "But like you said, you won't be busy forever. I made a mistake, Evelyn. I was frustrated, but that's no excuse. I know that. Please, don't let one mistake ruin our future. Please."

It felt like the universe was having a laugh at her expense today. All Evelyn wanted was to be left alone to get on with her work. Was that so much to ask for?

"Look Min, can we table this? I'm not saying no, but I need to get through today and then I'll have some space to think about it some more."

"But you're saying there's a chance we can try again?" The hope in Mindy's eyes was soul crushing. Mindy wasn't her forever person, but she was nice enough, if you discounted the whole cheating thing. Had Evelyn been too rash?

"I'm saying I need to think on it, okay?"

"Okay, okay, that's fine. I'll leave you to think. Not too long though, Evie. I'm not sure how long I can go without touching you," Mindy purred next to Evelyn's ear. Not giving her a chance to react, Mindy skipped out of the room. Evelyn wasn't impervious to Mindy's charms. The woman was hot, but the effects weren't as strong on Evelyn anymore. Mindy had broken the trust between them, and there was no going back. How was she going to get that through to Mindy, though?

With the office finally silent, Evelyn took a second to breathe. There was still a full list of things she needed to attend to, but she just needed a few seconds of calm. Walking over to the window, she dropped down to her knees next to the little dog. Resting her head against the cool window, she gazed out upon London, her hand stroking gently across the dog's back.

As the minutes ticked by, Evelyn felt her stress slowly dissipate. The beep of her email notification signalled the end of their time together, though. Evelyn looked down into the soulful eyes of the pup. Smiling, she gave him one last pat and went back to her desk.

"Mags, can you bring Terry back in, please?"

"Ms Crawford," Terry nodded.

"Right, Terry, sorry about that. Let's get back to why that little one and twenty-five others like him are in the building."

"I think you need to talk to Ms Fox," he replied.

"Okay, and who is that?" Evelyn knew all her employees by name and there was no Ms Fox among them.

"She runs the dog sanctuary."

"Right, and which dog sanctuary is that?" Good Lord, it was like pulling teeth.

"The one that's here," he said matter-of-factly. Evelyn was about to burst, her frustration with this particular conversation was driving her insane.

"Okay, can you send Ms Fox up here then?"

"Certainly, Ms Crawford."

Evelyn watched him leave before addressing Maggie. "Have you any idea what the fuck is going on?" Evelyn was completely exasperated.

"Nope, I tried to get an answer, but he just repeated what he said to you."

"Christ, I hope whoever this bloody Ms Fox is has some sodding answers. I'm about ready to commit murder."

"I hope I'm not the one you're going to off," a low velvety voice said from Evelyn's doorway. Jumping in surprise, Evelyn nearly fell out of her chair. "I'm Ms Fox, the one with some sodding answers."

Evelyn could feel her cheeks burning. Not only had this woman overheard Evelyn grumbling, she'd also just witness her nearly pole vault out of her chair.

Excellent.

6

Escape Artists and Condescending Arseholes

ALYSSA

The morning had started off wonderfully. All of Alyssa's worries were for naught. The team overseeing the handover of the dogs did a great job with no cockups. A minor miracle in Alyssa's eyes.

The one and only doozy of an issue arose before lunch. With all the dogs successfully buddied up, Alyssa was left with one pup. Bug, a three-year-old English Cocker Spaniel, who was supposed to have been partnered with Cyril Jones again. Unfortunately, Cyril had taken a nasty fall the night before and was in hospital, having his hip replaced.

"Bugger," Alyssa muttered when she heard the news. Cyril Jones had been paired with Bug specifically. "What shall we do with you now?" she asked Bug, who sat by her feet looking into her eyes. Alyssa would never admit this out loud, but Bug was her favourite dog. There was just something about him that made him special.

"What's up, buttercup?" Lil called. Lil had spent most of the morning checking up on everyone, fielding questions and concerns.

"Bug hasn't got a partner."

"Oh, no. Where's Cyril?" Lil looked around the crowded office for the older gentleman.

"In the city hospital, receiving a titanium hip apparently."

"Bugger!" Lil exhaled loudly.

"That's what I said. What do we do now? I don't want him to be the only one without a friend." Alyssa really hated the idea that Bug was going to miss out.

"You'll just have to take him, Al. Anyway, he will be back with the others in the evening."

"I'm going to be in and out of here though, Lil. I have meetings across the city. I can't take Bug with me."

"Obviously. He can stay with me when you have to go out. It's no big deal."

It felt like a big deal to Alyssa, though. Bug had been with the sanctuary for two years now and it pained her to see him overlooked time and time again. Why was it always this little fella that got left behind?

"Okay, I'll take him with me today. I'm just going to wander around the offices, making sure everyone is good to go."

"What do you think I've been doing all morning, Al?" Lil rolled her eyes. She was more than used to Alyssa and her controlling ways.

"I know, I know. Just let me do it for my own peace of mind, okay?"

"Go on, off you go, your ladyship. Check on your lowly workers."

"You're an arse." Alyssa laughed. Alright, so she could do with learning to let go of the reins a bit more, but it was hard. Four Paws was Alyssa's baby, her dream come true, and she would do anything to make sure it succeeded.

This relationship with Crawford's was a huge step. The connection she'd forged with Richard Crawford meant tremendous opportunities for the sanctuary, and Alyssa wasn't about to fluff that up.

Richard had talked about fundraisers and adoption parties. Everything Alyssa dreamed of was in her grasp. That's why these two months had to go perfectly.

"Okay, Bug, let's...Bug?" Alyssa turned on her heel and frantically searched her immediate surroundings. The spot where Bug had been sitting was now empty. "Lil, where is he?"

"Bug?" Lil called. Both women split off, searching around the feet of office workers. There was no sign of him.

"Shit, shit, shit," Alyssa hissed. How in god's name had she managed to lose him?

"Don't panic, Al. He couldn't have gone far. It's not like he can open doors. He's two feet tall on his hind legs. You'll see, we will find him curled up next to a radiator or something.

The next half an hour was a frantic search of the office floor. Crawford's HQ occupied the entire tower, and Alyssa had dogs spread over all twenty floors.

"Start on the other levels. I know it's unlikely that he left this office, but we have to check. He's definitely not here right now." Alyssa was panicking. Of all the stupid things she could have done today, misplacing a dog that was in her care was not something she thought would happen, but here she was. Shaking her head at her idiocy, Alyssa set off to comb Crawford's HQ.

Alyssa's legs were on fire. Any other day, she would have thought she was in decent physical shape. Not now though. Running up and down stairs gave Alyssa a painful reality check. Breathing was also becoming a problem, but she couldn't stop. Alyssa's mind came up with terrible scenarios. What if Bug had been snatched? What if he was scared and alone, trapped somewhere? Sheer dread settled over her body like a weighted blanket.

Lord knew how much time had passed, but Alyssa finally found herself on the topmost floor. By the look of the décor and furniture, it was the floor where all the higher ups worked. Expensive leather sofas and glass walls occupied the entire area.

The office was empty save for Terry, the security guard who had just exited an office in the far corner. "Ah, Ms Fox, just the person. Ms Crawford wants to see you."

"I can't right now, Terry. I'm on the lookout for our resident escape artist."

Bug had been known to disappear now and then. In the rescue centre it wasn't a big deal. There were only so many places he could go, and he never went far. Usually it was to the sunny spot in Lil's office. That dog was a sun worshipper through and through.

"Are you looking for a little Cocker Spaniel by any chance?"

Alyssa rounded on Terry, grabbing his very thick arms. "Yes, I am. Have you seen him?"

"He's alright. In fact, that's why Ms Crawford wants to speak to you. She found him in her office."

Oh crap! How the hell had he got all the way up here?

"Right, okay, I'll just..." Alyssa pointed to the office Terry had exited moments earlier.

Straightening her shirt, Alyssa approached the door to the office, which was slightly ajar. Voices mumbled inside, and Alyssa couldn't help but overhear. Ms Crawford did not sound happy at all.

"Christ, I hope whoever this bloody Ms Fox is has some sodding answers. I'm about ready to commit murder." Alyssa heard Ms Crawford say. That was her cue to enter.

"I hope I'm not the one you're going to off. I'm Ms Fox, the one with some sodding answers."

Alyssa had clearly taken the woman—who was downright stunning—behind her desk by surprise. So much so that Alyssa had to stop herself from laughing when the gorgeous Ms Crawford almost fell out of her chair.

Whilst the grumpy CEO straightened herself out, Alyssa took a moment to drink her in. Ms Crawford was the epitome of elegance and good taste. Her perfectly styled blonde hair sat just above her collar, tucked behind her ears, shining like gold rays of sunshine. Diamond studs twinkled from either lobe. Hazel eyes, so rich they looked like pools of chocolate, bored into Alyssa as she studied the woman.

Heat rose in Alyssa's body. A heat which had been absent for far too long. The top two buttons of Ms Crawford's shirt teased Alyssa's imagination. If the swell of her breasts were anything to go by, Alyssa knew that the body underneath the shirt was breathtaking.

Swallowing thickly, Alyssa cleared her throat. No point ogling the woman, not when the CEO was so clearly pissed off.

"Ms Fox, I'm sorry, I didn't see you there," Ms Crawford stuttered. "Please come in and take a seat."

Alyssa took a step towards the empty seat directly in front of Ms Crawford, but stopped when she saw Bug sitting by the window. Her instinct was to scoop him up and squeeze him.

"Where have you been?" she whispered into his ear. Bug gave her a quick sniff before licking her face. Alyssa giggled. Oh shit, I just giggled like a child in front of Ms Crawford and whoever that other woman is.

Releasing Bug, Alyssa turned back to the women and smiled. "Sorry about that. I was just worried, we've been looking for him for a while now."

"Right," Ms Crawford stated, studying Alyssa.

"So, you said you needed some answers?" Alyssa took the offered seat and waited.

"Indeed Ms Fox. You can imagine my surprise when I found that little one sitting in the middle of my office floor."

"Yeah, sorry about that. Bug likes to wander."

"Bug?"

"Yes, the dog." Alyssa pointed to Bug, who had resumed his perusal of London City.

"Right. So can you tell me why there are twenty-six of your dogs wandering around my office building?"

Alyssa didn't like Ms Crawford's tone at all. "I assumed your father would have filled you in."

"My father?"

"Yes, Richard Crawford."

"I'm well aware who he is, thank you."

Wow, snarky much?

"Then you should know why I'm here with my twenty-six dogs. I don't make a habit of turning up uninvited, you know."

"Well, you have today," Ms Crawford shot. A different kind of heat was taking over Alyssa's body now. Gone was any kind of pleasant feeling towards the uptight cow sitting on her stupidly expensive-looking chair and ostentatious desk.

"I assure you, Ms Crawford, I have not. May I suggest you call your father and talk to him?"

"I'm talking to you, Ms Fox."

"No, you're being a condescending arsehole to me, Ms Crawford." With that zinger of a sentence hanging between them, Alyssa stood, scooping Bug into her arms, and left the office without another word.

Well, that could have gone better.

Alyssa made her way down to the bottom floor with Bug snuggly tucked into her body. Her heart rate was still cruising along at warp speed.

"Well, she was horrible," she muttered into Bug's fur. "This is why I prefer dogs to humans, Bug."

"Where have you been?" Lil screeched when the elevator doors slid open.

"Looking for this one." Alyssa jiggled Bug playfully. "And I found him."

"Where was he?" Lil didn't wait, relieving Alyssa of the dog immediately, then smushing her face into his. Alyssa smiled. Lil was a big ol' softy sometimes.

"He was in the bloody CEO's office."

"Oh, bugger!"

"Yeah, you can say that again."

"Did you talk to her?" Lil was rocking Bug back and forth like a baby, kissing his head every few seconds.

"I did, and it did *not* go well." Alyssa recalled the fierce expression on Ms Crawford's delicious face.

"What does that mean, and why are you looking like that?"

"I'm not looking like anything. Turns out Ms Crawford is the complete opposite of Richard. As in, she has a stick up her arse and a chip on her shoulder."

"Explain." Lil finally sat Bug down on the floor, clipping on his lead so he couldn't make another great escape.

"I mean, she had no idea we were here. Until she found him—" Alyssa pointed to Bug "—in her office.

Looks like Richard didn't fill her in on our partnership before leaving."

"Well, what does that mean? Can she cancel it? Send us home?"

"Lil, I have no idea. I mean, I have a written agreement with Richard, so that must mean something. I told her to ring her dad and talk to him…" Alyssa trailed off because she didn't want to blurt out that she'd called the CEO a condescending arsehole. Lil wouldn't be too pleased with that.

"What aren't you telling me, Al?"

Damn it!

"I may have called her a condescending arsehole," she muttered under her breath.

"What?" Lil bellowed. "Alyssa, have you lost your mind?"

"Lil, you should have heard the way she was talking to me," Alyssa argued. "I didn't deserve it and she was being an arsehole!"

"That doesn't mean you point it out to her, you prat!"

"It just slipped out. I was angry."

"I wish, just once, you would curb your temper. See, this is what I get for working and being friends with a bloody Aries."

Alyssa rolled her eyes. So what if she fit her astrology sign to a T? It didn't make her wrong! Ms Crawford was a miserable cow who shouldn't be allowed to speak to people like that unchecked.

"Relax, Lil. I'll apologise later."

"You better, Al. We haven't got a back-up plan."

Alyssa wasn't stupid. She knew she had to apologise and make nice, but she wasn't in the headspace to do it just now. Definitely better for everyone involved if Alyssa had time to cool off first. Otherwise, the apology would turn into another argument.

"So what's she like, apart from being an arsehole?" Lil asked, dragging Alyssa along to the vending machines.

"Well, she's...she's..."

"Ha! She's fit, isn't she? You're all stuttery, meaning Ms Crawford has to be a looker."

"Oh for God...she's pretty. I'll give her that. Shame her personality sucks so much, though." There was no chance she was going to tell Lil that the wretched Ms Crawford gave her all the feels in her intimate areas. Nope.

"C'mon, fess up, she's hot and you want to do unspeakable things to her," Lil cackled. Alyssa laughed along because her friend was ridiculous.

"Shut up and get me a coffee...oh, and a muffin."

"There's a muffin waiting for you in the office upstairs," Lil winked.

"What?"

"Ms Crawford's muffin." Lil laughed harder this time.

"That was such a bad lesbian joke it's almost funny."

"I'm freakin' hilarious." Lil wiped the stray tear from under her eye. Alyssa had to give it to her best friend: there wasn't anyone else she knew who found themselves as funny as Lil Barnes.

"You're off your freakin' rocker, more like. Anyway, enough chitchat. Any updates?"

"All's well, fearless leader. Most of the team have gone back to the centre to do a deep clean. Thought it would be a great opportunity to spruce the place up a bit whilst the residents are out."

"So who's left here, then?"

"You're looking at 'em, love. Just me and you. I was going to do one more check before heading out to lunch."

"I'll do that. You go grab some food. Bring me back a sandwich or something."

"Roger that. See you soon." Lil handed Bug's lead to Alyssa and skipped out the room. The manky apple slices in the vending machine weren't particularly appealing. No wonder everyone went looking elsewhere for sustenance.

"Just me and you now, Bug. C'mon, let's go visit some of your pals."

Alyssa led Bug around the offices, stopping to chat with as many people as possible. After checking the fenced-off play area outside, Alyssa sat back and relaxed with Bug in a particularly sunny spot by the office entrance.

Closing her eyes, Alyssa basked in the heat of the winter sun. "Global warming is a real bitch, Bug," she mumbled. They should *not* be having temperatures like this in November. The chatter of two people caught Alyssa's attention.

"I heard she went off on the woman who brought the dogs," a woman said.

"Are you surprised she didn't know? The woman never leaves that bloody office," the man walking next to her replied. Alyssa heard the two workers fiddle with a packet and then the distinct sound of a lighter being flicked. The woman took a long draw of her cigarette in.

"She needs to relax. Richard was never like this. I'm getting secondary stress from just being near her."

"What the bloody hell was Richard thinking running off like that? I suppose we have to give her some credit for stepping in at the last minute. Right before Christmas as well. I wouldn't want to be her." The man said.

"God, and did you hear about her ex strolling in earlier?" Alyssa's ears perked up. "That woman was awful. What Evelyn ever saw in her is beyond me."

Woman. Her. Did that mean...

"Yeah, I get that. Mindy was a bitch from the start. Everyone knew she was just after the money. Shame, really, it's not like Evelyn isn't a looker. I'd have thought she'd have the pick of anyone on the London lesbian scene."

"Tom, what the bloody hell would you know about the London lesbian scene?" The woman laughed.

"I know things. I'm just saying, Evelyn surely has more options than that gold digging cow," Tom replied.

Alyssa's mind was spinning. Evelyn Crawford was a lesbian, or at least dated women. Not that it changed anything. The woman was still condescending and mardy. Not Alyssa's type at all.

Still, Alyssa found herself thinking of Ms Crawford for the next few hours. Even though she had things to do, her mind wandered back to the infuriating CEO.

"Did you apologise yet?" Lil asked later that afternoon. They hadn't broached the subject, and Alyssa foolishly thought Lil had forgotten all about it.

"Not yet, but I will."

"Alyssa, go and do it. Maybe take the time to actually tell the woman why we're here. It is her company, after all."

"It's Richard's company as far as I'm concerned."

"Stop being antagonistic and just go apologise. Think of the centre. Think of what we're trying to achieve. All of that can and will go away if you piss off the woman in charge."

"Fine, I'm going."

Lil was right, this wasn't about her or Evelyn Crawford. It was about her dogs, and they were the only thing that mattered. If Alyssa had to put up with Ms Crawford and her catty attitude, she would. Alyssa Fox would do anything for her pups.

The ride up to the executive floor was silent bar the hum of the elevator. Alyssa counted down the floors as she ascended higher. A weird lump formed in her stomach, but she couldn't quite work out if it was because she was going to have to apologise and grovel if necessary to Ms Crawford, or if it was because Ms Crawford's beauty was unnerving. Either way, the next few minutes were going to suck.

7

Bug's Grand Tour (and the Art of Strategic Delay)

ALYSSA

The elevator dinged its ascent, a tinny carol leaking from the speaker like a slow drip of eggnog through a cheesecloth. Alyssa stood in the back corner, clutching Bug's lead in one hand and rehearsing her apology in her head for the hundredth time. Her nerves jangled with every floor.

At least she wasn't the only one feeling the tension; Bug glared at the ceiling with all the silent judgment of a Victorian magistrate, completely ignoring the trio of sales reps who tried to pet him on the fifth floor.

"Don't take it personally," Alyssa whispered to one of them. "He's a bit...senior management."

The woman gave a tight smile, then shuffled out, casting a wistful look back at Bug's stumpy tail. Alyssa tried to smooth her hair in the polished steel doors and gave up. There was no smoothing anything about this day, this situation, or—if she was being honest—her entire adult life.

The elevator stopped on the twelfth floor. Alyssa pressed the button for the top floor again, but Bug had other ideas. The moment the doors opened, he yanked the lead from her hand and bolted.

"Bug! No!" Alyssa lunged after him, nearly colliding with a woman carrying a precarious stack of files that looked like they'd been photocopied sometime during the Major administration.

"Sorry! So sorry!" Alyssa called over her shoulder as she chased Bug down the corridor.

Bug, for his part, seemed to have a very specific destination in mind. He trotted with purpose past the open-plan office, ignoring the calls of "cute dog!" and "come here, puppy!" from various employees who clearly hadn't read the memo about not distracting working animals. Alyssa followed, breathless, as Bug made a sharp right turn into what appeared to be a break room.

Inside, the accounts team huddled around a table that looked more like a battlefield of spreadsheets and half-eaten lunches. The fluorescent lighting gave everyone the complexion of someone who'd been underground for several months. Bug made a beeline for a dropped sandwich crust, his stealth operations worthy of a corporate espionage expert.

"I am so sorry," Alyssa panted, finally catching up. "He's not supposed to—"

A lanky guy, who introduced himself as Tom, with thick-rimmed glasses and a calculator watch that probably had more computing power than the building's server, interrupted her. "Are you kidding? We've been the forgotten department all year. Last month, they forgot to invite us to the fire drill. We only found out there'd been one when someone mentioned it in passing."

After Tom introduced himself, it was like a line of dominoes fell as Alyssa tried to remember all their names.

Priya, a woman with intricate henna tattoos peeking out from her sleeves and an expression that suggested she'd seen every creative accounting trick in the book, nodded. "Every other team gets a dog. Marketing? Golden Retriever. HR? Adorable Corgi. Us? Spreadsheets and the lingering scent of despair."

Sarah, who looked like she'd been born with a red pen in her hand and had probably corrected her own birth certificate for grammatical errors, was already scratching Bug behind the ears. "We're not 'too busy,'" she air-quoted with the precision of someone who'd spent years highlighting discrepancies. "We're just...strategically overlooked. Like that corner of the office where the printer goes to die."

Alyssa recognised that tone. These were people who knew exactly how important they were, even if no one else did. The unsung heroes who kept the lights on while everyone else took credit for the electricity.

"Accounts keeps this place running," she said. "Without you, no one gets paid."

Tom's eyes lit up. "Exactly! We're the unsung heroes. The backbone. The—" He paused. "Actually, we're more like the spleen. Vital, but no one really knows what we do."

Bug, sensing an ally, dropped the sandwich crust and sat directly on Tom's shoe, looking up with what could only be described as professional solidarity. Or possibly just the hope of more sandwich.

"I think," Alyssa said, watching Bug settle in like he'd found his spiritual home, "Bug would like to be your official morale officer. Lunch breaks only. Non-negotiable."

The trio exchanged looks of pure, unbridled joy—the kind usually reserved for discovering the vending machine had been restocked or that the quarterly meeting had been cancelled.

"We'll take him," Priya said solemnly. "We'll treat him better than some of our senior managers treat us."

"Which is to say, we'll remember his name," Tom added.

Alyssa had a sneaking feeling the "senior management" knew *every single* name in the accounting department. They were more than likely treated a *lot* better than most departments.

Bug wagged his tail, as if he'd just closed a multi-million pound deal. Or at least secured a reliable source of sandwich crusts.

As Alyssa left the break room, Bug in tow, she felt a small glow of satisfaction. Maybe this partnership was working better than she'd thought. Maybe the dogs were doing exactly what they were meant to do: reminding people that work was just work, and that sometimes the most important thing was a moment of uncomplicated joy.

But her satisfaction was short-lived. Bug had apparently decided that today was the day for maximum chaos. As they passed the marketing department on the fifteenth floor, he spotted something through the glass wall and froze, ears perked like satellite dishes receiving a transmission from the Dog Star.

"Bug, no. We need to—"

Too late. Bug launched himself at the glass, barking frantically at a poster of a German Shepherd advertising Crawford's premium dog food line. The poster dog looked impossibly glossy and professional, the kind of dog that had never eaten its own sick or rolled in something unspeakable.

"Bug! That's not a real dog! It's been Photoshopped to within an inch of its life!"

Several marketing employees looked up from their desks, some amused, others wearing the expression of people who'd been in back-to-back meetings since dawn and were no longer entirely sure what reality was.

A woman in a sharp blazer that probably cost more than Alyssa's monthly grocery budget approached, her heels clicking with the authority of someone who'd survived at least three corporate restructures.

"Is he okay?" she asked, not unkindly.

"He's fine. Just...passionate about advertising, apparently." Alyssa tugged Bug away from the poster. "Sorry for the disruption. I'm sure you were all doing very important...marketing things."

The woman laughed, a genuine sound that seemed to surprise even her. "Don't be. This is the most entertainment we've had all week. Last excitement was when someone used the wrong font in a presentation. There were tears. I'm Claudia, by the way. Legal, technically, but I wander."

"Alyssa. Four Paws. Also a wanderer, but usually with more purpose."

"Oh! You're the one who brought all the dogs." Claudia's expression shifted to something more conspiratorial, the look of someone about to share classified information. "Everyone's been talking about you."

Alyssa winced. "I'm guessing not all positive?"

"Mixed reviews. The dog people love you. The people who think animals belong in fields and not near their ergonomic keyboards are less enthusiastic." Claudia glanced around, then lowered her voice. "I heard you had a bit of a run-in with the top floor this morning."

Alyssa felt her face heat. "Word travels fast."

"This is a corporate office. Gossip is our primary form of communication. That and passive-aggressive emails." Claudia leaned in. "For what it's worth, the general consensus is that you weren't entirely wrong. Things have been...tense since the transition."

She didn't elaborate, but Alyssa caught the subtext. New leadership. Old expectations. The kind of pressure that turned reasonable people into walking stress fractures.

"Are you heading up to apologize?" Claudia asked.

"That obvious?"

"The fact that you're dragging a reluctant dog toward the executive elevator is a bit of a giveaway. Also, you have that look. Like you're about to walk into a performance review you know won't go well."

Alyssa laughed despite herself. "Any advice?"

Claudia considered. "Be direct. Don't grovel. And maybe lead with the dog. Hard to stay angry at someone holding a Cocker Spaniel." She paused. "Good luck. You'll need it."

As Claudia walked away, Alyssa felt a knot tighten in her stomach. She'd faced down angry donors, hostile board members, and once, a particularly aggressive goose that had taken up residence at the sanctuary. But somehow, the thought of facing Evelyn Crawford again made her more nervous than all of those combined.

Bug, apparently sensing her anxiety, had decided he'd had enough. He planted his bottom firmly on the floor and refused to move, his expression suggesting he'd found this spot perfectly acceptable for the foreseeable future.

"Bug, come on. We need to do this."

Bug looked at her with those soulful brown eyes and yawned, a performance of indifference that would have impressed a teenager.

"You're not helping," Alyssa muttered.

A passing janitor, pushing a cart that squeaked with the rhythm of someone who'd been doing this job for decades, chuckled. "That one's got a mind of his own, doesn't he?"

"You have no idea. I'm starting to think he's conducting some kind of social experiment."

"Dogs usually are," the janitor said sagely. "They're smarter than most of the people in this building. Present company excluded, of course."

After five minutes of coaxing, bribing with treats that Bug examined with the scepticism of a food critic, and finally just picking him up like a furry, judgmental sack of potatoes, Alyssa managed to get Bug into the executive elevator.

As the doors closed, she caught sight of her reflection in the polished steel. Her hair was a mess, her shirt was wrinkled, and she had what appeared to be a paw print on her jeans. Perfect. This was exactly how she wanted to look when apologising to the Ice Queen.

Bug, cradled in her arms, licked her chin with what might have been affection or might have been an attempt to taste-test her anxiety.

"Thanks, buddy. At least one of us has confidence."

The elevator climbed higher. Alyssa's stomach churned in sympathy with the ascending numbers.

Eighteenth floor.

Alyssa took a deep breath. "Okay, Bug. This is it. We're going to march up there, I'm going to apologize like a professional adult who definitely didn't call her a condescending arsehole, and then we're going to get out of there before I say something else stupid."

Bug sneezed, which Alyssa chose to interpret as agreement rather than commentary on her life choices.

"Yeah, I don't believe me either."

The doors opened on the nineteenth floor. A woman in a pencil skirt that looked like it required an engineering degree to walk in stepped in, took one look at Bug, and immediately started cooing in a voice that suggested she'd been suppressing this urge all day.

"Oh my goodness, is this one of the Four Paws dogs? I've been dying to meet them! Everyone on my floor has one except me. I think HR hates me."

"This is Bug," Alyssa said, grateful for the distraction and the delay.

"He's adorable! Can I pet him? I promise I washed my hands after the tuna sandwich incident."

"Sure."

The woman scratched Bug behind the ears with the enthusiasm of someone who'd been denied this simple pleasure for far too long. Bug immediately melted into her hands, tail wagging, his earlier resistance completely forgotten. Traitor.

"I tried to sign up as a volunteer, but all the spots were taken," the woman said wistfully.

"That's unfortunate," Alyssa observed. It would be too easy to offer Bug, considering he was a "buddy" down, but Alyssa had selected Cyril for a reason. Bug wouldn't be compatible with just anyone.

"I live with unfortunate all the time. Last month, someone took my yogurt. It had my name on it. In permanent marker."

They chatted for the rest of the elevator ride, and by the time they reached the twentieth floor, Alyssa had given the Hillary, the elevator woman, her contact information and promised to set up a meet-and-greet. Alyssa had several dogs in mind that she thought might be compatible for a permanent home with Hillary. She'd just have to wait until January to apply. Bug had also managed to charm his way into receiving approximately seventeen ear scratches and what looked like half a digestive biscuit from the Hillary's pocket.

As Hillary stepped off on her floor, she turned back. "Good luck with whatever you're doing up here. And thanks for bringing the dogs. It's made this place feel a lot less...just thanks."

The doors closed, and Alyssa was alone again with Bug and her impending sense of doom.

"Alright," she said, setting him down. "No more distractions. We're doing this."

Bug looked up at her, then promptly sat down and started licking his paw with the concentration of a surgeon performing a delicate operation.

Alyssa sighed. "Of course you are."

She glanced down the corridor toward Evelyn's office. The frosted glass door loomed at the end like the entrance to a particularly unforgiving headmaster's office.

Lil's words echoed in her head: "Think of the centre. Think of what we're trying to achieve."

Alyssa squared her shoulders, tightened her grip on Bug's lead, and took a step forward.

Then Bug spotted something—a dust bunny, a shadow, possibly the ghost of corporate dreams past—and lunged sideways, nearly pulling Alyssa off her feet.

"Bug!"

He ignored her with the practiced ease of someone who'd been ignoring people his entire life, trotting purposefully toward a water cooler, where he proceeded to investigate it with the intensity of a health and safety inspector who'd found a serious violation.

Alyssa groaned. "We're never getting to that office, are we?"

Bug looked up at her, tail wagging, completely unbothered by her existential crisis. His expression clearly said: your human problems are not my concern. This water cooler, however, is fascinating.

Maybe, Alyssa thought, that was the point. Maybe Bug was trying to tell her something. Maybe she needed to stop overthinking this and just...be. Or maybe Bug was just a dog who liked water coolers and she was projecting meaning onto his complete lack of interest in her emotional state.

Either way, Alyssa decided to take a breath. She'd get to Evelyn's office eventually, but for now she'd let Bug be Bug.

After all, wasn't that what this whole partnership was about? Letting the dogs remind everyone to slow down, to be present, to find joy in the small things? Like water coolers. And sandwich crusts. And the lingering hope that maybe, just maybe, work didn't have to be quite so relentlessly work-like all the time.

Alyssa sat down on the floor next to Bug, who had now moved on to sniffing the baseboards with the dedication of someone conducting a very important survey.

"Alright, buddy," she said. "Five more minutes. Then we face the music."

Bug wagged his tail in what Alyssa chose to interpret as agreement, though it might have just been because he'd found a particularly interesting bit of dust.

And for those five minutes, Alyssa let herself just be. No apologies, no stress, no Ice Queens waiting behind frosted glass doors.

Just her, Bug, and a water cooler on the twentieth floor of Crawford's headquarters.

8

Second Chances and Soft Hands

EVELYN

"**W**hat the hell was that?" Evelyn barked once Ms Fox had stormed out with her dog.

"That was you getting told off by a fine piece of ass," Maggie laughed.

"Never say 'fine piece of ass again,' Mags, seriously."

"Whatever. She *was* fine. Did you see her hair? I would give my yearly paycheck for that mane."

Evelyn rubbed her forehead. Why had that gone so badly? Had she spoken to the woman condescendingly?

"Mags, was I out of order?"

Maggie brought her forefinger and thumb close together. "A little, Evie. I mean I know today has been stressful, and you weren't expecting to deal with a bunch of dogs on top of everything else, but you didn't really give the woman a chance to tell you who she was or what she was doing here."

"Hey, she told me to call my dad. How is that explaining things?" Evelyn protested.

"I think she only said that because you came out of the gate swinging. Your body language didn't exactly scream warm and friendly."

"Maggie, come on."

"No, you come on. It's been a bit of a running joke between us lately about your stress levels. You think I'm just nagging, but I'm worried, Evelyn. Ever since you took over from Richard you have been going full steam with no breaks. How many times have you come to the office before dawn?"

Evelyn went to open her mouth to mount some sort of protest, but Maggie wasn't in the mood.

"Don't answer that because we both know it's one time too many. Yes, there is a lot of work to do, but nothing that's out of the ordinary. Nothing you weren't accustomed to before you became CEO. Everyone knows you were practically running the place well before your dad buggered off. Ask yourself why you have taken it upon yourself to carry all this extra weight?"

"You think I like this?" Evelyn shot. How dare Maggie accuse her of putting this on herself?

"Yes, I do. You have done the Christmas period many, *many* times. You have overseen budget reports and meetings. All that shit you've done for years. Yet now those three letters are attached to your name, you've become work obsessed. And before you try to argue: don't!"

Evelyn was stunned into silence.

"When was the last time you took a weekend off? Or finished work before midnight? Gone out for drinks with your friends? Friends, I might add, that sorely miss you. Before you became 'Evelyn Crawford CEO,' you had a good balance between work and home. Now? Nothing, you're making yourself ill, working every god given hour."

"Maggie, I haven't got my dad to fall back on this time. The buck stops with me. That's what comes with having those three letters attached to my name."

"Three letters you never wanted," Maggie shouted. And there it was, the thing Evelyn hadn't voiced in months: the truth.

Before Richard decided to go on an extended trip with the floozy, Evelyn was contemplating resigning from the family company. Maggie was her confidante and knew that for a few years, Evelyn had become steadily more unhappy in her job.

The thing that always held her back was her loyalty, which increased tenfold after her mother passed away. The thought of abandoning her dad and the company her mother had created felt too much. Her mum and dad had worked hard to provide her with a stable income, a family legacy.

For the most part, Evelyn loved working at Crawford's Pet Supplies, but as she got older, she felt the need to branch out. Try something she had to work for without having her parents there to hold her hand. Because that's how it felt. Even though Evelyn worked harder than most people, she still felt the unease of having a company practically handed to her. A career path laid out since she was a toddler.

"I couldn't just leave, Mags."

"Why the hell not? Your dad should have checked in with you before saddling you with his company."

"It was my mum's company too!" Evelyn shouted.

"But your mum isn't here, Evelyn. I'm sorry, honey. I'm not trying to piss you off or hurt you. Hell, you're doing a good job of that yourself. But be honest with yourself. Would your mum want to see you this stressed out, tired and on the verge of collapse?"

"It's just until after Christmas," Evelyn tried to reason. Was she reasoning with Maggie or herself, though? Why was she clinging so tightly to a company she didn't really want to be a part of anymore? The answer was simple...that's what she was used to doing. If she let go of Crawford's, what would she have? No girlfriend, no other career options. Evelyn would have nothing, and that wasn't acceptable.

"You won't get all the things you want in life, Evie, if all you have is this office," Maggie said, as if reading her thoughts.

"How did this turn into a beat on Evelyn conversation, hm?"

"Okay, you don't want to hear it. Call your dad, ask why we have a bunch of dogs running around, and then apologise to that woman. She didn't deserve the way you spoke to her."

"Maggie…" Evelyn began, because she hated hearing the dejection in her friend's voice.

"No, Evelyn, I'm done trying to convince you to look after yourself. I'll see you later. I have some files to get to."

Evelyn huffed out a breath. Today sucked. Like, really, *really* sucked. With the budget meeting looming over her, Evelyn pulled open her bottom drawer and grabbed two chocolate bars. Ideally, she would like to have a shot of something strong, but she wasn't quite at the drinking at work stage yet.

"I love you," she mumbled to her Double Decker.

With an entire day's worth of calories consumed, Evelyn picked up her mobile. It was over two months since her dad left, and she'd only received one message from the man. Well, now she needed him to pick up and explain who and why this sexy Ms Fox was in the building.

"Ms Fox," she said to no one. Hearing the name roll off her tongue sent shivers down her spine. Evelyn could imagine playing a few naughty games with that woman. Pulling herself back to the present, Evelyn hit the call button. Straight to voicemail. Great. Instead of calling again, she sent a message asking her dad to call ASAP.

The office felt too big and way too quiet. Maggie's words bounced around her brain as she sat in silence. What could she do, though? Even if she *wanted* to look into a different career path for herself, Richard had put pay to that by leaving.

Outside, Evelyn could hear her colleagues returning from their lunch. That meant the day had to go on. Whether or not Maggie agreed, there was still a lot to get done. The damn budget meeting for a start. Taking some meditative breaths, Evelyn readied herself for the afternoon ahead.

"Well, that went down like a bag of crap," Evelyn muttered as she sat behind her desk after a gruelling two hours in the conference room. All the managers were angry because they didn't get the money they requested. It was a no-win situation, and Evelyn was glad it was over. Budget meetings were Satan's playground.

A sharp rap on the door nearly caused Evelyn to catapult her coffee across the room. Maybe more caffeine wasn't such a good idea after all.

"Come in," she called, secretly praying it wasn't someone else who wanted to shout at her. The door opened slowly, and Evelyn audibly gasped when she locked eyes with Ms Fox.

"Don't worry, I'm not here for round two," the gorgeous woman chuckled. "I came to apologise."

Evelyn stared at Ms Fox, unable to form a sentence. Maggie called her a fine piece of ass—crude, but not wrong. Evelyn, however, would call her exquisitely beautiful. Ms Fox had thick, dark hair, which she had bundled into a ponytail. Though her hair looked as if it could burst its restraints at any moment. Evelyn could imagine Ms Fox's hair hanging down in luscious locks around the woman's shoulders. There must be some Italian in her lineage. Not only was her hair fantastic, but her skin, face, body, hell, you name it, Ms Fox had it. Even in worn jeans and a flannel shirt, she was delectable. Last but in no way least were Ms Fox's eyes. Not brown, but almost golden. In a word, she was breathtaking.

"Ms Crawford?"

Evelyn jumped a little at the sound of her name. "Right, right, um...yes...sorry."

Nicely handled, Evie.

"Can I?..." Ms Fox pointed to the seat in front of Evelyn's desk.

"Sure, yeah." Evelyn replied, watching the little dog who'd caused all the trouble in the first place wander over to the windows, sigh, and promptly fall asleep.

"Ms Crawford."

Evelyn snapped her attention back to Ms Fox. "Please call me Evelyn."

"Okay, Evelyn. Please let me say how sorry I am for the way I reacted this morning."

"I should apologise too, Ms Fox—"

"Alyssa."

"Alyssa. Yes, as I was saying, *Alyssa*. I shouldn't have let my bad mood out on you."

"How about we start again?" Evelyn watched as Alyssa leaned over the desk, offering her hand to shake.

"That sounds good," Evelyn replied, taking the proffered hand. Holy moly, Alyssa had soft skin. "So, now we're back at square one. Could you tell me about the partnership you formed with my father? I have tried to call him, per your request." Evelyn gave Alyssa a little smile.

In return, she got a smirk. Alyssa had a very sexy smirk. "However, he is unreachable and God knows when he'll return my calls."

"Fair enough. Okay, so I run Four Paws Dog Sanctuary—"

"Oh, I know that place. My next-door neighbour got a beautiful little terrier from there last year."

"Monty?"

"Yes, how did you know that?"

"I remember every dog that has been in the centre. Last year we had two terriers. One female and one male. The little girl got adopted by a woman in Scotland. So that left Monty."

"Wow, impressive." Evelyn really was impressed.

"So, this year I closed the centre from November to the beginning of January."

"That's risky business," Evelyn commented, earning a nose flare from Alyssa. Oops, she'd said something wrong already.

"It would be if the sanctuary was a business. It's not."

"My apologies. I didn't mean to offend you."

"It's fine. You weren't to know. Anyway, once I decided to close, I contacted your father."

"Can I ask why you closed it?"

"I was sick of dogs being adopted for Christmas and returned in the New Year once their shine had worn off."

"That happens a lot?"

"More than you realise. Two-thirds of the dogs adopted last year were returned."

Two-thirds—that was an outrageous amount. "That's awful," Evelyn murmured.

"Yes, it is. Even though we spend an absurd amount of time drilling home the reality that owning a dog is hard work, and requires time and patience..." Evelyn watched Alyssa huff out a frustrated breath. The woman was too worked up to even finish her sentence.

"So why the partnership?" Evelyn wanted to move the conversation along. Not because she was bored, but because she didn't like to see Alyssa upset.

"The dogs still need stimulation and socialisation. My partner came up with the idea of approaching Richard. Honestly, I didn't go to him with any kind of plan. That sort of just happened. Your dad got so excited." Alyssa chuckled.

Evelyn rolled her eyes playfully. That was her dad all right. Put a dog in front of him, and he was a kid at Christmas. Maybe not the best phrase to use. Definitely not something to say in front of Alyssa. "So, what did he offer?"

"Basically, we paired each dog up with a volunteer. Your dad made sure that everyone involved knew their responsibilities. They signed forms. Anyone with an allergy where a dog would be present was moved to a different floor, or offered to work from home if possible."

"Okay, that doesn't sound too bad, I suppose."

"We collect the dogs at the end of the day and return them to the sanctuary."

"The volunteers can't take them home?"

"Not yet. We decided to give everyone a month. When December rolls around, any volunteer who wishes to take the dog can do so for a night during the week or the weekend."

"But not all week?"

"Nope. I don't want the dogs thinking they have found their forever home. It's not fair to them. That's why I will be the one to decide if a dog can be taken for a night. Some of the pack are more sensitive than others."

"Sounds reasonable. And everything is going well so far?" Now that Evelyn had calmed down and spoken to Alyssa like a rational human being, she was delighted with the partnership. Her dad knew what he was doing. She trusted his judgement, even if she wished he had told her first.

"Everything has gone brilliantly. Except for the minor hiccup with Bug." Alyssa chuckled.

Ah, yes Bug. The little runaway.

Evelyn laughed. "It was a surprise, I must admit. At first I thought I was hallucinating."

"Oh, no. Bug is definitely real."

"Who is his volunteer?"

"It was a fella called Cyril—"

"But Cyril is in the hospital—"

"With a broken hip, yes. Well, there isn't anyone else who matches Bug, so he will stay with me during the day. Or Lil, when I need to go to meetings."

"Lil?"

"Yes, my partner." Evelyn's heart dropped to her stomach. Of course, Alyssa had a partner.

"I feel a bit bad for the little guy now."

"Don't feel too bad. Lil and I will spoil him."

The conversation hit a lull. Evelyn watched Alyssa gaze around her office.

"It's not the most exciting of offices, I'm afraid." Evelyn suddenly felt conscious of the stark coldness her workspace offered. Alyssa seemed like a warm and colourful kind of person. Not corporate bland.

"Hey, whatever floats your boat. My office is a sixth of the size of this, covered in dog hair and piles of paperwork."

"Sounds heavenly," Evelyn laughed.

"So…"

"So?" Evelyn arched her eyebrow and then blushed because she was using her signature sexy eyebrow move on this woman, the one with a partner and not in the least bit interested in her.

"Are we okay…the partnership, I mean?" Did Alyssa have a little tinge of red on her creamy cheeks? If so, was that because of Evelyn's fabulous eyebrow game?

"Yes, of course. I think it will be great for morale around the building, and the dogs get some human time. Win-win."

"Oh, thank God," Alyssa laughed. "I really didn't have a backup plan."

"Let me know if you need anything. I'm only an elevator ride away."

"Will do. Thanks, Evelyn. I appreciate what your dad offered us and I appreciate you upholding it."

Evelyn gave Alyssa a shy smile.

With the partnership debacle cleared up, there wasn't anything else to discuss. Evelyn wanted more than anything to keep the conversation going, learn everything she could about Alyssa, but that would have seemed weird, right? Unprofessional. Yes, definitely. Anyway, there was still a good chunk of the day left.

Bidding Alyssa goodbye, Evelyn sat a while processing. Not about the alliance between Four Paws and Crawford's. No, she needed to process Alyssa. Sweet, beautiful, sexy Alyssa Fox. Partnered Alyssa Fox.

She's a no-go, Ev, keep it in your undies, girl.

The sun had long set over London. Evelyn checked the time on her laptop, surprised to find it was only half five. The rest of the afternoon had been crammed as usual. Plenty of people needing her time. The last of those people was Roger, the IT guy. Evelyn hated talking to Roger because Roger only spoke to Evelyn's cleavage. He also left the bloody door open after leaving. An open door meant people thought they could pop their heads in and chat. Evelyn was not about that at all. Not anymore, anyway.

Standing, getting ready to close said door, Evelyn chuckled when she met the little brown eyes of Bug, who sat squarely in the middle of her office again.

"Well, what are you doing here, young man?"

This time there was no stand-off, no staring competition. Evelyn manoeuvred herself round the desk and sank to her knees in front of him. Bug lifted his left paw, placing it delicately on Evelyn's lap.

"Good God, you're a charmer," she giggled. Unable to resist any longer, Evelyn took his face in her hands and kissed his head before ruffling his cheeks. This seemed to be the magic action because Bug immediately moved closer, ramming his head into her belly, demanding more, which only caused her to laugh again.

"Alyssa is going to be worried sick about you again, Bug. You can't keep running off." Evelyn should take him back downstairs, but the thought of Alyssa paying her another visit was too enticing. Maybe they could chat a bit more.

The sound of footsteps hurrying down the hall gave Evelyn a spike of excitement. The rapid knock on her door made her smile.

"Come in," she called.

The door pushed open, but it wasn't the illustrious Alyssa Fox. No, this woman was a little shorter, with spiky brown hair and dark makeup. Her black dungarees had rips in the knees, and her top looked as if it was twenty years old.

"Oh, thank Christ," the woman bellowed. Her hands dropped to her knees as she bent over, trying desperately to catch her breath.

"Can I help you?" Evelyn asked, getting to her feet.

"Sorry. Lil Barnes. With Four Paws."

Ah, Alyssa's partner. Evelyn couldn't stop the zing of jealousy that shot through her body. Silly really, considering she'd only met Alyssa twice and the first encounter wasn't exactly something to write home about.

"Of course. I take it you're looking for this one?" Evelyn smiled, pointing at Bug, who hadn't moved.

"Yup, gave me and Alyssa another heart attack. Thanks for that, mate." She chuckled. "Sorry, he keeps breaking in."

"The door was open so…" Evelyn shrugged good-naturedly.

"Well, I'll be getting him back downstairs. The van is waiting for him."

"Oh, you're all done for the day?" Evelyn felt a pang of disappointment, knowing that Alyssa would be leaving.

"Yeah, it's half five. Most of your staff are packing up to head home."

"Of course. Well, see you tomorrow then, I guess."

9

Glass Towers and Tangled Lights

EVELYN

Evelyn had never understood the phrase "bone tired" until she slumped into the back of the company town car and let her head thunk against the chilled window. The city was all taillights and glass, the traffic crawling up the Thames like a mechanical artery. The car radio, too polite to break the silence but too timid to play anything interesting, murmured barely above the idle. She rolled her temple against the glass, willing herself not to close her eyes. The city always felt different after hours, like it belonged to someone else—a version of London for the insomniacs, the shift workers, the ones who were always just a little bit out of sync.

She recognised a stretch of illuminated office blocks on the other side of the river. There: the Crawford building, the one she'd finally left for the night, its logo a backlit badge of familial expectation. The lights on the top floor burned brightest. Evelyn pictured herself, slouching over spreadsheets, bickering with Maggie, trying to ignore the yawning chasm of her inbox. Her name, in a sense, floated twenty stories over the city, a daily dare to not fuck things up.

The driver dropped her in front of the glass lobby of her apartment tower. She could have walked the last few blocks, as usual, because Evelyn was conscious she had to fit some sort of exercise into her daily routine, but her feet still ached from yesterday's shoes, and she was already dreading the ascent to her apartment. There was something obscene about the speed of these lifts, how they whipped you from lobby to penthouse before you'd even formed a thought. Sometimes, on the way up, she counted the seconds. Tonight she just let her head loll, wishing briefly that the elevator would stall so she'd have an excuse not to keep going. Evelyn knew that even though she was home, she would still work if given the opportunity.

When the doors pinged open, the silence of the penthouse swallowed her whole. It was an architectural marvel—glass everywhere, sharp lines, the distant hum of the city faint as tinnitus. There was no evidence of Mindy now, no makeup smeared on the master bath counter, no abandoned trainers in the hall. Evelyn wasn't sure if she preferred it that way.

She didn't bother with the lights, just dropped her bag near the entrance and padded barefoot across the hardwood. The city's glow spilled in from the full wall of windows, all blue and orange and white, making the apartment look like a showroom. She went straight to the kitchen, opened the fridge, and stared inside as if waiting for a message from God to appear between the almond milk and a half-empty jar of Polish pickles.

There was an unopened bottle of Sauvignon Blanc on the top shelf. She took it out, found a glass, and filled it higher than she normally would. Only then did she notice her hands were shaking.

Evelyn was not the type to wallow. She'd been taught, by genetics or by parental example, to process emotions at a dead sprint and leave them panting in the dust. The trick was to stay in motion, to always have something new in front of you—another task, another problem, another reason to keep your hands busy. But now, with no emails and no Maggie and no Bug (God, Bug), the apartment pressed down on her, a suffocating bubble.

She sipped her wine, wandered over to the windows, and stared out at the city. From this height, it was impossible to distinguish individuals, let alone lives. The London Eye rotated with measured grace in the distance, a useless clock for tourists. She pressed her forehead against the glass, letting the cold bite her skin.

She should have been thinking about the next day's staff meeting, or the interminable board conference, or the half-done Christmas campaign plan on her laptop. Instead, her mind kept drifting sideways, snagging on the day's oddest moments. The dog, for starters. Bug. He'd just sat there in the centre of her office like he owned it, like he'd been waiting for her his entire life. He hadn't barked or whined, just looked at her as if he knew exactly what she needed and was prepared to wait forever.

Then, of course, there was Alyssa Fox. The woman had walked into Evelyn's office like a summer storm—sudden, warm, impossible to ignore. And sure, Evelyn was attracted to women; she'd never hidden that, even from her father, who'd simply shrugged and asked if she needed help finding a date for the annual charity ball. But this was different. She couldn't stop thinking about Alyssa's smile, the way she'd called Evelyn out—"condescending arsehole"—without flinching. She'd apologised later, but the words had stuck, vibrating in Evelyn's skull for hours. No one talked to her like that. Maybe that was why she couldn't let it go.

Evelyn drained her glass and poured another. She imagined what Maggie would say if she could see her now: "You're supposed to be out living, not marinating in white wine." But the idea of another empty restaurant meal or a night at a bar, surrounded by strangers and their faux intimacy, made her want to crawl out of her own skin.

She made a half-hearted attempt to open her laptop, stared at the login screen for a solid minute, and then snapped it shut again. Instead, she roamed the apartment, glass in hand, flicking on lights as she went. The master bedroom was as pristine as she'd left it. She passed the guest room—formerly Mindy's "office," now just a clean space with a dead plant and a pile of unopened letters on the desk.

The bathroom was clinical, all stone and glass and luxury fittings. Evelyn took a perverse comfort in the fact that even her toothbrush looked military-precise in its placement. She studied herself in the mirror: the flawless hair, the subtle makeup, the suit jacket that still looked sharp despite the hour. But there were circles under her eyes, and the tension in her jaw was starting to look permanent.

She thought of her mother, as she often did when the hour was late and the apartment quiet. Roslyn had always been the strong one, the genius who'd built an empire out of a few shopfronts and a dream. Evelyn remembered her mother's laugh—loud, undignified, full-bodied. She wished she could conjure it now, just for a second, but her memory only served up a few ragged snippets, faded like old Polaroids.

Sometimes she wondered what her mother would say if she saw her now. Probably something like, "You work too hard, Evie. You have to let yourself be loved." But that had never come easy, not for any of the Crawfords.

After removing her makeup and climbing into comfortable pyjamas, Evelyn retreated to the sofa, tucking her knees up beneath her. She switched on the television, scrolled through the endless menu, and settled on a cooking show hosted by a man with a suspiciously orange tan. She watched as he flambéed a stack of bananas, narrated with a theatrical cadence that made Evelyn roll her eyes.

The day kept replaying: her confrontation with Alyssa, her own embarrassing inability to act normal in the face of an attractive, competent woman. What would she have said if she could do it again? Would she have been less defensive, more open? Was it possible, even now, to backtrack and try again?

The thought made her stomach flutter, which was ridiculous. She barely knew the woman. Still, something about Alyssa had set off a quiet alarm in her head—equal parts caution and curiosity.

And then there was Bug, the improbable Cocker Spaniel who had clearly decided, in his dog wisdom, that Evelyn was his new project. He had an aura about him, a kind of steady-eyed patience she found both alien and soothing. It was almost funny, the idea of Evelyn—Ice Queen of the Executive Floor—getting attached to a dog, especially one with a name like Bug. She could already hear the jokes from the board members. But the truth was, the dog made her office feel less like a cell and more like a place where something real could happen.

Maybe she would bring him up again tomorrow. Just for an hour, to see what it was like. It couldn't hurt.

She finished her wine and set the glass on the table. Her phone buzzed, a notification from her email. She ignored it.

Instead, she padded over to the window, leaned her cheek against the glass, and looked out at the city—her city, her company, her life. A thousand windows, each hiding its own story. She wondered, for a moment, what it would be like to belong to someone again. Not just in a superficial, two-people-sharing-space kind of way, but really belong.

The thought scared her more than she cared to admit.

She wandered back to the kitchen, put the bottle away. As she flicked off the lights and headed for bed, she allowed herself, just for a second, to imagine Alyssa's warm hand in hers, the pressure of Bug's sleepy head on her lap.

Evelyn did not sleep easily, not these days. The doctor had offered her a prescription—small white pills in an orange bottle that sat untouched in her medicine cabinet, a kind of threat. Evelyn preferred her own method: lie as still as possible, ignore the distractions, let her mind spiral into exhaustion and finally cave. Most nights she managed it.

Tonight, the city's noise was a comfort rather than a curse. She lay in bed, duvet pulled up to her chin, and watched the ambient glow from the skyline crawl across her ceiling. For a while, she listened to the distant sirens, the low drone of a night bus rounding the corner.

But sleep, ever evasive, only sharpened her thoughts. And so her mind drifted back, as it often did, to her mother.

Roslyn Crawford had been the kind of woman who could walk into a room and immediately absorb all the chaos, harness it, and whip it into purpose. She'd always seemed to know what everyone needed—her clients, her family, the staff at Crawford's Pet Supplies, and, most of all, Evelyn. After the cancer diagnosis, Evelyn had expected her mother to shrink, to become a shadow of the force she'd always been. But no: if anything, Roslyn grew sharper, more deliberate, as if her remaining time on earth was something she had to deploy with surgical precision.

Evelyn remembered the Christmas before Roslyn died. She'd come home from work—exhausted, trying to balance her new role at Crawford's—and found her mother on the floor, knee-deep in tinsel, untangling a mess of lights with a patience that bordered on religious.

"Sometimes the best way to solve a problem," her mother had said, "is to stop thinking so hard about the problem and just let your hands do the work." Evelyn, sceptical, had tried it, and had been shocked when the strands yielded in moments. It wasn't about brute force or even cleverness; it was about not giving up, and maybe, she thought now, about not doing it alone.

She wondered, as she often did, what advice her mother would offer her now. Maybe nothing so direct. More likely, Roslyn would have found a way to push Evelyn into something that felt like her own idea, to prod her gently into seeking what she really wanted rather than what she thought she was supposed to want.

Evelyn grabbed and stared at her phone, her finger hovering over her father's contact. She'd been avoiding this call for weeks, the weight of her professional struggles pressing down on her.

Before she could second-guess herself, she pressed 'call'.

Four rings. Five rings. Voicemail.

"Dad," she began, her voice tight. "I know you're probably on some tropical island, but I need to talk to you. The board is breathing down my neck, and I'm struggling to keep Crawford's running the way Mum would have wanted. I don't know if I'm doing this right."

She paused, taking a deep breath.

A text pinged almost immediately after she hung up.

Richard

Can't talk now, love. But I hear you. We'll catch up soon.

Evelyn stared at the message, a familiar mixture of frustration and resignation washing over her. Soon never seemed to come.

Just then, another text arrived.

Richard

Your mother would be proud of you. Always.

The message hung there, simple yet profound. For a moment, Evelyn felt a weight lift from her shoulders, but the uncertainty remained.

Did she want to run a multinational company? Not particularly. Did she want to be remembered as the "Ice Queen," the automaton who broke records and never broke a smile? *Definitely* not. Evelyn realized, with a pang, that she wanted to be a force for something—maybe even something a little messy, a little unpredictable, like a sanctuary for unwanted dogs. Or a relationship that didn't fit perfectly into the prescribed Crawford narrative.

She rolled onto her side, pulling the duvet tighter. It was embarrassing how much comfort she took in thinking about a Cocker Spaniel with a patch over one eye. And it was more embarrassing still to think of Alyssa's face, all warm eyes and wild hair, and to realize that, for the first time in years, she felt an itch for more than just another task, another win.

The partnership with Four Paws, she decided, would be her project. Not the sanitised, marketable version, but the real thing—a shot at meaning, at connection. Maybe she'd even bring Bug home one day, if Alyssa was agreeable. She could almost imagine his paws clicking on the hardwood, his tail thumping against the baseboard, his gentle brown eyes watching her with the same patient expectation she'd seen in Alyssa's.

She would call Maggie in the morning, tell her to set up a lunch with Alyssa. Not for business, not even for PR, but just because she wanted to. Evelyn wasn't sure what would happen, or even what she hoped would happen, but the not knowing was, for once, exciting.

She closed her eyes, exhaled, and let herself drift. In the half-dream state between wakefulness and sleep, she found her mother waiting for her in a room full of tangled Christmas lights. Roslyn didn't say anything. She just handed Evelyn an end of the strand and smiled.

10

Sunlight, Schedules, and Selective Socialising

EVELYN

The morning after was, predictably, awful.

Evelyn woke with a wine headache that felt like someone had taken a cheese grater to the inside of her skull. She'd slept through her alarm—an unprecedented failure—and had to skip her usual routine of coffee, breakfast, and the twenty minutes of silent dread she usually devoted to preparing for the day ahead.

She arrived at the office at eight-fifteen, which was late by her standards and practically lunchtime by her father's. Maggie was already at her desk, looking annoyingly fresh and holding a takeaway cup that smelled like salvation.

"You look like death," Maggie said cheerfully, handing over the coffee. "Rough night?"

"Wine," Evelyn muttered, accepting the cup with both hands like a supplicant at an altar. "Too much wine."

"Well, at least you're consistent." Maggie followed her into the office, clipboard in hand. "You've got the budget review at nine, the marketing presentation at eleven, and lunch with the board at one. Also, someone from IT wants to talk to you about the server migration, but I told them you'd rather set yourself on fire."

"Accurate," Evelyn said, collapsing into her chair. The office felt too bright, too loud, too everything. She closed her eyes and tried to remember why she'd thought running a company was a good idea.

"Oh, and the dog situation seems to be settling in nicely," Maggie added, her tone casual but her eyes sharp. "Apparently half the building is already in love. The other half is pretending to be annoyed but secretly taking photos."

Evelyn felt a flutter of something in her chest—anticipation, maybe, or curiosity about how the partnership was progressing. She thought about Bug, about Alyssa, about the apology she'd accepted yesterday.

"Good," Evelyn said, trying to sound professional and not at all like someone who'd spent last night thinking about a certain sanctuary owner. "That's...good."

Maggie gave her a look that suggested she wasn't fooled for a second, but mercifully said nothing.

The morning passed in a blur of spreadsheets and passive-aggressive emails. Evelyn powered through the budget review on autopilot, nodding in the right places and making the occasional comment that sounded vaguely intelligent. By eleven, her headache had downgraded from "cheese grater" to "mild concussion," which she considered a win.

She was halfway through the marketing presentation—something about social media engagement and influencer partnerships that made her want to lie down in a dark room—when there was a soft scratching at her door.

Evelyn ignored it. Probably someone from accounts, or a delivery, or the ghost of corporate ambition past.

The scratching continued, patient and persistent.

"Come in," she called, not looking up from her laptop.

The door didn't open. The scratching intensified.

Evelyn sighed, stood, and crossed the office. She pulled the door open, fully prepared to deliver a withering comment about the importance of opposable thumbs in a professional environment.

Bug sat in the corridor, looking up at her with an expression of mild reproach, as if she'd kept him waiting an unreasonable amount of time.

"Oh," Evelyn said.

Bug tilted his head, one ear flopping forward in a way that should not have been as devastating as it was.

"You're...here," Evelyn continued, feeling foolish. "Again."

Bug stood, trotted past her into the office, and made a beeline for the expansive floor-to-ceiling windows. He sat directly in the patch of sunlight streaming through the glass, his black and white fur catching the light, and settled down with a soft sigh.

Evelyn stared at him. Then she stared at the open door. Then she stared at Bug again.

"Right," she said to no one in particular. "This is happening."

She closed the door—gently, so as not to disturb him—and returned to her desk. Bug didn't move. He just lay there, a small black-and-white comma of contentment, soaking up the November sun like it was his job.

Evelyn tried to focus on her laptop. She really did. But her eyes kept drifting to the window, to the dog, to the way his chest rose and fell with each breath.

It was...peaceful. Absurdly so. It's why she'd thought about bringing him to her office again last night as she pondered life whilst trying to capture the perpetually elusive sleep she so desperately needed.

Lasting ten minutes before giving up entirely. Evelyn stood, walked over to the window, and sat on the floor beside Bug. He opened one eye, regarded her with what might have been approval, and went back to sleep.

Evelyn leaned her head against the wall and let herself just...stop. No emails. No meetings. No expectations. Just her, a dog, and the city sprawling out below them.

"You're a terrible influence," she told Bug.

Bug's stubby tail thumped once against the floor.

Evelyn smiled.

By the end of the week, Bug's visits had become routine.

He arrived every morning around ten, scratched at her door with the patience of a saint, and let himself in the moment she opened it. He always went straight to the window, always claimed the same patch of sunlight, and always stayed for exactly two hours before trotting back out again.

Evelyn had no idea how he knew when two hours were up. She suspected he had an internal clock more accurate than anything Swiss engineering could produce.

On Tuesday, she'd tried to work through his visit. She'd lasted forty-five minutes before abandoning her laptop and joining him on the floor. They'd sat together in companionable silence, watching the city move below them, and Evelyn had felt something in her chest loosen—a knot she hadn't realized, or at least admitted, was there.

On Wednesday, she'd brought a cushion. Bug had immediately claimed it as his own, circling three times before collapsing with a sigh that suggested he'd been waiting his entire life for someone to provide proper bedding.

On Thursday, Maggie had walked in to find Evelyn lying on the floor, one hand resting on Bug's back, staring at the ceiling.

"Should I be concerned?" Maggie had asked.

"Probably," Evelyn had replied.

Maggie had nodded, set a cup of tea on the desk, and left without another word.

On Friday, Alyssa came to collect him.

Evelyn heard the knock and felt an irrational surge of disappointment. She'd grown used to Bug's quiet presence, to the way he made the office feel less like a prison and more like a place where she could breathe.

"Come in," she called, trying to sound professional and not at all like someone who'd spent the last two hours lying on the floor with a dog.

Alyssa stepped in, her hair pulled back in a messy ponytail, her flannel shirt dusted with what looked like kibble. She looked tired but happy—the kind of tired that came from doing work that was a passion more than a career.

"Hey," Alyssa said, her smile warm and easy. "Just checking in on Bug. Making sure he's not causing too much trouble."

"He's been perfect," Evelyn said, and meant it.

Alyssa's smile widened. "He likes you."

"How can you tell?"

"He doesn't visit just anyone. Trust me, I've tried to get him to socialise with half the building. He's very...selective."

Evelyn felt absurdly pleased by this. "Well. He's welcome here. Anytime."

"Good to know." Alyssa crossed the room and crouched beside Bug, scratching behind his ears. He opened one eye, gave her a look that clearly said you're interrupting, and went back to sleep.

Alyssa laughed. "Yeah, you're definitely his person now."

"I'm not—" Evelyn started, then stopped. Because maybe she was. Maybe that wasn't such a terrible thing.

They stood there for a moment, the silence stretching between them, comfortable and strange all at once.

"So," Alyssa said, straightening up. "How's the partnership going? From your end, I mean. Any complaints? Concerns? Employees threatening mutiny?"

"Quite the opposite, actually," Evelyn admitted. "Morale's up. Productivity's...well, it's about the same, but people seem happier. Less stressed."

"That's the magic of dogs," Alyssa said. "They don't care about your job title or your quarterly targets. They just want to be near you."

Evelyn thought about Bug, about the way he'd chosen her office, her window, her company. "It's nice," she said quietly. "Having him here."

"He thinks so too." Alyssa hesitated, then added, "You know, if you ever want to visit the sanctuary, you're welcome. See where he comes from. Meet the rest of the pack."

Evelyn's heart did something complicated. "I'd like that."

"Yeah?" Alyssa's face lit up, and Evelyn felt that flutter again, stronger this time.

"Yeah."

"Cool. I'll, uh, I'll text you some dates. We can figure it out."

"Sounds good."

Alyssa lingered for another moment, then seemed to remember herself. "Right. I should...I've got about fifteen other dogs to check on. But I'll see you Monday?"

"Monday," Evelyn confirmed.

Alyssa left, and the office felt emptier without her. Bug, sensing the shift, opened his eyes and looked at Evelyn with what might have been sympathy.

"Don't start," Evelyn told him.

Bug yawned.

The weekend passed in its usual haze of work and wine and staring at the city. Evelyn tried to focus on the quarterly reports, on the budget projections, on anything that wasn't the way Alyssa's smile had made her feel like a teenager with a crush.

It was ridiculous. She barely knew the woman. They'd had, what, three proper conversations? Four if you counted the apology, which Evelyn was trying very hard not to think about.

But there was something about Alyssa—something warm and solid and real—that made Evelyn want to be around her. To talk to her. To see what would happen if she let herself be something other than the boss for five minutes.

On Sunday night, she texted Maggie.

Evelyn stared at her phone for a long time after that, Maggie's words echoing in her head.

Scared of being happy.

Was that it? Was that why she kept everyone at arm's length, why she worked herself to exhaustion, why she'd let Mindy cheat on her without even putting up a fight?

She thought about her mother, about the way Roslyn had loved fiercely and without reservation. About the way she'd filled every room with warmth and laughter and the kind of joy that made people want to be near her.

Evelyn had spent so long trying to be strong, to be untouchable, that she'd forgotten how to be soft.

But Bug had reminded her. And Alyssa—God, Alyssa—had made her want to try.

She fell asleep that night with her phone in her hand, a half-written text to Alyssa glowing on the screen.

She deleted it. Tried again.

Deleted that too.

In the end, she sent nothing. But the wanting was there, bright and terrifying and impossible to ignore.

Monday morning arrived with the usual dread, but this time it was tempered by something else: anticipation.

Evelyn got to the office early, made herself a coffee, and left her door slightly ajar. Just in case.

At ten o'clock exactly, Bug scratched at the door.

Evelyn rolled her eyes at the pup's insistence that he be formally greeted, instead of just walking through the gap Evelyn had left him. Smiling, she opened the door further and gestured for him to enter, which he seemed to appreciate. He trotted in like he owned the place, heading straight for his spot by the window.

"Morning," Evelyn said.

Bug stepped onto his cushion, turned in a circle, and flopped down with a contented sigh.

Evelyn sat beside him, her back against the wall, her coffee growing cold in her hands.

Outside, the city hummed with its usual chaos. Inside, everything was still.

"You know," Evelyn said quietly, "I think you might be the best thing that's happened to me in a very long time."

Bug opened one eye, looked at her, and closed it again.

Evelyn smiled.

11

Guinness, Glutes, and Grumpy Snuggle Bugs

Alyssa

November was flying by. The partnership with Crawford's was sailing along brilliantly. All the dogs were being spoiled by their volunteers, and it made Alyssa's heart sing to watch some of her more timid dogs come out of their shells.

The offices were now decorated to the nines in Christmas apparel. Crawford's Pet Supplies really took the festive season seriously. Best of all, Evelyn had gifted each of Alyssa's dogs a brand new coat, fresh off the production line. The only pooch not happy about the new winter wear was Bug. He was not impressed at all, which shouldn't have come as a surprise. Bug liked things a certain way, and getting jammed into a fluffy coat was not how he wanted to spend his time.

"Al, have you seen Bug?"

For the past three weeks, that sentence was asked daily by Lil. Alyssa had long stopped worrying about Bug's Houdini act. She knew exactly where to find him, and she wasn't about to stop him from going there.

Evelyn had said nothing about the little dog travelling up to her office daily. In fact, Alyssa had noticed Evelyn had started to leave her door ajar, which made her smile.

Sure, Alyssa could just ask Evelyn outright if she wanted to be Bug's new volunteer, but that meant Alyssa wouldn't have much of an excuse to go up to the twentieth floor daily. As it stood, Alyssa would let Bug go for a few hours, then wander up to Evelyn's office to "check in."

Nine times out of ten, Alyssa would catch Evelyn on the floor with Bug, rubbing his head or belly. Sometimes they would be standing together looking out over London. Occasionally, Alyssa worried Evelyn probably didn't have the time to be entertaining Bug, but then she'd stop and flip it over. Maybe entertaining Bug was exactly what Evelyn needed. Who was Alyssa to decide otherwise?

"You know where he is," she chuckled, shaking her head at Lil.

"I know, I just like asking it. It's like our thing now," Lil grinned. "Are you going up to get him?"

"I suppose I should." Alyssa tried to sound nonchalant.

"Oh, look at the time. It's almost lunch. You could grab something for Evelyn before going to retrieve Bug. Wouldn't that be kind?" Lil's shit-eating grin was just too much. For the past few weeks, Alyssa had put up with Lil's comments and suggestions.

"You know what? I think I will."

So Alyssa might have a tiny crush on the CEO, and sure, she was pretty crap at hiding it from her best friend who liked to tease her mercilessly, but that wasn't going to stop her from admitting how she felt. Evelyn Crawford was intriguing, funny, kind, sometimes stern, but overall utterly magnetic.

Alyssa and Evelyn chatted daily. They spent their time talking about this and that. Only covering surface topics, but it allowed them to get to know each other.

For example, Alyssa now knew that Evelyn had a major man crush on Jason Statham. Hawaiian pizza was her favourite food. The argument of whether pineapple should belong on pizza was a doozy. Eventually, they had to agree to disagree. Evelyn's favourite colour was emerald green, and her favourite band was The Red Hot Chili Peppers.

Alyssa told Evelyn about her first crush on a girl. About her first date with a guy. How her parents threw her a coming out party at sixteen. Most importantly, Alyssa filled Evelyn in on her pet history. All the dogs and cats she'd had as a kid. It surprised Alyssa to find out Evelyn had only ever had one pet, and that was a hamster.

"Knock, knock." Trying to push open Evelyn's heavy ass door with her hands full of takeout food and coffee wasn't the easiest of things.

"Jesus, hang on, let me help," Evelyn said, rushing over to relieve Alyssa of the bags. "You brought lunch?"

"Well, yeah. Is that okay? I just figured I was going to eat, and I knew I would have to come up and make sure Bug was here so..."

"Alyssa, it's perfect, thank you. I thought I was going to have to skip lunch today. The meeting with the board ran over by an hour, leaving me no time to grab food."

"Well, fear not. You have a chicken mayo baguette with your name on it. Literally." Alyssa laughed, holding out the wrapped sandwich that had Evelyn's name scrawled on it in black pen.

"Did you go to Marco's?" Evelyn gushed. Alyssa loved how excited the woman got. Alyssa nodded with a big smile. "That place is my favourite. How did you know?"

"I've seen Maggie bring you food from there before, so I made a leap."

"God, I could kiss you." Alyssa froze. Evelyn obviously didn't register what she'd just said. No, she was too busy stuffing her face, moaning. Moaning! Dear Lord, Alyssa wanted to be that sandwich.

"Do you want to come out for a drink tonight?" The question was out of Alyssa's mouth before she could overthink it. A few employees went to the local Irish pub down the street once or twice a week and had asked Alyssa and Lil to join them. Now Alyssa wanted Evelyn to be there. More time outside of the office environment and all that.

"Oh," Evelyn coughed, swallowing her baguette. "I...I probably have to work late."

"Nonsense. Come on, just for one drink. It is the holiday season, after all." Alyssa watched Evelyn roll her eyes. "Don't you like Christmas?"

"I like it enough."

"Wow, way to convince me there, Evie." Alyssa laughed.

"Christmas is fine. It just means more work for me."

"Then going to the pub for a drink is the perfect excuse to unwind a little. Come on. For me? A bunch of us are going." Alyssa gave Evelyn her best puppy eyes. Her grin spread widely when she saw the CEO's resolve falter.

"Fine, one drink, but then I have to get on."

"Shake on it," Alyssa smirked, thrusting her hand to shake Evelyn's. Laughing, they sealed the deal. "Now, eat up. You've got a long afternoon ahead. I'll take Bug back downstairs."

"Oh...alright then."

Alyssa didn't miss the flash of disappointment that ran over Evelyn's beautiful features.

"I'll swing by your office at half five. Be ready!" Alyssa didn't stick around long enough for Evelyn to answer. With her half-finished sandwich in one hand and Bug tucked under her arm, Alyssa made her exit. Bug didn't help the situation by trying his damndest to nibble the sandwich as she ran the gauntlet of office workers, who had a habit of jutting out their chairs randomly.

After a short ride down, the elevator doors slid open. Bug wriggled himself free, determined to get over to the patch of sunlight shining through the lower office window. Alyssa had ten minutes to wolf down her lunch before she had to head out for the afternoon.

Just as her lips met the bread, a shadow loomed over her. Looking up, she was pleasantly surprised to see Josh, one of the building's security officers.

"Hi," he said with a grin. Josh was tall, blonde and stacked. Alyssa could see his muscles through his shirt, which did rather naughty things to her.

"Hey, Josh, how's it going?"

"Great. Sorry to interrupt your lunch. Just wanted to make sure you were coming along tonight?"

"Yup, that's the plan. Is Terry coming too?"

"Yeah, says he needs a cold one after the week he's had with his fella."

"Oh no, trouble in paradise?" Alyssa liked Terry a lot. He came across as a little gruff, but he was a big ol' teddy bear. His long-term boyfriend was the sweetest man she'd ever met. Funny, really, because he and Terry were like chalk and cheese, but it worked for them.

"Ned threw a wedge of brie at him because he left his underwear on the kitchen table again."

Alyssa threw back her head, laughing. "I would have, too," she tittered.

"So, tonight, you'll be there."

"Yeah, I just have a few things to do, but I'll be back here before half five."

"Cool, see you then."

Alyssa watched Josh walk away. Those bum muscles were incredible.

"Earth to Alyssa," Lil sang.

"Yes, dear," Alyssa answered, still looking at Josh's fine glutes.

"You're terrible, do you know that?" Lil wheeled a chair over and sat next to Alyssa.

"Why am I terrible?"

"Because you're salivating over Josh whilst simultaneously drooling over Evelyn."

Alyssa failed to see the problem. "I'm young and single. What's the issue?"

"Would it kill you just to...nevermind, you do you!"

"I shall," Alyssa smirked.

"What did Josh want? Has he finally asked you out yet?"

"Nope, not outright anyway. He wanted to know if I was going to the pub tonight. I said yes. So are you, right?"

"Sure. Charlotte's taking the dogs back tonight. Pete's coming too and he's driving so we can grab a lift home from him."

"Fabulous. Right," Alyssa slapped her hands on her thighs. "I've got to go see a man about a dog."

Working with dogs was Alyssa's dream. It had been since she was small. What she didn't like about the job was having to deal with the heartache that inevitably came with it. This afternoon had been tough. One of the other local shelters had a litter of puppies brought in. Seven little fluff balls found in a garbage bag on the side of a busy road. The shelter was full and had reached out to Alyssa. The puppies were in awful shape. Each of the babies had fleas and worms.

Of course, Alyssa immediately agreed to take them on. As soon as they were treated by a vet, Alyssa would set them up in her home. That meant she had approximately three days before she would have to stop visiting Crawford's as much. The puppies would need her attention.

Five-thirty arrived and Alyssa was bang on time to collect Evelyn, who looked as if she was going to try to get out of the pub drink.

"Before you say anything, Ms Crawford, I have had a hideous afternoon and could do with a friendly face and a chat. Yes, there are other people I could chat to, but I want to chat with you, so get your coat."

Alyssa hid her grin as Evelyn opened and closed her mouth several times before closing her laptop and grabbing her coat. The commute to the pub was short. Several coworkers joined them in the lobby and walked with them. Ideally, Alyssa wanted Evelyn alone, but tonight wasn't the night for that.

The pub was busy, packed with office workers trying to shed the stress of the day. The Crawford's group had snagged a large table at the back of the pub. Alyssa sat down and removed her jacket. She was ready for a cold beer. Before she could utter a word, a pint of Guinness was placed in front of her. Josh leaned over and winked.

"Glad you made it," he said. Then he realised Alyssa wasn't alone. Evelyn was sitting there looking between them. "Oh, Ms Crawford, I didn't see you there."

"Hello, Josh," Evelyn replied with an almost cold indifference.

"Would you like a drink?" Josh was stuttering; his face had flushed.

Alyssa couldn't help but chuckle.

"I'll have what she has, please."

"On it." Josh raced over to the bar.

Alyssa turned, amused. "Do all your employees react like that around you?"

"Of course not. Josh was just embarrassed because he wanted to sit here hitting on you all night and instead he gets to sit next to his boss." Evelyn quirked her eyebrow, equally amused as Alyssa.

"Has he ever hit on you?" Alyssa didn't know why she was asking. It was none of her business.

"Nope, everyone knows I'm gay."

"So, what about female employees flirting then?"

"No, I was seeing someone and everyone knew. Crawford's a gossip mill."

"I'm sorry, was it a bad split?"

"Well, she cheated on me, but it's fine?"

What sane woman would cheat on Evelyn Crawford?

"Here you go, Ms Crawford," Josh panted, putting Evelyn's drink down a little too hard, causing some of it to slosh over the top and onto her skirt. "Oh shit, I'm so sorry," Josh spluttered.

"It's fine," Evelyn sighed, batting away his hand. "I'll be right back."

Should Alyssa go after her? Help her with the spill? No, that was stupid. Tonight was *not* turning out how she wanted. As much as she liked Josh and his assets, Alyssa really wanted to spend her time chatting with Evelyn.

"Crap, I can't believe I just did that," Josh mumbled, sitting in the seat Evelyn vacated.

"Stop worrying, Evelyn's cool. It was an accident."

"Yeah, but she's the boss." Josh shook his head, admonishing himself. "So, how was your day?"

Alyssa got lost in conversation with Josh, only realising that Evelyn hadn't returned from the toilets a while later. Looking around the pub, she couldn't see the woman anywhere. "Hey, Terry, did you see Evelyn?"

"Yeah, she left. Said something about needing a change of clothing or something."

Damn it. Being sure Evelyn was gone for the night, Alyssa couldn't hide her surprise when the CEO waltzed back in twenty minutes later in a pair of black jeans that clung to every inch of her legs and arse.

"Sorry about that, I just had to grab something dry to wear."

Alyssa looked up at Evelyn, unable to speak. Evelyn looked back down at her and then at Josh. Her eyebrow rose slowly, and her eyes bored into his.

"Oh, do you want your seat back?" he asked.

"Yes, please."

Alyssa was in awe of the woman. Sleek and elegant. Powerful, yet soft. Commanding people with the arch of an eyebrow was amazing and very hot. Josh scuttled out of the seat. Unfortunately for him, the only other vacant spot was down at the other end of the table.

"I'll...see you later then?" Josh mumbled. Alyssa offered him a little wave.

"Did I interrupt?" Evelyn asked, sitting down. Alyssa grew jealous of the pint Evelyn put to her lips.

"Not at all. We were just chatting."

Evelyn nodded and wiped a bit of foam from her top lip. "So you said you had a bad day? Tell me."

With her Guinness in hand, Alyssa walked Evelyn through her afternoon. It felt good to unload. Evelyn didn't offer an opinion, she just sat and listened. She made Alyssa feel heard.

"Can I ask about Bug?" They had been quiet for several seconds after Alyssa finished ranting about her day.

"Of course. What do you want to know?"

"Well first, why Bug? I mean, it's an odd name, don't you think?"

Alyssa laughed. It wasn't the first time she'd heard that said. "Bug is a perfect name for him. It sums him up."

"What do you mean?"

"Okay, first, when he gets to know you and is comfortable, he is a massive snuggle bug. I'm talking world-class cuddler. So that's the first connection: Snuggle Bug. Second, he was born a grumpy old man at Christmas. He was never an overly excited puppy. He liked to just sleep and grumble anytime we tried to get him to walk or play. So with him being a December baby and a miserable sausage, you can understand why we linked his Scrooge-like behaviour to his name. You know Bah Humbug. Third, he is black and white. Just like the hard-boiled sweet humbugs."

"I'm starting to see the pattern." Evelyn laughed.

Alyssa smiled. Evelyn's low, sultry laugh was outstanding.

"Last but not least, he bugs the crap out of me most days."

"How?" Evelyn snickered.

"Bug has a few interesting habits and traits. I'm not going to tell you because I think it's something you have to discover on your own. But! When you do, some of those traits will bug you. Even though he is totally adorable. That dog is special. Only the lucky get to really know him."

"I hope I'm one of those lucky ones," Evelyn sighed.

"You are. He hasn't visited anyone else in the building since the day we arrived. Whether you like it or not, he's made you his friend."

"I like when he comes to my office."

Alyssa wanted to reach out and cup Evelyn's cheek. She was so sweet and almost shy as she spoke.

"Do you want to set up a time to visit the centre? We never got around to it." Alyssa blurted.

"Really, you still want me to come?"

"Yeah, totally. I think it would be really good for you to see what we do. Especially if we work together in the future."

"I'd love that." Silence settled between them. Alyssa was very aware of Lil's eyes drilling into her from across the table.

"Has Bug been with you since he was a baby?"

"Since he turned one. He was born on a working farm, but he was the runt of the litter and scared of gunshots. The farmer spent a few months trying to train him, then gave up and dumped him on my doorstep."

"Poor boy."

"Yeah. I thought he would get adopted quickly, but it never happened. For some reason, he always gets overlooked."

"I don't know how anyone could overlook him. Have you seen his face and those bloody sad eyes he makes when he wants something?"

Alyssa burst out laughing. "So you are getting to know his traits then, huh? That lad can manipulate the hardest of people. It's a gift."

"Could...?"

Alyssa waited for Evelyn to continue, but the CEO had become quite timid, her hand rubbing the back of her neck.

"Could?" Alyssa urged.

"Could I be his volunteer from now on? I mean officially. He spends his day with me anyway. Or maybe we could share him. You know, if I have a board meeting or something, then you could have him...but otherwise he can stay in the office with me?"

"Evelyn, that would be wonderful! Yes, yes, yes, of course you can be his volunteer." At that moment, Alyssa knew something good was on the horizon. Whether it be for Bug or for her, she wasn't sure, but she knew Evelyn Crawford was the key.

12

Fleas Navidad and Festive Feelings

ALYSSA

Alyssa's workweek, like all good things, had to come to an end. Not that she wanted it to—especially not with the office so full of dog hair and Christmas lights and, more importantly, the regular appearance of one Evelyn Crawford, who had a way of looking both exhausted and annoyingly flawless at the same time. Not that Alyssa was paying special attention or anything. She just...noticed things. Like how Evelyn's laugh, when it snuck out, sounded like someone daring the universe to be less serious for once. Or the way she'd flick a pen between her knuckles when she was thinking, fast and rhythmic, until a good idea came and she'd set it down like a gavel.

It was Thursday, the day before the sanctuary's big holiday fundraiser at the local Christmas market, which Crawford's Pet Supplies was sponsoring. More dogs than ever, more holiday decorations, more people darting from desk to desk with stacks of last-minute paperwork that needed to be filed before the market officially opened. Even though the sanctuary would be closed until January, the fundraiser was crucial—it would help cover operating costs for the year ahead, and there was no better place to host it than the Christmas Market.

Alyssa had just finished wrangling a set of mismatched, enthusiastic mutts back into their respective pens—new volunteers were always so optimistic about "open office" time, until the puppies started chasing their own tails and then each other's—and she was looking forward to her reward: sneaking up to the executive floor to check on Bug, who was presumably sprawled out on Evelyn's couch like the world's least productive assistant.

"Hey, Lee, can you finish up here?" Alyssa called, already halfway out the door.

Lee, who was busy retrieving a half-chewed stress ball from under the couch, gave her a thumbs up. "Are you seeing the boss lady again?" he asked, not bothering to lower his voice.

Alyssa rolled her eyes, but she didn't slow down. The truth was, she'd seen more of Evelyn Crawford in the last month than she had her own reflection. It was not a hardship.

She took the stairs two at a time—Bug had, after all, proven himself capable of not only finding the CEO's office but also the break room's secret biscuit stash, and Alyssa figured any destruction would be proportional to the length of her absence. She slowed as she reached the top floor, trying not to look too eager, and peeked through the glass panel of Evelyn's door.

There they were. Evelyn and Bug, both in identical states of intense focus: Evelyn hunched over her laptop, typing with controlled aggression, and Bug splayed at her feet, snoring like a chainsaw in sleep mode. The scene was so peaceful that Alyssa hesitated to knock, but she did anyway, then entered without waiting for an answer.

"Hi," she said, aiming for casual and landing somewhere near "weirdly cheerful substitute teacher."

Evelyn's head snapped up. She blinked twice, then relaxed when she saw it was Alyssa. "Oh, thank God. I thought it was the finance team again."

Bug lifted his head, looked at Alyssa with soulful reproach, then burrowed deeper into the rug, clearly unimpressed.

"How's my little runaway?" Alyssa grinned, dropping to her haunches to ruffle Bug's ears. Even though Bug was officially Evelyn's buddy, Alyssa still liked to play on his well-earned moniker.

"He's single-handedly responsible for at least two spreadsheets being erased today," Evelyn replied. "Not that I'm complaining."

It was the first time Alyssa had seen Evelyn in anything other than a suit, and even though the woman's "casual" was still a cashmere sweater and tailored trousers, she looked...softer. Less "CEO" and more "person you'd want to share a pizza with."

"Sorry to barge in," Alyssa said, pushing herself upright and dusting imaginary dog hair from her jeans. "I just wanted to remind you about tomorrow night."

Evelyn's brows knitted. "Tomorrow night?"

"Yeah, the Four Paws fundraiser at the market."
Alyssa paused, suddenly worried she'd miscalculated.
"You...are coming, right?"

"Oh, right, yes!" Evelyn's face coloured, just a touch.
"Sorry. My brain's at capacity right now. Tomorrow night,
the Christmas market, yes. I'll be there."

Alyssa watched as Evelyn's lips curled up, almost like
she was looking forward to it. That was new.

"Do you want to go together?" Alyssa asked, trying to
sound casual.

"Together?" Evelyn said, with a hint of playful
dryness.

Alyssa's face heated for some reason. "I mean, we
could just arrive together and then do our own thing.
Or—"

"Alyssa. Breathe." Evelyn's eyes twinkled, a sure sign
she was teasing. "I'd love to go together."

Alyssa grinned, sudden and wide. "Great. I'll, um,
pick you up. Or we can meet there, if you want. Whatever's
easiest."

"Pick me up," Evelyn said. "It'll give me an excuse to
get out of here early."

"Six thirty?" Alyssa ventured.

"Six thirty's perfect."

There was a beat of silence. Bug snored, oblivious. Evelyn looked at Alyssa, then at Bug, then back at Alyssa, like she was trying to solve a particularly challenging puzzle.

"I'll bring the dog," Alyssa said.

"Please do," Evelyn replied.

Alyssa left before she could say something embarrassing. As the door closed behind her, Alyssa heard Evelyn laugh, soft and unguarded.

The morning of the market fundraiser, Alyssa woke up before dawn, heart pounding with a combination of excitement and anticipation. She ran through her usual routine: feeding the early riser dogs, driving into the city, making sure the temporary outdoor kennels were set up near the market. She was halfway through organising a donation crate when Lil appeared at her side, wielding a clipboard and an expression of pure mischief.

"Tell me you have an outfit for tonight," Lil said, not even bothering with a greeting.

Alyssa squinted at her. "I'm going to be wrangling dogs and hauling equipment. I'll be covered in drool by eight p.m., tops."

"Excuses," Lil said. "This is a social event, not a cage cleaning. Look, I even got you a top."

She held up a slightly-too-small red jumper decorated with a grinning reindeer and the words "Fleas Navidad." It was aggressively festive.

Alyssa made a face, but took the knitted monstrosity. "You're the worst."

"I know," Lil grinned, then sobered. "Seriously, though, are you okay about tonight?"

"Why wouldn't I be?"

Lil's eyebrows shot up. "Alyssa, you've been vibrating like a jackhammer since Tuesday. You like her."

"So?" Alyssa tried for nonchalance and failed spectacularly.

"So, don't overthink it. Just go, have fun, maybe flirt a little."

Alyssa was about to retort, but Bug chose that moment to butt her in the calf, demanding a scratch. She obliged, rubbing his head until he melted into a puddle of pleasure at her feet.

"See, Bug's got the right idea," Lil said, wandering off to scold a volunteer for putting a dog harness on upside down.

Alyssa watched her go, then looked down at Bug. "It's just a market, right?"

Bug wagged his tail in what Alyssa could only interpret as reluctant encouragement.

At six fifteen, Alyssa stood outside Evelyn's building, sweating under her borrowed "Fleas Navidad" jumper and a slightly-worse-for-wear parka. Bug was beside her, dressed in a sensible tartan scarf.

"He's not wearing the antlers, don't even try," Alyssa had warned Lil.

The city was awash in holiday light, headlights and Christmas decorations and the glow of a hundred corner shops, all blending together into a kind of festive haze.

She checked her phone—early, but not too early. She texted "Outside!" with a bug emoji and waited.

Two minutes later, the front doors opened and Evelyn emerged. She was wearing a long navy peacoat, a black scarf, and the sort of high-heeled boots that Alyssa suspected had never once touched a puddle. She looked every inch the CEO, except for the way she was clutching a battered reusable shopping bag and smiling as soon as she spotted Alyssa.

Bug trotted forward, tail wagging so hard his whole body wobbled. Evelyn bent to greet him, murmuring, "Hello, troublemaker," and ruffling his ears.

"You're early," Evelyn said, straightening and fixing her gaze on Alyssa.

"So are you," Alyssa replied. She realized she was smiling like an idiot and tried to dial it back, but it didn't work.

"Shall we?" Evelyn said.

They walked side by side through the city's early winter darkness, Bug weaving a lazy figure-eight around their ankles. The market was only a few blocks away, but the closer they got, the more the air vibrated with music, the scent of roasted chestnuts, and the shouts of people hawking everything from mulled wine to novelty baubles.

"I don't remember it always being this packed." Evelyn said as they pushed through the first wave of tourists.

Alyssa considered. "It's London at Christmas. I think this is normal." She steered them toward the less-crowded side street, the one lined with stalls selling handmade soaps and scented candles.

Bug, predictably, made a beeline for the bakery tent. Alyssa followed, and Evelyn followed Alyssa, which made Alyssa's heart jump a little. They sampled cinnamon rolls and then something called a "mince pie doughnut," which Evelyn declared "offensively good."

They stopped to watch a busker playing "Last Christmas" on a violin. The woman's hair was a mass of black curls that rivalled Alyssa's own, and for a moment, Alyssa caught Evelyn looking at her, eyes soft and maybe a little vulnerable.

"What?" Alyssa asked.

Evelyn shook her head, smiling. "I was just thinking how nice it is to see this place from your side of things."

"My side?"

"There's something about you here. You're more...grounded, I guess. Like your mind isn't somewhere else, thinking of a million problems that might crop up."

Alyssa blinked. No one except Lil had ever said that to her before. "Is that a good thing?"

"Absolutely."

"Well, you're not so bad yourself, Ms Crawford."

Evelyn laughed, deep and clear. "Do you want to see my favourite stall?"

Alyssa raised an eyebrow. "You have a favourite?"

"Of course. I've been coming here for years. We've sponsored the market for over a decade now."

Evelyn led the way, weaving confidently through the crowd until they reached a small, dimly lit tent at the edge of the market. Inside, paper lanterns in varying shades of green and gold hung overhead, casting a warm glow. The air was heavy with fresh pine and something sharper—citrus, perhaps.

The vendor, an older woman with a shock of white hair and a knowing smile, looked up as they entered. "Evelyn, darling it's so wonderful to see you again!" she called, her Brixton accent unmistakable. "I saved you one, like I do every year. I'm so glad you're finally here."

Alyssa wondered what the woman meant by that. Evelyn's face lit up in a way Alyssa had never seen before. "You're the best, Imelda."

The woman produced a wreath made entirely of rosemary, bay leaves, and dried oranges. Evelyn took it with both hands, inhaling deeply. "It smells like my mum's kitchen."

Imelda turned her attention to Alyssa, looking her up and down with frank appraisal. "Who's this then?"

Alyssa could feel herself blushing. "Alyssa Fox. I run the dog sanctuary up the road."

Imelda looked from Alyssa back to Evelyn with a smirk. "You two have a lovely evening, yeah?"

Alyssa glanced at Evelyn, who was looking at her with an expression halfway between pleased and slightly embarrassed.

"We will," Alyssa said, and meant it.

They left Imelda's stall with the wreath in tow, Bug making friends with every child and pensioner who offered him a scratch. Alyssa bought a pair of gingerbread men, one with an evil-looking grin, and they ate them while watching a troupe of middle-aged carollers perform "All I Want for Christmas is You" with alarming sincerity.

As the evening wore on, the crowd thinned, the lights glowed warmer, and Alyssa found herself walking closer to Evelyn than she had planned. She liked the way Evelyn's arm brushed hers every few steps, liked the way their conversation meandered from work to childhood stories to the most embarrassing things they'd ever done on a first date.

Evelyn's was impressively mortifying. "I once dropped a full glass of Merlot in a woman's lap and then tried to mop it up with my sleeve."

Alyssa tried to top that, but the best she could do was, "I once lost a bet and had to take someone out to a fancy restaurant wearing a ridiculous Christmas jumper. In July."

Evelyn choked on her mulled wine. "Please tell me there are pictures."

"There are, and you'll never see them."

They looped around the market one last time, then wandered down a quieter street toward a small public garden, just for the sake of walking.

"This was good," Evelyn said, voice soft.

"Yeah," Alyssa replied. "It was."

Bug circled them once, then sat, looking expectantly at Alyssa's pocket. Alyssa snorted and nudged Evelyn's shoulder with her own.

"You know," she said, "I was worried you'd cancel on me tonight."

Evelyn smiled, but there was a sadness under it. "I almost did."

"Why?"

"Because this—" Evelyn gestured to the two of them, to Bug, to the whole bright, messy night, "—is new. I'm not great with new things. I've been stuck in a routine for so long, feeling like I'm barely keeping my head above water."

Alyssa nodded, letting the silence settle. She wanted to say something reassuring, something cool and memorable, but the words wouldn't come.

"I think you're doing great, Evelyn. And I happen to like new things," Alyssa replied, hoping she didn't sound lame.

They walked in comfortable silence until they reached the edge of the garden, where the city's noise faded to a dull hum.

They returned to Evelyn's building, Bug padding contentedly behind them, and rode the elevator up to the Evelyn's floor. Neither spoke much; the city lights outside said enough. At Evelyn's door, they hesitated—caught between the night's momentum and the awkwardness of real life.

"I've got tea," Evelyn said.

"Sounds good," Alyssa replied.

Evelyn shed her coat, then stood there, suddenly shy. "I don't usually do this."

Alyssa smiled, stepping closer but maintaining a respectful distance. "That makes two of us."

They spent the next hour on the sofa, sipping tea and sharing stories—about their families, about their favourite holidays, about everything and nothing. At some point,

Alyssa's hand came close to Evelyn's, hovering just near enough to feel the warmth between them.

Eventually, the conversation wound down. Bug curled at their feet, sighing with contentment. Alyssa watched the city lights flicker through the window, and for the first time in a long time, didn't feel the need to be anywhere else.

13

Caravans, Confessions, and Clarifications

EVELYN

The first week in December was the only time Evelyn could carve out some space for a visit to Four Paws. The night in the pub still played on a loop in Evelyn's mind. Normally, she would have made every excuse under the sun to stay in the office and get a little more work finished—Maggie could attest to that. But when someone like Alyssa Fox invites you for a drink, there is no other answer than yes. Knowing there would be other people there had been a tad disappointing. Evelyn wanted to continue their chats. Getting to know Alyssa was Evelyn's favourite thing to do now, apart from looking after Bug.

Ah, Bug, that little charmer!

Bug had a way to let Evelyn know it was time to take a break. People would think she was a sandwich short of a picnic if they heard her thoughts, but Evelyn was sure of it: Bug had special powers. He was the only creature that had got her to take a step back in months. Even Maggie had commented.

In just a few weeks, Evelyn had gone from workaholic, hell bent on spending every waking hour chained to her desk to something...different. It was hard to put a finger on what exactly had changed, but one thing was for sure, Evelyn found herself taking more breaks—even if it was just to stare out of the window with her furry friend. The pressure to be perfect and do everything herself had lessened.

That's why Evelyn knew she had to make time for the tour around Four Paws. Like Bug, the sanctuary was special. Evelyn felt it in her bones. Plus, she would get a little one-on-one time with a certain raven-haired beauty.

A solid frost clung to the ground. Evelyn's car tyres crunched loudly as she made her way down the winding gravel driveway to Four Paws. The clock read seven-thirty, which was a hideous time to be awake on a Saturday, but Alyssa had asked her to arrive early.

Pulling into the empty car park, Evelyn took a second to look at the centre. The building looked brand new. A lot of money had been invested in it, that was for sure. Evelyn got to wondering how Alyssa had secured the finances for such a place. It was well known that animal rescue centres found it hard to survive. Usually because they relied on charity.

The façade of the building was ninety percent glass. Decals stuck on the windows in the shapes of bones and dog paws softened the harshness of the glass and chrome. Smoothing down her jumper, Evelyn headed for the entrance. Her hand had just touched the handle when the door flew open and a thrilled looking Alyssa ushered her inside.

"Hey, how was the drive over?" Alyssa was dressed in her usual worn jeans and flannel shirt. Evelyn wondered if her entire wardrobe comprised jeans and shirts.

"Easy peasy. It's been a while since I've left the city."

"As soon as you're out of the hustle and bustle, it's quite a pleasant drive over, I think." Alyssa was walking as she spoke. Evelyn followed, trying to take everything in. The reception was all clean lines and chrome. On the lefthand side was another wall of glass. Through it, Evelyn could see a playroom.

"That's where we take the dogs to meet potential owners." Alyssa remarked.

"It looks wonderful." The room was set up with toys and beds. Hidey holes and adventure equipment.

"We try to cater for all our dogs. Some need to hide away for a little while before they are comfortable meeting people. That's why we have the hidey holes. Other dogs are full of energy and want to zoom around the adventure course. It's important the potential owners get to see the dog's actual personality."

"It's brilliant, Alyssa."

"Want to feed some puppies?" Alyssa grinned, her eyes sparkling.

"Are you joking? Of course I want to feed some puppies...but first can I say hello to Bug?" Evelyn had missed the little guy. It had been just over twelve hours since she'd seen him, but already she could feel his absence.

Alyssa chuckled. "He's waiting for you in my office."

Sure enough, as soon as Evelyn walked into Alyssa's office—which *was* piled high with files and dog hair—Bug came waddling over. He wasn't fat, it's just that when he wagged his stumpy tail, his whole body moved with it. He looked as if he was doing some strange version of the twist.

"Hey, little man," Evelyn crooned as she got to her knees. "Missed you, buddy," she whispered into his ear. Bug dropped his head and rammed it into Evelyn's stomach, trying to get as close as possible to her.

A good ten minutes went by of Bug demanding Evelyn's attention. It was only when Alyssa laughed and tugged on his collar the moment was broken.

"He'd have you doing that all day. Come on, we have jobs to do. You can come too, Bug."

Evelyn smiled sheepishly. She'd forgotten about everything as she massaged Bug's fur. It was just as therapeutic for her as it was for him. Getting to her feet, Evelyn shot a wink down at her favourite pooch and followed Alyssa into another room. This one had several crates with heat lamps in them.

"This is where we bring dogs that need some TLC. Right now, it's just the pups. Thankfully, all our other residents are fighting fit."

Evelyn moved quietly to the crate at the back of the room. Bending down slightly, she gazed at the mountain of fur wiggling and squeaking.

"There are seven of them," Alyssa whispered.

"It's hard to see them, they're so tightly packed together." Evelyn looked closer and could see tiny pink paws and little blue eyes.

"Let's get them fed."

Evelyn didn't move. She waited for Alyssa to return with seven bottles of milk.

"Watch what I do and then give it a go." Alyssa opened the crate and untangled one of the puppies. Evelyn gasped at how small and adorable the puppy was. All brown, with a smushed face, its eyes shining bright. She had to laugh when the little dog fought for all it was worth to get to the bottle Alyssa was dangling close to its mouth.

"He's hungry," Evelyn chuckled quietly.

"This one always is. She's going to be a tank." Alyssa laughed, finally letting the dog suckle.

Evelyn watched carefully until she was sure she knew what to do. Together, they fed each puppy until they were full to bursting.

"I'm going to stimulate them so they poop. Normally the mother would do it, but..."

Evelyn nodded, understanding the seven dogs were orphans. Evelyn regarded Alyssa with wonder. She was so fluid in her motions, so knowledgeable and sure of herself. Every dog in the centre was loved and adored. That was plain to see. For Alyssa this wasn't a job, it was a lifestyle, a passion, and Evelyn admired her for it.

"What's next, boss?"

"Let me give you the grand tour." Alyssa beamed.

Evelyn's favourite part of the tour had to be the kennels. It was obnoxiously loud, but so full of life. The dogs at Four Paws were happy and excitable. Taking the entire pack out to the playing field was certainly an experience. Together, Alyssa and Evelyn took turns running with a football, throwing tennis balls, and playing tug.

Once the fun was over, Evelyn happily helped feed and water all the dogs. It was hard work, and Evelyn wondered how much time—if any—Alyssa got to herself. Back in Alyssa's office, they sat with a fresh coffee and a box of donuts. Bug dutifully guarded them with his life. Evelyn had to laugh. He was staring at the box so hard, as though he expected to move the donuts into his mouth by sheer will...or the force, one or the other.

"This is a really impressive set-up, Alyssa. I can honestly say I've never seen a rescue centre so well equipped or managed."

"Thank you. This place is my life. All I ever wanted to do was help and work with dogs."

"Can I ask how this place is funded? Is that too personal?"

There was no way the sanctuary was funded on charity alone. Everything in the place was new and top of the line.

"It's fine. I won the Euro lottery when I was twenty-one."

Evelyn almost choked on the sip of coffee she'd just taken.

Alyssa laughed. "That's usually the response I get."

"Wow, I mean, that's awesome. Lucky you."

"Yeah, I won more money that I could ever spend and I'm not about personal materialism. My parents are new age hippies. I was practically brought up in a campervan."

"I can see that," Evelyn smiled.

"We had a house. It was only small. But my parents wanted me to experience things. They didn't want me to spend my time in front of a TV. We were always travelling around; even if it was just day trips, we were always visiting somewhere. I learned all I needed to be happy was my family and my pets."

"That's beautiful."

"It was different. I didn't have loads of friends, but I didn't mind. Anyway, when I won the lottery I knew straight away what I wanted to do, so I sunk my winnings into this place, and I've never looked back."

"I'm so impressed with you right now, Alyssa Fox."

Could this woman be any more perfect?

"Thanks. What about you? What's your story? I feel like I know you, but not the deep stuff."

Evelyn blew out a breath. "It's not exciting, really. Mum and dad started Crawford's when I was small. I remember the first shop they opened. It was like a wonderland for me. I loved helping them out and learning about animals. I grew up in the business, so it was a foregone conclusion where I would work. Even though dad is the face of the company, it was really my mum who was the driving force."

Evelyn needed to take a steadying breath. Anytime she spoke of her mum, her heart broke all over again. She gave a watery smile as Alyssa took her hand. "We were really close. I am with my dad too, but I had a special bond with my mum. Probably because we were so alike. Dad is the easygoing kind of person whereas my mum was serious. Not all the time, mind you. She knew how to let go, but she just had a focus about her."

God, I miss you, Mum.

"When dad started seeing his floozy, I found it hard." Evelyn hadn't told anyone this except for Maggie. "I felt like he just abandoned Mum. I know she was gone, but he just found someone else so fast. That's where he is now, on some tropical island with her."

"The floozy."

Evelyn chuckled. "Yes, the floozy. She's my age, for god's sake."

"Have you told your dad how you feel?"

Jesus, this was turning into a therapy session. Evelyn didn't want Alyssa to see her as a weak and vulnerable mess.

"Enough about my sad life." She replied with a half-hearted laugh.

"Is it sad? I mean, outside of losing your mum?"

Bloody hell, Alyssa was going for gold with these questions.

"I..." Should she confess how she really felt about being CEO? "Before dad went away, I was considering leaving the company."

"Wow, and now you're CEO."

"Yeah, not by choice. Dad didn't exactly give me an option."

"Why did you want to leave?"

"I love the company, don't get me wrong. It was built from hard work and love. My parents gave everything they had to it. And then they gave it to me. Well, that's how it feels. I haven't earned it...I was given it and that irritates me."

"Are you kidding me?" Evelyn was taken aback by Alyssa's sudden outburst. "Evelyn, I've known you for a month and I already know you well enough to see how bloody hard you work. How can you say you haven't earned it?"

"I had a job waiting for me since the day I could walk. How's that me earning it?"

"Alright, yes, you were given the opportunity, but I bet you worked your arse off. I'm guessing you went to university, aced business, and then steadily worked your way up through the company." Alyssa was right. Evelyn had done that. "If you weren't CEO, what would you do?"

"I have no idea. I think I would prefer to work in the charity side of the company. Like I said, I admire you for doing what you do. I'd like to do something in the same field."

"So you don't really want to leave Crawford's, just change up your position?"

Evelyn sat and thought for a minute. She'd always imagined that if she wanted something different, she would have to leave the family business behind. After all, how disappointed would her dad be that she didn't want to be at the helm, but in a lower position?

"I love Crawford's. I just need a change. Something I've done on my own."

Alyssa shrugged. "So do it then. Find something you want to do and get on with it. Evelyn, I've seen you work. I know for a fact that you could find that thing you love and make it a success. Take some time to figure out exactly what you want and go for it."

Could she really do that? Tell her dad she didn't want to be CEO? Find something within Crawford's that was just hers? Alyssa was the first person to tell her outright to go for it. Maggie was supportive, but she listened more than advised. Well, she lectured at times, but that was Maggie's love language.

"It's hard not to get swept up in you sometimes," Evelyn laughed, then stilled. Their eyes held, and Evelyn swore she saw more than friendship on Alyssa's face. It was a building heat, a crackle, and Evelyn wanted to do something about it. But she wouldn't—not when Alyssa had a partner.

This wasn't the first time Evelyn had felt the pull. There had been stolen moments at the office, afternoons when it was just the two of them, times when Evelyn had caught herself flirting and had to pull back. She'd felt guilty about it too—about how much time she spent with Alyssa when Lil wasn't around, about how easy it was to forget that Alyssa was spoken for. What struck her most was how little Alyssa and Lil actually seemed to spend together. Or talk about each other, to be honest. Evelyn could've sworn Alyssa had flirted back on more than one occasion, but she'd never acted on it. She wouldn't now, either.

Clearing her throat, Evelyn swallowed the last bit of coffee, hoping the break in eye contact would also break the tension.

"Want to stay for dinner?"

All Evelyn had to do was politely turn down Alyssa's offer to stay for dinner. Did she do that? Nope. Of course not, because she was an idiot. Even though Evelyn knew she couldn't pursue Alyssa, that didn't stop her body from wanting to be close to her.

As she helped Alyssa hand over the nightly duties to a man called Gary, her nerves kicked up a notch. It's not like they'd never shared a meal before. Blimey, they ate lunch together most days, but this felt different. Evelyn was going to be invited into Alyssa's private space, her home. A home that took Evelyn a quick minute to process.

"You live in a caravan?"

"No, I live in a mobile home. What part of that," Alyssa pointed, "looks like a caravan?" Thankfully, she was laughing as she spoke, so Evelyn didn't worry that she'd offended her.

"No, sorry, I know. I'm just surprised."

"Most people are. Come on, I'll show you around."

Evelyn had stayed in mobile homes before. Her mum and dad took her to Cornwall every year for their family holiday. Some of her best memories were in mobile homes.

Inside was deceptively large. All open plan, top of the range equipment and fittings. Evelyn instantly felt at home. Unlike her penthouse, which had always felt lonely. Even though she decorated to her own taste, it never felt cosy and homely.

"I love it, Al."

"So do I. It's super convenient for the shelter."

"And the views are superb. I bet you get a lovely sunrise from your deck."

"Indeed I do. That's why I wanted a model with a full wrap around deck. I can sit outside and enjoy the sunrise and sunset. Not that I've done it in a while."

"You should make the effort, Alyssa."

"You're right."

There it was again, that undeniable tension between them. The eye contact had to stop because it was driving Evelyn bonkers.

"Drink?"

"Please." Evelyn dropped her purse by the door and took a seat on the couch. Alyssa handed her a bottle of beer and sat beside her. Everything in Evelyn was screaming to reach out and kiss Alyssa. What she wouldn't give to run her hands through Alyssa's gorgeous hair.

The atmosphere was heady. If Evelyn didn't look away soon, she was going to do something stupid. Luckily, there was a knock at the door, which made both women jump a little. Evelyn closed her eyes and took a few steadying breaths as Alyssa moved to greet her guest.

Probably her girlfriend, you moron.

"Hannah, what brings you here?"

Evelyn looked over at the door. A very attractive woman stood with her hands in her pockets, looking at Alyssa like she hung the moon.

"I wanted to see if...look, Al, I want you to reconsider."

"Reconsider?"

"Yes, us, Al...reconsider us. I miss you. I miss your bed."

Well, that was interesting information. Evelyn didn't know where to look. She was sure Alyssa wouldn't want her privy to this conversation. Not when it implicated her cheating on Lil.

"Hannah, I told you how I feel."

There was an awkward silence. Evelyn wanted to crawl under the coffee table.

"Oh, I see," this Hannah woman sneered, peering over Alyssa's shoulder and shooting daggers Evelyn's way. "You've moved on to the next one."

"Hannah, this is Evelyn. I work with her company. I was just giving her a tour of Four Paws," Alyssa replied calmly.

"Yeah, right. You're unbelievable, Alyssa."

"No, Hannah. Stop. I was honest with you from the start. What I do in my personal life has nothing to do with you. I don't have to explain myself. Please leave."

"Maybe I should…" Evelyn began. She would be more than happy to extricate herself.

"No, Evelyn, sit down."

Sitting back on the sofa, Evelyn gave both women a tight smile. This was friggin' awkward as hell.

"Alyssa," Hannah began.

"No, I need some time to cool off. I'll call you Hannah. Good night." And that was that. Alyssa shut the door and came back to the settee.

"That was…" Evelyn began with no idea how to finish the sentence.

"Embarrassing. Awkward?" Alyssa grinned.

"Yep, all that."

"Sorry. I thought Hannah and I were on the same page. Obviously not."

Evelyn peeled the label off her beer bottle. It wasn't any of her business, but she couldn't stop herself from asking. "Does Lil know about her?"

"Yeah, of course? Why?"

That was not the answer she expected. "Oh, right. And she doesn't mind?"

"Why would she?" Alyssa asked, furrowing her brow.

"Well, I…I wouldn't want to share you, that's all."

Was that too honest?

"Why would…Evelyn, do you think Lil is my girlfriend?" Alyssa asked, her eyebrows shooting to the sky.

Evelyn felt her face heat. "Yes, you told me she was."

Alyssa made some sort of scoffing slash choking sound. "When?"

"When we first met. You said Lil was your partner," Evelyn rushed out.

"Business partner, Evelyn. Business partner. Lil has never been, and will never be, my life partner."

Well, shit! She'd got that wrong. Now she really regretted not making a move after the Christmas market.

14

Pizza, Plans, and Puppy Dog Eyes

ALYSSA

B eing made to feel like a liar was not Alyssa's idea of a good time. Three days had passed since Evelyn's visit to Four Paws—the one that had been so spectacularly disrupted by Hannah showing up. The epic miscommunication that followed. The awkward hug goodbye after Alyssa had explained that Lil wasn't her girlfriend.

Hannah had accused Alyssa of moving on to her next notch on the bedpost. Normally, an accusation like that was water off Alyssa's back. But when that comment was aimed at Evelyn, it irked her. Evelyn wasn't a notch on the bedpost. She was a friend—a very sexy friend that Alyssa wanted to do naughty things with, but not just for one night.

And that's where the lie came in. Or was it? During her time with Hannah as friends with occasional benefits, Alyssa had been straightforward, honest about her intentions—or lack thereof—because she wasn't lying when she told Hannah they could never be more than what they were.

Alyssa didn't have the time or inclination to be in a relationship. Four Paws was her chief priority. But now? Shit, there was something about Evelyn Crawford that made Alyssa, for the first time ever, want more.

Why did Bug have to go wandering off to Evelyn's office? If he'd just stayed in the lower offices, this wouldn't be happening!

Those were the kinds of thoughts that had been circulating around Alyssa's head since Evelyn's visit. Not only had they been interrupted by Hannah, but Evelyn had thought she was a cheat. How could they have gotten their wires crossed so badly? The evening had ended with an awkward goodbye and a promise for lunch on Monday.

It was Tuesday now, and no lunches had happened. Evelyn apparently couldn't stop for an hour, too swamped to eat lunch. Bug still got to visit, which sounded petulant, but that's where Alyssa's state of mind was at. Jealous of Bug getting to spend time with Evelyn.

Now Evelyn was Bug's official volunteer, Alyssa didn't have an excuse to go to the CEO's office every day. But she wanted to! Boy, did she want to—even if she could only see the woman for five minutes. What was happening to her? How had Evelyn got under her skin so easily? For the first time…ever, Alyssa was struggling to concentrate on the sanctuary. Sure, she got the jobs done, but her focus was on the twentieth floor.

"What is wrong with you?" Lil huffed, jabbing Alyssa in the arm. They were spending the afternoon at Four Paws combing over their finances. It wasn't a fun task, but not something they could shirk.

"Nothing," Alyssa huffed back. Her mood had soured over the past forty-eight hours and Lil had noticed.

"Wanna try that again? Jesus, Al, you've got a face like a wet weekend."

"Just had a thing with Hannah."

"What does that mean? Bloody hell, Alyssa, spit it out."

"She came over unannounced on Saturday. Asking me to reconsider having a relationship with her."

"Right, and how did that go?"

"I told her I'm not the relationship type and that she always knew the score."

"Okay, and?"

"Then she left." Not the entire story, but Alyssa wasn't sure she could explain what had happened without trying to make sense of her frustrating feelings.

"Tell you what, I'm going to go make a coffee and give you time to settle down. Then you can tell me the rest of the story and I can help." Lil didn't wait for Alyssa's response.

Closing her eyes, Alyssa growled under her breath. This is why she didn't do relationships and feelings. All those things ever brought was frustration.

"Can we not talk about it?" Alyssa pleaded when Lil placed her coffee in front of her five minutes later.

"Nope. You've been in funk and I don't like it. C'mon, spill."

"You're so annoying." Lil nodded in agreement and smiled sweetly. Alyssa rolled her eyes. "Evelyn was with me when Hannah arrived. I'd given Evelyn a tour of the shelter and asked her to stay for dinner."

Chancing a look at Lil, Alyssa wanted to growl again. Lil wore a satisfied grin that rubbed Alyssa up the wrong way.

"Go on," Lil urged.

"Hannah accused me of moving on to my next fling, which I don't really care about, but..."

"You don't want Evelyn to see you that way."

"Yeah, I suppose. But it got worse. When I finally got rid of Hannah, Evelyn asked if you were okay with me sleeping with other women."

"Why the bloody hell would I care who you're shagging?" The look of bewilderment made Alyssa laugh.

"She thought you and I were a couple?"

"Why?" Lil laughed. "That's ridiculous, and gross."

"Hey!" Alyssa laughed.

"It's gross," Lil repeated.

"It is. Anyway...when we first met, I introduced you as my partner. I meant business partner, but Evelyn thought I meant life partner."

"So all these weeks she's been flirting with my girlfriend?" Lil gasped, holding her hand to her heart.

"Oh stop. She has not been flirting."

"Alyssa, don't be a moron. Of course she has. And why wouldn't she? I knew the two of you were into each other."

"Lil, c'mon, it's not like that."

"Oh, give me a break. Why are you in such a tizzy then, if it's 'not like that'?"

Bloody Lil. Ugh. "Okay fine. I have been feeling stuff."

"God, you're so deep and enlightened, Alyssa. You should think of doing some life coaching on the side," Lil deadpanned.

"Look, I stand by what I said to Hannah. I don't do relationships, I haven't got the time—"

"But...?"

"But," Alyssa sighed, "I can't get Evelyn out of my mind. I want to spend time with her. Get to know her more than I already do and it's frustrating me. I can't concentrate on the things I need to. I feel like a liar, like I misled Hannah."

"Alyssa, sweetie, you didn't mislead anyone. You can't help who you fall for."

"Hold your horses, lady, no one said I was falling for anyone."

"Didn't you? I mean, you've just described everything that happens when you meet and fall for someone. Tell me. When you wake up, do you think of her first or the centre?"

Alyssa's face flared red. Over the course of the past few weeks, Evelyn had been invading her mind more often. To the point Alyssa thought of her when she woke up, or grabbed a coffee, or lunch. It didn't seem to matter the time of day. Evelyn Crawford was never far from Alyssa's mind.

"Shit," she hissed.

"Stop fretting. It's not the end of the world to like someone, Al. Look, you know I have respected your choices regarding relationships and all that jazz, but I'd be a shitty friend if I didn't give it to you straight."

Well, this sounds ominous.

"The shelter isn't going anywhere, Alyssa. You have a crack team of people behind you, all willing to put in the hard work. I think we've all proven how valuable we are. I totally understood your aversion to relationships when you first got Four Paws up and running. There was a lot to do, and you needed to focus. But the thing is, you don't need to focus that hard anymore."

"This place is my home, Lil," Alyssa argued.

"Of course it is, and no one is saying otherwise. But the truth is you could, if you wanted to, dedicate some of your fierce focus on a woman. Obviously, the right lady has never come along, but I think that's changed. Evelyn likes you, that's plain to see, and you like her. Refusing to do anything about it is just stubbornness on your part. But it's your choice."

"Christ, tell me how you really feel, Lil," Alyssa groaned. She was feeling pissy because her friend was right.

"I always will. Now, will you stop moping and help me get this finance shite out of the way so I can go home?"

"Who's collecting the dogs?"

"You are. Get the pack and talk to Evelyn whilst you're there."

"Ricky, what are you doing here?" It was almost half five, and Alyssa had just arrived to collect the dogs.

"I'm taking the dogs back. Lil called me earlier, asked if I could stop by. Said you would drop the van off and she'd give me a lift into work tomorrow."

Lil, you conniving so and so!

"Oh, my mistake. I thought I was taking them back." Lil had set her up knowing full well that without the excuse of getting the dogs, Alyssa would *not* have come to Crawford's today.

"No worries. I'll get them loaded. You okay getting home?"

Lil hadn't thought it through at all. How was Alyssa supposed to get home? Well, she could take Ricky's car, she supposed. Oh, hang on a minute, Alyssa understood now. Lil expected her to talk to Evelyn with the hope that more would happen and that she would either go back to Evelyn's or ask her for a lift home. Neither one was going to happen.

"I'll drive your car back if that's cool. You get everyone ready and I'll meet you back there. Don't worry about Bug, I'll bring him with me."

"Roger Dodger! See you later, Al."

Alyssa waited for Ricky to leave. She needed a moment to gather herself. Even though she had no intention of going anywhere with Evelyn tonight, she wanted to clear the air between them. When Evelyn found out Alyssa was not with Lil, she acted a little oddly. Alyssa couldn't quite put her finger on it. However, the fact Alyssa felt Evelyn was avoiding her was enough to warrant a discussion. They were becoming fast friends, and no matter how Alyssa's feeling evolved, she didn't want to lose that friendship.

As usual, the top floor was quiet when Alyssa arrived. Only a couple of employees lingered, but they were chatting amongst themselves, too busy discussing EastEnders to take notice of her.

Evelyn's raised voice echoed through the door to her office. "Daniel, I don't care. I have no time to plan a bloody Christmas event. It should have been done months ago."

Alyssa stopped and listened.

"Dad might have always organised it, but he isn't here and this is the first I'm hearing about it."

Alyssa could make out the garbled noise coming from the other end of the phone.

"Whatever, Daniel, I'll sort it out. Goodbye." The sound of a phone being slammed into its cradle signalled the call's end.

"Hey," Alyssa called quietly. Approaching Evelyn cautiously. The CEO looked wired, maybe a little manic.

"Alyssa," Evelyn barked, causing her to jump. "Sorry, didn't see you there. Have we got an appointment?"

The hot poker of disappointment jabbed Alyssa in her gut. They'd never needed an appointment before.

"No, sorry, I just came to grab Bug." Not a lie. Yes, she hoped they could chat, but this clearly wasn't the time. Evelyn's face visibly dropped, which confused Alyssa. Was Evelyn upset she was taking Bug, or because Alyssa hadn't come up to see her specifically? Blimey, all this falling for someone was ridiculous and complicated.

"He's in his usual spot," Evelyn replied despondently, her fingers massaging her temple. Should Alyssa just grab the pup and hightail it out of there? Probably. That's what commitment-free player Alyssa would do. But this was Evelyn, and Alyssa's heart ached at the sight of this beautiful woman struggling.

Instead of picking up Bug, Alyssa sat in the chair opposite Evelyn, who had her head down, staring at her desk. "Is everything okay, Evie?"

Stupid question. Clearly everything was not okay, but this was way outside Alyssa's wheelhouse. If Evelyn was strictly a friend, Alyssa would be shit hot at advising, but as soon as the line blurred from friendship to something more, Alyssa was lost.

Evelyn let out a sharp laugh. "Oh, the usual, you know." Finally Evelyn looked up. Alyssa was shocked at how tired the CEO looked. Dark circles marred Evelyn's perfect face.

"Evelyn, when was the last time you ate? Or slept, for that matter?"

"What time is it now?"

"Half five."

"Then yesterday. I ate yesterday. Couldn't sleep, so I came in around four."

Alyssa let out a surprised gasp. "Evelyn Crawford," she admonished.

"I know, I know. I've already had a bollocking off of Maggie."

"Good. Now, want to share the reason you were so angry at the phone you almost put it through your desk?"

Evelyn chuckled. "Apparently my father, the perfect boss, organised an HQ Christmas Party each year. Obviously I knew about the party, but I never realised it was him who threw it. Dan, the douchebag, was just informing me the responsibility for said party falls to me now. And he decided to let me know that nugget of information two weeks before the party is supposed to happen. I have no time to eat, let alone plan a fucking party."

That was probably the first time Alyssa had heard Evelyn swear.

"I can help."

Oh look, another case of verbal vomiting, Alyssa. Maybe one day you will think before you open your trap?

"You can't help, you have the centre to run. You're just as busy as I am."

Alyssa heard Lil's earlier words. *The truth is you could, if you wanted to, dedicate some of your fierce focus on a woman.*

Lil was right, Alyssa had plenty of help. There was no reason she couldn't lend Evelyn a hand, as she was clearly struggling. What would that mean, though? Alyssa never chose a woman over Four Paws. Never.

"I have time, Evelyn, and I can help you."

"What about Four Paws?"

"Lil is there and I have a full team to help. Let me do this for you. Let me help." Alyssa saw Evelyn's eyes swim with unshed tears. This was unfamiliar territory. How should Alyssa handle it?

Standing up, Alyssa rounded the desk and hauled Evelyn into her arms for a bone-crushing hug. Alyssa's mum always gave her a hug when she was feeling a little overwhelmed, and it always helped.

"Thank you," Evelyn mumbled into Alyssa's shoulder. They stayed glued to each other for a few moments longer. Alyssa broke the hold because she was getting some pleasant feelings in pleasant places that were wholly inappropriate for the circumstances.

"Okay, here's the game plan. You're going to shut off your laptop and pour us a drink of something. Do you have alcohol?"

Evelyn shook her head.

"Bummer. Okay, new plan. I'll order a pizza and beer. We'll sit on the sofa with Bug glaring at us while we eat." That earned her a laugh. "Then we will have a quick chat about what needs to be done for this party, and then you're going home to sleep. Deal?"

"Well, how could I say no to that?"

Alyssa grinned. "You can't. It's impossible."

With the pizza ordered, Alyssa and Evelyn settled on the sofa. Bug trundled over, ignoring Alyssa completely. Popping his front paws on the sofa, Bug looked at Evelyn expectantly. Alyssa regarded the pair with curiosity.

What's going on here then?

Evelyn didn't skip a beat. As if this was something they did regularly, Evelyn scooped Bug on to the sofa by his bum. Bug circled twice and then lay down, his upper body leaning over Evelyn's leg. Evelyn carried on like nothing was amiss. Alyssa wanted to laugh out loud. What else did this pair get up to? It was clear as day that they had formed a bond and now had a routine.

"Oh, pizza's here," Evelyn announced when her phone pinged. Jumping up, Alyssa headed to the elevator to wait for the delivery man. She was determined to get Evelyn to relax, and if that meant sitting on the sofa with Bug lounged on her, then so be it.

"Oh, my God, this is heaven," Alyssa mumbled through her first bite of pizza.

"This is just what I needed, thank you Al."

"No worries. I am worried about you, though, Evelyn. You can't keep going like this."

"I know," she sighed. "I'll just be glad when bloody Christmas is done."

"Whoa, whoa, whoa. We need to rectify this dislike of Christmas. You're as grumpy as Bug about it. Have you never enjoyed it?"

"Not at all. I loved Christmas. Decorating, watching movies, eating junk. Waiting for Santa. What isn't there to like as a kid?"

"But not now?"

Alyssa watched Evelyn deflate. "My mum was the one who made Christmas extraordinary. Every year seemed to get bigger and better than the last. Then she died."

Alyssa wiped a tear from Evelyn's cheek.

"Dad didn't know how to make Christmas what it was without her and then he met the floozy. There was no way I wanted to share Christmas with him and her, so I worked. That's when I realised how much larger my workload was over the festive period. I had less and less time to enjoy it."

"I'm really sorry to hear that, Evie."

"It's okay. Times change."

"But that doesn't mean you can't enjoy Christmas again," Alyssa said gently, taking Evelyn's hand. All she wanted to do was make the woman feel better. Wrap her up in cotton wool and make everything okay.

"What's the point? My dad will be away. Maggie has her family. I have an empty penthouse. I might as well forget about it and carry on as normal."

No chance in hell Alyssa was going to let that happen. She had some planning to do.

"Well, let's forget about that tonight. We still have pizza. Bug is practically drooling in anticipation. I'm guessing this isn't the first time he's got food from you with those big puppy eyes. Am I right?"

Evelyn grinned.

"Thought so. So let's eat, drink, and plan for this party."

"I can do that. And, to show you I'm not quite the grinch you think I am, I'll treat you to some festive music."

The opening bars of "Fairytale of New York" played softly through speakers dotted around the office. With the light low and the beer flowing, Alyssa had to be on guard. Those complicated feelings were becoming less complicated as the minutes wore on. Evelyn Crawford had captured her attention, and it was becoming painfully clear that somehow she'd captured Alyssa's heart, too.

15

Party Planning and Impossible Deadlines

ALYSSA

Three days had passed since Alyssa found Evelyn stressed out in her office, having just been informed by Dan the Douche that she had to organise the traditional Crawford's HQ Christmas Party. The task had seemed impossible then: plan a corporate event for all of

Crawford's staff in under two weeks. Alyssa had offered to help, thinking it would be a quick afternoon project.

She'd been spectacularly wrong.

Planning a corporate Christmas party was, Alyssa discovered, approximately 7,000 times more complicated than managing a sanctuary full of dogs with varying digestive issues and personality disorders.

"So," she said, spreading a massive spreadsheet across Evelyn's conference table, "we need to categorise your employees like we do our rescue dogs."

Evelyn looked simultaneously horrified and intrigued. "Excuse me?"

"Different personalities require different party strategies," Alyssa explained, pulling out color-coded Post-it notes. "Marketing types need disco. Accounting needs structured fun. IT needs...well, basically a LAN party with festive hats."

Since the beginning of the partnership with Crawford's, Alyssa had gotten to know the various departments within the company pretty well. She'd learned that Tom from graphic design was meticulous and creative, that Polly in accounting had a dry sense of humour that could cut glass, and that the marketing team thrived on energy and spectacle. Each department had its own rhythm, its own culture, its own needs. Understanding that was half the battle.

Bug, who had been supervising from his designated conference room chair, gave a soft "woof" of apparent agreement.

"Did the dog just validate your organisational strategy?" Evelyn asked.

"Bug is an excellent consultant," Alyssa said seriously. "His instincts are legendary at Four Paws."

The next two hours were a masterclass in corporate event engineering. Alyssa mapped out theoretical seating arrangements depending on the venue they would finally settle on, potential dietary requirements, and probable drama zones with the precision of a military strategist.

The venue search had become their biggest challenge. With Christmas less than two weeks away, most spaces were already booked solid. Every call Alyssa made was met with the same response: "Sorry, we're fully committed through the new year." They'd narrowed it down to a handful of possibilities, but nothing felt quite right yet. Still, Alyssa refused to let logistics derail the planning. They could adapt the seating, the flow, the entire layout once they had a space locked down.

"You've colour-coded potential romantic tension," Evelyn observed with an arched brow, pointing at a section marked in bright yellow.

"Workplace dynamics are complex," Alyssa replied. "Much like dog pack hierarchies."

Bug thumped his tail in agreement.

By midday, they'd transformed Evelyn's pristine conference room into a war room. Sticky notes covered every surface, each colour representing a different department, potential challenge, or critical consideration.

"This feels like a tactical operation," Evelyn said, looking slightly overwhelmed.

"Welcome to event management," Alyssa grinned. "It's basically herding cats. Or in our case, dogs."

The catering section was particularly complex. Alyssa had created an intricate matrix that considered dietary restrictions, potential allergies, and what she called "hangry prevention strategies."

"You've got a column here that says 'Potential Meltdown Risk,'" Evelyn noted, pointing to a bright red section.

"Some people get very serious about their Christmas pudding," Alyssa explained. "It's like watching dogs protect their favourite chew toy."

Bug lifted his head and gave a pointed look that suggested he took toy protection very seriously.

"How did you become so good at this?" Evelyn asked, genuinely curious.

Alyssa shrugged. "Running a sanctuary means being part event planner, part therapist, part detective. You learn to anticipate problems before they happen."

They broke for lunch—pizza again, because apparently it had become their planning fuel. Bug sprawled across the floor between them, his head resting on Alyssa's foot, occasionally lifting his eyes toward the pizza box with shameless hope.

"He's manipulating me for pizza," Evelyn said, rolling her eyes, but she was smiling.

"Of course he is," Alyssa agreed, "but he's very charming about it."

The afternoon brought more detailed planning. "What's this section?" Evelyn pointed to a detailed flowchart.

"Potential drama mitigation," Alyssa explained. "Like how we prepare dogs for new environments. Slow introduction, positive reinforcement, clear boundaries."

Evelyn snorted, which made Alyssa feel a hundred feet tall. She loved making Evelyn laugh.

By late afternoon, they'd developed a plan that was part corporate strategy, part psychological intervention, and part festive celebration.

"I can't believe we've managed this," Evelyn said, looking at the meticulously organised documents.

"Teamwork," Alyssa said, offering a high-five. Bug immediately shoved his head between their hands, demanding inclusion.

"And canine supervision," Evelyn added, scratching Bug behind the ears.

As the sun began to set, casting long shadows across the conference room, Alyssa felt something shift. This wasn't just about organising an event anymore. This was about helping Evelyn rediscover something she'd lost: the joy of bringing people together.

"We should test some of the games," Alyssa suggested. "Make sure they're actually fun and not just team-building torture."

Evelyn raised an eyebrow. "You want to practice party games? Now?"

"Why not?" Alyssa said. "Bug can be our impartial judge."

Bug wagged his tail, clearly delighted to be assigned such an important role.

And just like that, the serious planning dissolved into laughter, sticky notes, and increasingly ridiculous game scenarios, with Bug as their most discerning critic.

The party was going to be perfect. Or at least, perfectly chaotic.

The next few days became a blur of last-minute problem-solving meetings and increasingly elaborate spreadsheets. Alyssa found herself spending more time at Crawford's than she'd initially planned, which was definitely not something she was complaining about.

"I'm pretty sure this is not what I meant by 'help with the party,'" Evelyn said, watching Alyssa rearrange the entire staff kitchen to create what she called a "festive flow zone."

"Trust the process," Alyssa replied, carefully positioning a set of reindeer-shaped mugs. "Spatial arrangement matters more than you'd think."

Bug watched from his perch on a nearby chair, looking like he'd be taking notes if dogs had opposable thumbs.

"That sounds made up," Evelyn said.

"Maybe," Alyssa grinned. "But it sounds convincing, doesn't it?"

The marketing department had been particularly enthusiastic. Tom from graphic design had created no fewer than seventeen potential party banners, each more elaborate than the last. The current favourite featured Bug wearing a Santa hat, which the dog himself seemed to find acceptable.

"I'm not sure this is professional," Evelyn said, looking at the design.

"It's exactly what your employees want," Alyssa countered. "Trust me. I understand pack dynamics."

Lil had been sending increasingly pointed texts, mostly variations of "Are you actually working or just flirting?", which Alyssa studiously ignored. The event was becoming a project of epic proportions, and she was determined to make it perfect.

"This is more intense than I expected," Evelyn said one evening, surrounded by sample Christmas decorations and sticky notes.

"This is how we prepare for puppy adoptions," Alyssa replied. "Except with fewer worksheets and more sanitiser."

As the days passed, the excitement became palpable. The Crawford's office transformed, with employees not-so-subtly asking Alyssa about details. Bug had become something of a mascot, with staff members stopping by to get his "approval" on various elements.

"I think he's enjoying the power," Evelyn observed.

"Total middle management energy," Alyssa agreed.

The event was becoming more than just a celebration. It was becoming a moment of reconnection for a company that had been struggling with leadership transition, with grief, with the challenges of the past year.

And somehow, in the middle of all the planning, Alyssa was creating something else. A connection. A possibility. Something that felt like it could be more than just a work project.

But for now, there were plans to finalise, and a very opinionated dog to consult.

The venue selection turned into an unexpected adventure—and a nail-biting one at that. They were now less than a week out from the party and still didn't have a confirmed location. With most spaces booked solid months in advance, Evelyn had suggested using the company's main conference hall as a last resort—practical, convenient, and utterly soulless.

"Absolutely not," Alyssa said, crossing her arms. "That room has all the festive energy of a tax audit."

"It's functional," Evelyn protested. "And it's available! Alyssa, we're running out of time. The party is in six days."

"So is a filing cabinet, but you don't throw a party in one."

Bug, who had accompanied them on the conference hall tour—their Hail Mary—sat down in the middle of the room and refused to move. His message was clear: this space was unacceptable.

"Even the dog hates it," Alyssa pointed out.

"The dog is biased," Evelyn replied, but she was already pulling out her phone to research alternatives. "Though I'm starting to think he has better taste than both of us."

That's when Alyssa found it: a converted warehouse space in Shoreditch. The listing had only gone up that morning—a last-minute cancellation. All exposed brick, fairy lights, and industrial charm. It was completely impractical, slightly over budget, and absolutely perfect.

"This is ridiculous," Evelyn said when they arrived an hour later, but she was smiling as she said it. "We're cutting this incredibly close."

"This is brilliant," Alyssa corrected. "Look at the natural light. The open floor plan. The potential for creative seating arrangements. And we can have it."

Bug trotted around the space, tail wagging, giving his seal of approval to various corners.

"He's doing a security sweep," Alyssa explained. "Very thorough."

The warehouse manager, a woman named Sienna with impressive sleeve tattoos and a nose ring, looked between them with barely concealed amusement. "So you want to book this for a corporate Christmas party? In six days?"

"Yes," Alyssa said firmly.

"Maybe," Evelyn said simultaneously, then sighed. "Yes. Definitely yes."

Sienna laughed. "You two are adorable. Lucky for you, the cancellation just came through this morning. The space is yours. I'll even throw in some extra fairy lights—and I'll waive the rush fee because I like your dog."

With the venue secured, the real work began—and the clock was ticking. Five days. They had five days to pull off what normally took months.

Back at Crawford's, Maggie had somehow gotten involved, bringing her own brand of organisational energy to the proceedings.

"I've created a system for tracking all the moving pieces," Maggie announced, dropping a comprehensive binder on Evelyn's desk. "Everything cross-referenced and colour coded. With timelines."

"That's...thorough," Evelyn said.

"That's genius," Alyssa corrected, immediately diving into the binder. "And we're going to need every minute accounted for."

Now that they had a venue, Alyssa could finalise the theme. She laid out colour swatches across Evelyn's desk, her vision finally coming together despite the compressed timeline.

"We settled on 'Crawford's Celebration of Connection,'" Alyssa said, "but now we need to make sure everything—decorations, invitations, even the playlist—actually reflects that. And we need to do it fast."

"You're very particular about cohesion," Evelyn observed. "Even under pressure."

"A theme isn't just words on an invitation," Alyssa explained. "It's the feeling people get when they walk in. It's what makes an event memorable instead of just...mandatory."

Evelyn nodded slowly. "My mother used to say something similar. That events should tell a story."

"Exactly," Alyssa said, feeling warmth spread through her chest at the mention of Roslyn. "This is about bringing people together. Reconnecting them to the company, to each other, to what Crawford's stands for."

"Bug would definitely approve of this philosophy," Evelyn said, glancing at the dog.

"He has excellent taste," Alyssa replied. "Now, catering."

The catering became its own saga—made more complicated by the fact that most caterers were already booked. Alyssa insisted on including options that went beyond the standard corporate fare. She'd somehow convinced a local chef—a friend of Lil's—to squeeze them in with only four days' notice, creating a menu that was part traditional, part adventurous, and entirely delicious.

"You've got 'Festive Fusion Tacos' on the menu," Evelyn observed.

"Trust me," Alyssa said. "They're going to be the highlight of the night."

"We're a pet supplies company, not a food truck festival."

"Exactly. Which is why this will be memorable."

The entertainment was another challenge—and another race against time. Evelyn wanted something subdued. Alyssa wanted something that would get people actually enjoying themselves.

"What about a DJ?" Alyssa suggested.

"Too loud," Evelyn countered.

"A string quartet?"

"Too boring."

They compromised on a live band that could do both—something with range, energy, and the ability to read a room. Miraculously, they had an opening.

"You're very good at this," Evelyn said one evening, watching Alyssa coordinate with the band manager over the phone.

"At what?"

"Making things happen. Bringing people together."

Alyssa felt heat rise in her cheeks. "It's just event planning."

"It's more than that," Evelyn said softly. "You're creating something that everyone wants to get behind. In less than a week."

The moment hung between them, charged with something neither of them was quite ready to name. Bug, sensing the shift, stood up and positioned himself directly between them, tail wagging slowly.

"Subtle," Alyssa muttered to the dog.

The final three days became a whirlwind. As the date drew closer, the energy at Crawford's shifted. People were excited. Genuinely excited. Not the forced corporate enthusiasm, but real anticipation—even though most of them had no idea how close they'd come to having the party in a soulless conference room.

"I think we might have actually pulled this off," Evelyn said one afternoon, looking at the final checklist. "With two days to spare."

"We?" Alyssa teased. "I seem to remember doing most of the work."

"You had an assistant," Evelyn gestured to Bug, who was currently napping on his designated planning chair.

"The best assistant," Alyssa agreed.

The final planning meeting was held in Evelyn's office the night before the party, with pizza—their traditional fuel—and a sense of accomplishment that felt hard-won. They'd created something together in record time. Not just a party, but a moment of connection for an entire company.

"Thank you," Evelyn said, her voice sincere. "I couldn't have done this without you. Especially not in under two weeks."

"You could have," Alyssa replied, "but it wouldn't have been nearly as fun."

Bug lifted his head, looked between them, and gave a soft, approving bark.

The party was tomorrow. And somehow, in the midst of all the planning and the pressure and the impossible deadlines, Alyssa had realized something terrifying and wonderful: she *was* falling for Evelyn Crawford. Hook, line, and sinker.

But that was a problem for another day. Right now, there was a final walkthrough to complete, and a very opinionated dog to consult.

Tacos and Tender Moments

EVELYN

E velyn stood at the entrance of the converted Shoreditch warehouse and tried to remember how to breathe.

The space had been transformed. Fairy lights draped across exposed brick walls, casting a warm glow that made everything feel softer, more intimate. Round tables dotted the open floor plan, each one decorated with centrepieces that somehow managed to be festive without being tacky—a minor miracle in corporate event planning. The live band was setting up in the corner, their equipment nestled among strategically placed poinsettias and evergreen garlands.

It was perfect. Absolutely perfect.

And Evelyn had no idea what to do with herself.

"Stop fidgeting," Maggie said, appearing at her elbow with two glasses of champagne. "You look like you're about to bolt."

"I'm not fidgeting," Evelyn protested, immediately stilling her hands, which had been smoothing down her dress for the third time in as many minutes.

"You're fidgeting," Maggie confirmed, pressing a glass into her hand. "Drink this. It'll help."

Evelyn took a sip, more to have something to do than because she wanted it. The champagne was good—Alyssa had insisted on upgrading from the standard corporate swill—and it did help settle the nervous flutter in her stomach.

"Where is Alyssa?" Maggie asked, scanning the room.

"Probably micromanaging the catering staff," Evelyn said. "She's been in full event coordinator mode since we arrived."

"She pulled this off in less than two weeks," Maggie said admiringly. "That woman is a force of nature."

Evelyn couldn't argue with that.

The first employees started trickling in, and Evelyn felt her shoulders tense. This was it. The moment she'd find out if all their frantic planning had been worth it. It was where she'd find out if she stacked up against her dad and his impeccable party-planning reputation.

Tom from graphic design was one of the first through the door, his eyes widening as he took in the space. "Holy shit," he said, then immediately looked mortified. "Sorry, I mean—this is incredible, Ms Crawford."

"Evelyn," she corrected automatically. "And thank you. Though I can't take credit. This was mostly Alyssa's vision."

"The dog lady?" Tom grinned. "She's brilliant."

More people arrived, and Evelyn found herself swept into a series of conversations that all blurred together. Everyone seemed genuinely excited, which was both gratifying and slightly overwhelming. She smiled, nodded, made small talk about the decorations and the menu and wasn't the venue just wonderful?

It was exhausting.

Her mother had been good at this—moving through a crowd, making everyone feel seen and valued. Roslyn Crawford could work a room like nobody's business, finding the exact right thing to say to put people at ease.

Evelyn had never quite mastered that skill. And after her mother died, she'd stopped trying.

"You're doing the thing," a familiar voice said behind her.

Evelyn turned to find Alyssa, looking unfairly gorgeous in a deep green dress that brought out the warmth in her eyes. Bug was at her side, sporting a festive bow tie that matched Alyssa's outfit.

"What thing?" Evelyn asked.

"The thing where you smile and nod but you're not actually present," Alyssa said. "Your eyes glaze over a bit. It's very subtle, but I've gotten good at reading you."

Evelyn felt heat rise in her cheeks. "I'm fine."

"You're overwhelmed," Alyssa corrected gently. "Which is completely understandable. This is a lot."

"I used to be better at this," Evelyn admitted. "Before—"

She didn't finish the sentence. She didn't need to.

Alyssa's expression softened. "Your mum would be proud of you, you know. This party, what you're building here—it's exactly the kind of thing she would have loved."

Evelyn swallowed hard against the sudden lump in her throat. "I'm not sure about that."

"I am," Alyssa said firmly. "Now come on. Let's go check on the Festive Fusion Tacos. I need to know if they're living up to the hype."

The catering station was mobbed. Evelyn watched in amazement as her normally reserved accounting department descended on the taco bar like a pack of very polite locusts.

"I told you they'd be a hit," Alyssa said smugly.

"You were right," Evelyn conceded. "About a lot of things, actually."

"I'm going to need that in writing," Alyssa teased.

The band started playing—something upbeat and jazzy that immediately got people moving toward the makeshift dance floor. Evelyn watched as her employees, people she saw every day in their professional capacity, transformed into actual human beings having actual fun.

It was strange. Wonderful, but strange.

"Dance with me," Alyssa said suddenly.

Evelyn blinked. "What?"

"Dance with me," Alyssa repeated, holding out her hand. "You've been standing on the sidelines all night. Time to actually participate in your own party."

"I don't really dance," Evelyn protested weakly.

"Neither do I," Alyssa said.

Against her better judgment, Evelyn took Alyssa's hand.

The dance floor was already crowded with people from various departments, all mixing together in a way that would have been unthinkable at a normal work function. Marketing was dancing with IT. Accounting was attempting some kind of coordinated line dance with HR. It was chaotic and joyful and completely ridiculous.

Evelyn loved it.

They danced through two songs before Bug decided he'd been patient long enough and inserted himself between them, demanding attention.

"Subtle as always," Alyssa muttered, but she was smiling as she bent down to pet him. "You should be at home with your friends."

Evelyn excused herself to check on the other aspects of the party, moving through the crowd with slightly more confidence than before. She stopped to chat with various employees, and this time, she actually listened. Actually engaged.

Tom cornered her near the dessert table, practically vibrating with enthusiasm. "The marketing team wants to do a photo booth," he said. "Can we? Please? I brought props."

"You brought props to a Christmas party?" Evelyn asked, amused despite herself.

"I'm always prepared," Tom said seriously. "I have reindeer antlers, Santa hats, and—" he pulled something from his bag with a flourish, "—matching ugly Christmas sweaters for anyone who wants them."

"That's..." Evelyn searched for the right word. "Extremely thorough."

"So can we?" Tom asked hopefully.

Evelyn glanced around, finding Alyssa across the room. Their eyes met, and Alyssa gave her a small nod of encouragement.

"Yes," Evelyn said. "Set it up near the entrance. And make sure Bug gets his own photo session."

Tom's face lit up like she'd just given him the best gift of his life. "You're the best boss ever!"

He scampered off, and Evelyn found herself smiling.

The party continued, and Evelyn found herself relaxing into it. She sampled the Festive Fusion Tacos (which were, admittedly, delicious). She judged an impromptu ugly sweater contest that Tom had organised. She even participated in a group photo where Bug sat front and centre, looking incredibly pleased with himself.

At one point, she found herself standing next to Maggie, both of them watching the dance floor.

"You did good, kid," Maggie said.

"Alyssa did good," Evelyn corrected.

"You both did," Maggie said firmly. "Your mother would have loved this. The energy, the connection, the way everyone's actually talking to each other instead of hiding in their departmental silos."

Evelyn felt that familiar ache in her chest, but this time it was accompanied by something else. Something that felt almost like peace.

"I miss her," Evelyn said quietly.

"I know," Maggie replied. "But she's here, in a way. In the way you're leading this company. In the way you brought everyone together tonight. That's her legacy, Evelyn. And you're honouring it."

Evelyn blinked rapidly, refusing to cry at her own Christmas party. "Thank you."

"Don't mention it," Maggie said. "Now go dance with that lovely woman who's been making heart eyes at you all night."

"She has not—" Evelyn started, but Maggie was already walking away, leaving her flustered and more than a little warm.

She found Alyssa near the catering station, deep in conversation with the chef about the success of the menu. Bug was at her feet, looking hopeful for dropped food.

"Everything okay?" Alyssa asked when she noticed Evelyn approaching.

"Everything's perfect," Evelyn said, and meant it.

The band announced their final song of the night, something slow and sweet that had couples pairing off across the dance floor.

"One more dance?" Alyssa asked, holding out her hand.

Evelyn took it without hesitation.

This time, when they moved together, Evelyn wasn't thinking about her employees watching, or what it might look like, or whether she was doing it right. She was just present in the moment, with Alyssa's hand warm in hers and Bug sitting nearby like the world's most attentive chaperone.

"Thank you," Evelyn said softly. "For everything. For helping with the party, for pushing me out of my comfort zone, for—" she hesitated, then continued, "—for reminding me how to be me again."

Alyssa's expression was impossibly tender. "You never stopped being you, Evelyn."

The song ended, and the band announced they were wrapping up. Employees started gathering their things, calling out goodbyes, thanking Evelyn for a wonderful evening.

Evelyn accepted their thanks with genuine warmth, surprised by how much she meant it when she said she was glad they'd enjoyed themselves.

As the crowd thinned, Alyssa started coordinating cleanup with the venue staff. Evelyn watched her work, marvelling at how effortlessly she moved through the space, how naturally she took charge.

"Stop staring," Maggie said, appearing at her elbow again. "It's obvious."

"I don't know what you're talking about," Evelyn said primly.

"Sure you don't," Maggie replied. "Just...don't overthink it, okay? Life's too short."

She left before Evelyn could respond, which was probably for the best.

The venue slowly emptied until it was just Evelyn, Alyssa, Bug, and a handful of staff breaking down tables and packing up decorations.

"We did it," Alyssa said, coming to stand beside Evelyn. "We actually pulled it off."

"You pulled it off," Evelyn corrected. "I just tried not to get in your way."

"You did more than that," Alyssa said. "You showed up. You connected with your people. You let yourself be present. That's huge, Evelyn."

Evelyn looked around the warehouse, at the remnants of the party they'd created together. The fairy lights still twinkled, casting warm shadows across the brick walls. A few stray pieces of tinsel glittered on the floor. The air still smelled faintly of pine and cinnamon.

It had been perfect.

As they helped with the final cleanup, Evelyn felt something shift inside her. Something that had been locked tight since her mother's death, slowly beginning to open.

Maybe Maggie was right. Maybe her mother would have been proud of tonight. Not just the party itself, but what it represented—Evelyn stepping out of her grief, reconnecting with her company, remembering how to lead with heart instead of just competence.

"What are you thinking about?" Alyssa asked, catching her expression.

"My mum," Evelyn admitted. "And how she would have loved this. The chaos, the connection, the terrible puns on the menu cards."

"Those were excellent puns," Alyssa protested.

"They were terrible," Evelyn countered, but she was smiling. "And she would have loved every single one."

They stood together in the slowly darkening warehouse, Bug between them, and Evelyn felt something she hadn't felt in a very long time: contentment.

"Ready to head out?" Alyssa asked eventually, as the last of the venue staff finished packing up.

"Almost," Evelyn said. She took one more look around the space, committing it to memory. The way the fairy lights reflected off the brick. The scattered chairs that would be collected in the morning. The faint impression of laughter still hanging in the air.

This was what her mother had meant about events telling stories. This space had held something important tonight—not just a party, but a moment of healing. For the company, yes, but also for Evelyn herself.

"Okay," she said finally. "I'm ready."

They walked toward the exit, Bug trotting ahead of them with his bow tie slightly askew. Sienna was waiting by the door, doing a final check of the space.

"Successful night?" she asked, grinning at them.

"Very," Evelyn confirmed.

"I could tell," Sienna said. "The energy in here was incredible. Whatever you two are doing, keep doing it."

Outside, the December air was crisp and cold, a sharp contrast to the warmth of the warehouse. Evelyn pulled her coat tighter, watching her breath form clouds in the night air.

"Need a lift?" Alyssa asked. "I've got Bug's crate, but there's room."

Evelyn hesitated. The sensible thing would be to call a car, go home, decompress from the evening. But sensible felt overrated right now.

"That would be lovely," she said.

They walked to Alyssa's car in comfortable silence, Bug leading the way like he knew exactly where they were going. The streets of Shoreditch were still busy despite the late hour, people spilling out of pubs and restaurants, their laughter echoing off the buildings.

"Thank you," she said again. "I know I keep saying it, but I mean it. Tonight was...it was important."

"I know," Alyssa replied. "I could see it. The way you started to relax as the night went on. The way you actually smiled when Tom showed you those ridiculous props."

"Those antlers were objectively ridiculous," Evelyn agreed.

"And you loved them," Alyssa teased.

"I tolerated them," Evelyn corrected, but she was smiling.

They lapsed into comfortable silence, Bug occasionally making small noises from the backseat. The drive wasn't long, but Evelyn found herself wishing it could last a bit longer. There was something about this—the quiet intimacy of the car, the soft music, Alyssa's profile illuminated by passing streetlights—that felt precious. Fleeting.

Too soon, they were pulling up outside Evelyn's building.

"Home sweet home," Alyssa announced.

Evelyn unbuckled her seatbelt but didn't immediately move to get out. "Would you...do you want to come up? For tea or something?"

The invitation hung in the air between them, loaded with possibility.

Alyssa's hands tightened on the steering wheel. "I should probably get Bug home. He's had a long night."

"Right," Evelyn said, trying to hide her disappointment. "Of course."

"But maybe another time?" Alyssa added quickly. "When we're both not completely exhausted from pulling off a miracle party?"

"I'd like that," Evelyn said softly.

She got out of the car, then bent down to look through the window. "Goodnight, Alyssa. Goodnight, Bug."

Bug wagged his tail, and Alyssa smiled. "Goodnight, Evelyn. Sleep well."

Evelyn watched them drive away, Bug's face visible in the back window, and felt that strange mix of contentment and longing settle in her chest.

Tonight had been perfect. The party had exceeded every expectation, her employees had genuinely enjoyed themselves, and she'd managed to step out of her grief-induced shell long enough to actually be present.

But more than that, she'd spent the evening with Alyssa. Dancing, laughing, creating something beautiful together.

And somewhere in the midst of all that planning and chaos and last-minute problem-solving, Evelyn had fallen completely, irrevocably for her.

She stood on the pavement long after Alyssa's car had disappeared around the corner, the December cold seeping through her coat, and smiled.

Her mother would have loved Alyssa. The thought came unbidden but felt right. Roslyn Crawford had always appreciated people who got things done, who cared deeply, who brought out the best in others.

Alyssa was all of those things and more.

Evelyn finally headed inside, riding the elevator up to her penthouse with a lightness she hadn't felt in months. Maybe years.

As she got ready for bed, she caught sight of herself in the mirror and barely recognised the woman looking back. Her eyes were bright, her cheeks flushed from the cold and the champagne and the dancing. She looked alive in a way she hadn't in far too long.

17

Butter Ratios and Bum-Shaped Hearts

ALYSSA

Alyssa had always been a sucker for holiday traditions. It was the one soft spot she'd allow herself, and only when it could be justified as "enrichment" for the dogs at the shelter. Gingerbread bones. Reindeer-shaped biscuits with carob noses. One year she'd even tried to make little edible Santa hats, but the icing glue had melted into a terrifying blood-red sludge that stained the entire puppy room. The photo made the rounds every Christmas, much to her eternal mortification.

But this time was different. This time, she was baking with Evelyn.

They'd arranged it at the Christmas party—or rather, after several glasses of champagne and a particularly successful round of dancing, Evelyn had mentioned she'd never baked dog treats before. Alyssa, riding high on the success of the evening and feeling bold, had immediately offered to teach her. Evelyn had agreed with that soft smile that made Alyssa's stomach flip.

That had been three days ago, and Alyssa had been second-guessing the invitation ever since.

She stared at her phone for a full minute, re-reading the text she'd just sent. "Kitchen's ready for you. Wear something you don't mind ruining." She almost added "xoxo," then deleted it in a panic. She wasn't a twelve-year-old. Jesus.

The clock barely hit seven when a knock rattled the mobile home's thin door. Alyssa opened it to find Evelyn clutching a roll of branded Crawford's Pet Supplies baking parchment and, inexplicably, a leather-bound portfolio.

"Tell me you're not here to make a PowerPoint about gingerbread men," Alyssa said, only half joking.

Evelyn's lips quirked. "If you'd seen the state of the last staff cookie day, you'd understand why I've drawn up an action plan." She stepped inside, trailing cool air and the faintest hint of sandalwood perfume. "Bug!" Evelyn crooned, spotting him sprawled in his customary patch of sunlight by the kitchen table.

Bug roused with a groan and padded over, eyes gleaming with that weird Cocker Spaniel mix of tragedy and calculation. He gave Alyssa's calf a perfunctory nudge, then sat at Evelyn's feet and thumped his tail.

"He's always been a traitor," Alyssa said.

"He knows where the best treats are." Evelyn dropped to her knees, ruffling Bug's fur. Alyssa's throat went tight, the way it always did when she saw people with their dogs, but this felt different. Maybe because Evelyn looked so at home, kneeling in her carefully pressed shirt, her hair coming loose already, talking to Bug like he was the only thing that mattered in the world.

"Wow," Alyssa said, shaking herself. "Okay. You're here to bake, not seduce my staff." She nudged Evelyn's hip with her foot, gently. "Let's get started."

The baking supplies were already lined up: flour, butter, sugar, ground ginger, cinnamon, treacle, half a bottle of vanilla because Lil had "liberated" the other half for an experimental eggnog. Alyssa handed Evelyn an apron—a spare from the shelter, emblazoned with cartoon corgis in Santa hats—and took a moment to admire how it looked on her. Ridiculous, is how. Ridiculous and, for reasons Alyssa couldn't articulate, heart-wrenchingly adorable.

"Have you ever actually baked from scratch?" Alyssa asked as she measured out flour.

"I once made a soufflé for my mother's birthday. It exploded."

"Exploded?"

"In the literal sense. Glass and hot egg custard everywhere. Mum found it hilarious. I cried for a week."

Alyssa snorted. "You'll be fine. These don't even require eggs, just lots of upper body strength." She pantomimed kneading dough.

Evelyn rolled her eyes but let herself be guided through the steps. The first challenge came with the butter. Evelyn approached it like a surgical procedure, cutting precise cubes with a knife she'd apparently brought from home—because of course she had.

"Are you measuring those?" Alyssa asked, watching Evelyn line up butter squares like tiny soldiers.

"They need to be uniform," Evelyn said, not looking up. "Otherwise the dough won't incorporate properly."

"It's just gingerbread."

"Everything deserves precision." Evelyn held up a cube, examining it critically. "This one's slightly larger. It'll throw off the ratio."

Alyssa bit back a laugh. "You're aware we're making cookies for dogs, right? They don't care about butter ratios."

"I care about butter ratios," Evelyn replied, and there was something so earnest in her voice that Alyssa felt her chest go warm.

Bug, sensing an opportunity, positioned himself strategically between them, eyes tracking the butter with laser focus.

"Don't even think about it," Alyssa warned him.

Bug's expression suggested he was thinking about it very much.

The rubbing-in process became a minor battlefield. Alyssa demonstrated first, fingertips working the butter into the flour with practiced ease. "You want it to look like breadcrumbs," she explained. "Nice and crumbly."

Evelyn's technique was methodical, working the butter into the flour with the concentration of someone defusing a bomb. Alyssa, watching her, couldn't help but smile at the intense focus on her face.

"You're overthinking it," Alyssa said gently.

"I'm being thorough."

"You're treating it like a science experiment."

"Baking is a science," Evelyn countered.

Alyssa reached over and placed her hands over Evelyn's, guiding them through the mixture. "Feel the texture? When it's like this, you're done. You don't need to be quite so...precise."

Alyssa was acutely aware of how close she was standing, the warmth of Evelyn's body next to hers, the faint scent of her perfume mixing with cinnamon and ginger. She swallowed hard.

"Right," Alyssa managed, stepping back quickly. "You've got it now."

Evelyn's cheeks were slightly flushed, though whether from the warmth of the kitchen or something else, Alyssa couldn't tell.

The treacle incident came next. Alyssa had warned Evelyn about the stickiness, but nothing could have prepared either of them for the chaos that ensued when Evelyn tried to measure it out.

"It's not coming out of the spoon," Evelyn said, shaking the utensil with increasing violence.

"You have to warm it first—"

Too late. The treacle released all at once, splattering across the counter, Evelyn's apron, and somehow, inexplicably, Bug's left ear.

There was a moment of stunned silence.

Then Alyssa started laughing—proper, gasping laughter that made her double over. Evelyn stared at the treacle carnage, then at Bug, who was attempting to lick his own ear with limited success.

"This is a disaster," Evelyn said, but her lips were twitching.

"This is baking," Alyssa corrected, still laughing. "Welcome to the chaos."

Evelyn picked up a tea towel and dabbed ineffectually at the treacle on her apron. "I'm going to smell like Christmas for a week."

"Could be worse."

"How?"

"Could be dog food. Trust me, that smell doesn't wash out."

They cleaned up the treacle—mostly—and continued. The dough came together eventually, despite Evelyn's continued insistence on precision and Alyssa's cheerful disregard for exact measurements.

"How do you know when it's ready?" Evelyn asked, poking the dough ball suspiciously.

"When it feels right."

"That's not an answer."

"It's the only answer I have." Alyssa pressed her thumb into the dough. "See? It springs back a bit, but it's still soft. That's perfect."

Evelyn tried it herself, her expression shifting from sceptical to surprised. "Oh. That is quite satisfying."

"Right?"

They wrapped the dough and put it in the fridge to chill. Bug, having given up on treacle opportunities, had relocated to his sunbeam and was watching them with the patient resignation of someone who knew the good bits were still to come.

"Twenty minutes," Alyssa said, setting a timer. "Want some tea?"

"Please."

They sat at the small kitchen table, mugs warming their hands, flour still dusting their clothes. The mobile home felt smaller with Evelyn in it, but not in a bad way. More like the space had rearranged itself to accommodate her presence.

"I haven't really done this before," Evelyn said quietly. "Baking, I mean. Not properly. Just that one disastrous soufflé."

"Not even at Christmas?"

"Especially not at Christmas. I always left it to the professionals—caterers, bakeries, whoever Mum hired." She traced the rim of her mug. "Mum used to make these elaborate gingerbread houses. She'd spend days on them—royal icing, sugar glass windows, the works. I'd watch, but I never actually helped. I was always too impatient. Wanted to skip to the decorating without learning the basics."

"Did she ever let you try?"

"Once." Evelyn's smile was soft, sad. "I made an absolute mess of it. The walls collapsed, the icing went everywhere. But she helped me salvage it, and we put it in the centre of the table like it was a masterpiece. She said it had character."

Alyssa reached across and squeezed Evelyn's hand. "It probably did."

"Maybe." Evelyn squeezed back, then seemed to realize what she was doing and pulled away, clearing her throat. "Anyway. That's why I'm rubbish at this. No experience."

"You're not rubbish. You're just...structured."

"That's a polite way of saying controlling."

"I was going for 'thorough,' but sure."

The timer went off, breaking the moment. They retrieved the dough and began rolling it out—another source of creative differences.

"It needs to be exactly five millimetres," Evelyn insisted, producing a ruler from somewhere.

"Where did you even—never mind." Alyssa shook her head. "It doesn't need to be exact."

"Everything needs to be exact."

"Not everything."

They compromised at approximately five millimetres, which Alyssa could tell physically pained Evelyn to accept.

The cookie cutters came out—Alyssa's collection was extensive and chaotic, ranging from traditional stars and trees to inexplicable shapes like dinosaurs and what might have been a deformed cat.

"Why do you have a cookie cutter shaped like a bum?" Evelyn asked, holding up the offending item.

"That's a heart."

"That's absolutely a bum."

"It's a heart that looks like a bum. There's a difference."

Evelyn's laugh was sudden and bright, transforming her whole face. Alyssa wanted to bottle that sound, keep it somewhere safe.

They cut out shapes—mostly traditional, though Alyssa snuck in a few bum-hearts when Evelyn wasn't looking. Bug supervised from his position of comfort, occasionally offering a bark of what Alyssa chose to interpret as approval.

The baking itself was surprisingly peaceful. They sat on the floor in front of the oven, watching the cookies rise and brown through the glass door, not talking, just existing together in the warm, ginger-scented air.

"This is nice," Evelyn said eventually.

"Yeah," Alyssa agreed. "It really is."

"Should we make them traditional gingerbread men?" Evelyn asked. "Or can we be more...creative?"

Alyssa grinned. "Define creative."

Evelyn set her jaw, like she was about to propose a hostile takeover. "Let's make a Christmas tree. But not just any tree. I want a replica of the one in Trafalgar Square. Complete with lights and pigeons."

"Lights?"

"We'll use silver balls. Those sugar things."

"I like the ambition, Crawford."

"I never do anything half-arsed," Evelyn said. She pressed her thumb into the dough, sculpting an approximation of the Norwegian spruce, then glanced up. "What about you? Have you always done this kind of thing?"

"Christmas cookies? Yeah. Mum and dad moved all the time, so I made my own traditions."

"You ever think about expanding? Opening another location?"

Alyssa shook her head firmly, focusing on rolling the dough. "Four Paws is exactly where it needs to be. I'm not interested in uprooting what we've built or spreading myself too thin."

"That's admirable," Evelyn said softly. "Knowing what you want and staying committed to it."

"It's not always easy," Alyssa admitted. "People assume I should want more—bigger facilities, multiple locations, that kind of thing. But Four Paws isn't just a business. It's home."

"I understand that," Evelyn said. "More than you might think."

They lapsed into silence, the good kind. Alyssa kept waiting for her usual restlessness to kick in, the urge to fill the air with some story or joke, but it didn't. It was enough to...exist. Next to Evelyn, hands sticky with molasses and flour, Bug wedged between their ankles, all of it felt embarrassingly right.

By the time they'd cut, baked, and decorated two trays' worth of cookies, the kitchen was a warzone. There was icing in Alyssa's hair and a powdered sugar handprint on Evelyn's arse that neither of them wanted to address.

Alyssa licked a dab of royal icing off her knuckle and handed a finished biscuit to Bug, who snatched it with surgical precision. "I think we made more of a mess than actual cookies," she said.

"Worth it," Evelyn replied, stealing a silver ball and popping it in her mouth. She chewed thoughtfully, her face unreadable.

Alyssa watched her, heart drumming in her chest. If Evelyn hated it, she'd laugh it off. If she loved it, she'd...well, Alyssa wasn't sure. This was uncharted territory.

Evelyn set her Christmas tree cookie on the table, then perched on the edge, wiping her hands on a tea towel. "Can I ask you something?"

"Sure."

"Is it hard, not having your parents around at Christmas?"

Alyssa shrugged. "They're living their best life, travelling the country. I talk to them all the time—video calls, photos of whatever beach or mountain they're currently exploring. It's nice, actually. They're happy."

"But you never feel like something's missing?"

Alyssa considered. "Sometimes. But they visit when they can, and I'm genuinely glad they're out there enjoying themselves. It's what they love. Besides, I've got the dogs. And Lil. And now..." she paused, meeting Evelyn's eyes, "...new friends who apparently can't measure butter without a ruler."

Evelyn was quiet for a long moment. "I thought I had the perfect family," she said. "Then Mum died. Dad turned into someone I didn't recognise. I kept trying to fill the hole, but the more I did, the more it grew."

Alyssa wanted to say something. To fix it. But the words tangled in her throat.

Evelyn smiled, brittle. "Sorry. That's dark. I didn't mean to bring down the mood."

"You didn't," Alyssa said, and meant it. "It's good to talk about it."

"Maybe." Evelyn toyed with a gingerbread star, spinning it on its point. "I've never been good at this stuff. Sharing."

"You're better at it than you think."

"Only with you, apparently."

Alyssa blushed. Bug chose this moment to leap onto her lap, presumably angling for more cookies, but it broke the tension. She scratched his ears and grinned at Evelyn. "He's not subtle, is he?"

"He knows what he wants," Evelyn replied, her eyes lingering on Alyssa for a moment longer than necessary. "Is this how you imagined your evening going?"

Alyssa tried not to imagine anything at all, lest she ruin the moment. "I thought there'd be more swearing. You seemed like the sort who'd cuss up a storm when covered in molasses."

"I'll save it for the clean-up."

They fell into comfortable silence, sipping their tea while Bug settled between them, finally content after his cookie heist. The kitchen was warm, the fairy lights Alyssa had strung up last week casting a soft glow over the flour-dusted chaos.

Once the tea was drunk and Bug lay snoring on the couch, they cleaned up together, mostly in silence, passing utensils and plates, moving around each other like they'd done it a hundred times. Every now and then their hands would brush, or one would reach for something at the same moment, but neither pulled away. When they finished, Evelyn leaned back against the counter, folding her arms.

"Do you want to walk?" she asked.

Alyssa glanced out the window. "It's freezing."

"I know. But it helps me think." Evelyn paused, then added with a small smile, "And I'm not quite ready to leave yet."

At the sound of the word "walk," Bug's head shot up from the couch, suddenly very awake. Within seconds he was at the door, leash in his mouth, giving them the hard sell.

"Well," Alyssa said, laughing. "Looks like we don't have a choice now."

The night was sharp and clear, frost curling at the edges of the windows. Alyssa pulled on her jacket and hat, then held the door for Evelyn, who'd managed to look perfectly put together despite her earlier icing-sugar baptism.

They wandered down the lane, Bug trotting ahead, tail up. Alyssa kept her hands jammed in her pockets, partly against the cold and partly to keep from grabbing Evelyn's. The urge was almost physical.

"So," Evelyn said, voice soft in the dark. "What are you doing for Christmas day?"

Alyssa shrugged. "Usual. Open the shelter for the volunteers. Give the dogs turkey treats. Watch *Home Alone* with Lil."

"That's it?"

"Why, what do you do?"

"Order Chinese, argue with my father over the phone, pretend to enjoy every second of it."

Alyssa laughed. "You could come here, you know. Have turkey with the dogs."

Evelyn was quiet, shoes crunching on the gravel.

"I'm serious," Alyssa said. "You're Bug's best friend now. And you make a mean gingerbread cookie. I bet you'd be an asset."

Evelyn looked up at her, eyes luminous. "If I come, you'll have to let me bring a bottle of something."

"Of course. I'm not a monster."

They walked on, not talking, not needing to. Alyssa thought of what Lil had said: *You can't help who you fall for.* For once, she didn't want to help it. She wanted to lean into it, let it catch her, just to see what happened next.

Bug veered off to sniff at a hedge. Evelyn slowed to a stop and turned to face Alyssa, hands tucked into the crooks of her elbows. The air between them went suddenly, wildly electric.

"Thanks for tonight," Evelyn said.

"You're welcome."

They stood there for a moment, close enough that Alyssa could see the flecks of gold in Evelyn's eyes, could count the freckles dusting her nose. Close enough that it would be so easy to lean in, to close the distance between them, to finally know what Evelyn's lips tasted like.

But Alyssa held back. Because as much as she wanted to kiss Evelyn—and God, did she want to—she had no idea how to navigate this. She'd never done this before. Not the slow build, not the uncertainty, not the wanting something more than just casual and easy. With Hannah and everyone before her, it had been simple: no expectations, no complications.

This mattered. Evelyn mattered. And Alyssa had no roadmap for that.

They walked the rest of the way back in easy silence, Bug weaving between them, anchoring their orbit. Alyssa thought about everything that had just happened—the mess, the laughter, the secrets—and realized that, for the first time in years, she was exactly where she wanted to be. And maybe, if she was very lucky, Evelyn was too.

18

Wine, Photos, and Finally

EVELYN

The middle of December arrived with a flurry of snow and biting, ice-cold wind. Of course, the British government went into meltdown, causing more trouble than the weather itself.

Although inundated with work, Evelyn was making a conscious effort to relax. All thanks to Alyssa and Bug.

"Hey, Evie," Alyssa called, walking into her office and plonking herself on the sofa.

"Hey, yourself. Good day?"

"Yeah, um, I actually came in to ask you a favour."

"Okay, shoot." Evelyn placed her fountain pen on the desk and waited. Why was Alyssa looking uncomfortable?

"So, um, you know the dogs are having their sleepovers tonight?" Evelyn nodded. Alyssa had granted most volunteers a night with their dogs. The ones she felt weren't ready for that were being treated to a sleepover with members of the Four Paws team. Bug was staying with Alyssa because Evelyn hadn't been sure she would be available to have him overnight.

"Yeah, everything okay? No issues, I hope."

"Um, no, not really. It's just...well, I was wondering if you could have Bug. I know you said you weren't sure if you were free, so it's totally cool if you can't."

"I can. I was going to ask you about it today, actually. I thought I would have to stay out of town, but the meeting got cancelled last minute."

"Oh great, thanks."

Evelyn smiled, warmth spreading through her chest at the thought of an evening with Bug. "Is there an emergency at the centre?"

"No, um...I have a date with Josh and...um, with everything being so busy lately, tonight is the only free time we have."

What the fuck?

A chorus of those three words played on repeat in Evelyn's head. Alyssa was going out on a date with Josh? The security guy Josh? The same Josh who'd thrown Guinness over Evelyn's lap at the pub?

Evelyn felt like the floor had dropped out from under her. Like she'd completely misread *everything*.

They'd spent *hours* together. The party planning, the baking night, the walks with Bug where they'd talked until the cold drove them inside. The way Alyssa's hand had lingered on hers when she was teaching her to knead dough. The looks that lasted just a beat too long. The almost-kiss that Evelyn had been replaying in her mind for days, wondering if she'd imagined the heat between them.

Apparently she had.

God, she felt foolish. Stupidly, embarrassingly foolish. She'd been building this up in her head, convincing herself that something was happening between them, that Alyssa felt it too. She'd been working up the courage to ask her out properly, to make her intentions clear.

But of course Alyssa was dating. Hadn't she said she didn't do relationships? That she kept things casual? Evelyn had heard her, had even understood it at the time. But then they'd grown so close, and Evelyn had let herself hope that maybe, just maybe, she was different.

What an idiot she'd been.

"Evelyn?" Alyssa's voice cut through her spiralling thoughts. "Is that okay? I can find someone else if—"

"No, it's fine," Evelyn said quickly, forcing her face into what she hoped was a neutral expression. "Of course I'll take Bug. Have a lovely time."

There, that sounded alright, right?

The words tasted like ash in her mouth.

How idiotic are you? Falling for her, when you didn't stand a chance of keeping her.

"You're...you're sure you don't mind?"

"Nope, you enjoy your date with...*Josh.*"

"Great...well, thanks."

An awkward silence descended. Evelyn wanted the floor to open up and swallow her. Could she fire Josh?

No, stop it Evie, don't be ridiculous.

"Well, I um...I should get on." Evelyn picked up her fountain pen and gave a mock salute, then wanted to die of embarrassment. Because who does that? Alyssa gave her a tight smile, waved, and left. After all the time spent together, how had they taken such a step back?

"What the hell was that?" Maggie bawled, rushing into the room, her face flustered.

"Sorry what?" Evelyn didn't have time to decrypt whatever Maggie was banging on about.

"That?" Maggie shouted, pointing to the door.

"Do you mean Alyssa?"

"Of course I bloody do. What are you playing at?"

"Maggie, can you stop yelling and start explaining what you're yapping on about?"

"Evelyn. That woman just told you she's going on a date with someone else and you did absolutely nothing!"

"Why would I do anything?"

Maggie shook her head. "Don't give me that nonsense. Anyone with two eyes can see you pair have been flirting up a treat. I thought you would have gone out with each other by now."

"Maggie, give me a break. We've had to work close together, that's—"

"Enough, Evie. Enough. Why can't you just admit you fancy the pants off her? Hell, I kind of do. She's smokin'."

Could this day get any worse? Hearing Maggie from Croydon say smokin' was just too much for one day.

"Listen, Alyssa can date who she likes. She doesn't do serious, so what's the point? I want more than a weekend shag."

"Maybe she hasn't been given a good enough offer in the past. You could be that offer. Look, I'm not saying you have to go full lesbian cliché. You can keep your U-Haul parked for now. I'm just saying that asking the girl out would be a good start. Give her the choice, you know?"

"You're full of opinions lately, aren't you?"

"I've always been full of opinions. Doesn't make me wrong. Come on Evie, grow some bloody ovaries and ask that sexy minx out."

The dam broke inside Evelyn. Alyssa *was* sexy, she was kind, and Evelyn had wanted to be more than friends from the beginning. What was she playing at? Why was she letting Alyssa get away?

"Oh, sod it. What have I got to lose, right?"

"That's the spirit. I'm going to get her back." Once again, Evelyn didn't have a chance to reply. Maggie zipped out of the room like her bum was on fire. Rolling her neck and shoulders, Evelyn prepared for what she thought would be humiliating rejection. Surely if Alyssa wanted more than friendship, she'd have asked Evelyn out already. It's not like Alyssa was shy or anything.

Evelyn almost jumped out of her skin when Alyssa spoke. She'd been so lost in her head she didn't see her enter the office.

"Hey, Maggie said you needed me."

Evelyn's heart drummed, her palms sweaty. "Hi, yes. Right."

Excellent start, Evelyn, top-notch!

"Sorry," she mumbled, taking a gulp of cold coffee. "Alyssa, would you have dinner with me?"

"Sure, when? I can grab takeout on Monday if you like."

"I mean a date, Alyssa, not an office dinner."

"A date?" Alyssa squeaked.

Oh, crap, had Evelyn made a terrible mistake and ruined their friendship? Why didn't she think of the repercussions of being rejected? How could they stay friends? That would be way too uncomfortable. Bollocks!

"Yeah, yes, a date. I can cook, or we could go to a restaurant. Or I could drive to Four Paws, so you're close by in case of an emergency. Whatever."

Shut up, you rambling pillock!

"Yes. To the date," Alyssa stuttered.

Evelyn smiled brightly. She'd said yes! *But she also said yes to Josh, so don't get too excited Ev.*

"Okay, great, we'll chat about it then. Soon." Evelyn gripped her pen, needing to channel her excitement into something that wasn't a happy dance.

"Okay." Alyssa smiled, her cheeks a little red.

Evelyn was a grown woman and yet she felt like a spotty tween who had just spoken to her first crush. Good Lord.

"Okay, so I'll see you soon. Don't worry about Bug, he's going to have a great time with me."

"I know he will. That dog adores you." They smiled sweetly at each other. "I'm gonna…" Alyssa said, hooking her thumb over her shoulder.

"Good night, Alyssa." Whoa, that sounded way too sultry.

Tone it down, Romeo.

As much as Evelyn hated saying good night to Alyssa, knowing she was off to get wined and dined by someone else, Evelyn couldn't stop the ember of hope growing in her belly. She also couldn't help watching Alyssa's lovely derriere leave the office. Hot damn.

Unsurprisingly, Maggie blew back into the room, sporting a grin as wide as the River Thames. "Nice one, Evie! Very well handled."

Evelyn laughed. "I think we need to have a chat about eavesdropping on my conversations, Mags."

"Don't be silly. Now, what's the plan? Posh restaurant? River cruise?"

"Nope, I think I want to cook for her. At my place, or hers. I want to talk to her properly and relax."

"Yep, good thinking. Plan the best date ever and Josh won't stand a chance!"

"I'm not competing with Josh or anyone, Maggie. Alyssa knows her own mind. If she chooses to be with Josh, that's her call."

"You are way too passé about this, Evie. I mean really." Maggie rolled her eyes.

"Well, now that's done, I'm going to go home. I have a house guest tonight and we need some sofa time."

"Have you got everything he needs?"

"Maggie, I run a pet supply company. I *literally* have everything he needs. I'll message Blake to deliver some stuff to my place."

"I'm proud of you, Evie."

"Don't be soft. I'm just looking out for him this evening."

"Not for that, and you know it. Whether it's because of Alyssa or that ball of fluff over there," Maggie pointed to Bug, who was curled up in a ball by the window. "You've been making some changes these past few weeks. Good changes. I'm proud of you for doing that."

Evelyn dropped her eyes to the table. It was Alyssa and Bug who had helped her. "They're good for me," she said, her voice just above a whisper.

"Then keep hold of them."

"Alright, Bug, we're home. Now, I just need a minute to get everything ready for you, so take your time. Have a wander round and make yourself at home."

Had Evelyn gone overboard with what she'd asked Blake to bring over? No doubt. Did she care? Not one bit.

It felt wonderful to spoil her little friend. He deserved it for being so caring.

Even though it was past the middle of December, Evelyn's penthouse remained Christmas-less. There was no garland on the fireplace. No tree twinkling in the corner of her living room. All signs that it was the festive season were nonexistent. Unlike her office, which had been transformed into a winter wonderland by Maggie.

She'd been surrounded by Christmas cheer for weeks now—the decorations at Crawford's, the magical evening at the Christmas market with Alyssa, the party at the warehouse with its fairy lights and festive warmth. She could appreciate it in those spaces, could even enjoy it, but bringing it into her home felt like a step too far.

No matter how hard she tried, Evelyn couldn't muster the enthusiasm for the holiday season in her own space. Everything just reminded her of her mum and how many things had changed. Even though she was an adult, Evelyn, her mum and dad always shared Christmas together. Roslyn hadn't cared that Evelyn was a grown woman. She'd still made the time magical, just like when Evelyn was a small child.

Home was where the absence felt sharpest—even though this penthouse wasn't where she'd grown up, wasn't where the majority of family Christmases had been spent, the memories followed her anyway. Here, she'd have to face the empty chair at the table, the missing voice singing carols off-key, the lack of elaborate gingerbread houses taking up half the kitchen counter. So the penthouse stayed bare. Neutral. Safe.

Those times were just memories now, though. Christmas was too hard without her mum, so Evelyn chose to skip it—and that was why she stood in her white and chrome penthouse with nary a bauble in sight.

Shaking her head, Evelyn set off to unpack the mountain of supplies shipped over for Bugs' stay.

"Now, I know you have dog kibble, but how about we have a treat?"

Evelyn took Bug's puppy eyes as a yes. Taking out two steaks from the fridge, Evelyn set about cooking them a feast of meat and maple-roasted vegetables.

"No one can complain, Bug. I've given you protein and veggies." She mumbled to him. Bug hadn't left Evelyn's side since getting home.

With a glass of red wine poured and a bottle of dog beer emptied into a bowl, the duo sat in the living room to eat. For the first time since Evelyn's mum had passed, she didn't feel completely alone.

Richard had tried his best, but he was grieving, too. Maggie tried to be there for her, but the woman had her own life to deal with. And Mindy…well, Evelyn should have known that was doomed from the start because Mindy never made her feel supported, not in the way she needed.

For three years, Evelyn had been lonely. But the little dog, quietly munching on his steak, had turned that around in a matter of hours. Since the first time he absconded to her office, Evelyn felt that want of companionship sated.

There were no conversations to be had, just Bug's presence. Evelyn was amazed at how intuitive he was. As if he could see all her feelings and know what she needed. Whether that was a break from work, in which case Bug would literally bug her until she stopped and petted him. Or when she was frustrated and Bug would whine at the window in her office until she joined him for a few calming minutes.

"Want to meet someone, Bug?" Maybe the third glass of wine was a mistake. Evelyn always got sentimental and emotional after too much vino.

Not waiting for the dog to answer—because she wasn't that sozzled—Evelyn took out her photo albums from a box at the bottom of her wardrobe.

Bug wandered over to her as she sat on the floor, her back against the sofa. "This is my mum," she mumbled.

The creak of the cover revealed how little the album had been opened. As with Christmas, staring at Roslyn's smiling face was just too painful at times.

"She was the best. I miss her."

Over the space of an hour, Evelyn showed Bug her family pictures. The pup sat diligently by her side and even though she knew it wasn't possible, Evelyn let herself believe he was looking at the photos, taking in everything she had to say. It felt good to talk about her mum. Sure, she wished she could do that with her dad, but Richard always shut the conversation down.

Hot tears streaked down Evelyn's face as she combed through the photos for a second time. Bug sidled up and leaned against her chest. "I miss her so much."

Bug abruptly got to his feet and dashed off toward Evelyn's bedroom. Wiping her face, Evelyn stood to investigate. The silence was worrying. The jingle of bells stopped Evelyn in her tracks. Bug appeared moments later with a Christmas tree decoration in his mouth. Stunned, Evelyn watched him walk back to the living room and drop the decoration at her feet.

"No, buddy, this isn't a toy," Evelyn chided, scooping the offending article back up. Striding into her room, Evelyn saw the box of stored Christmas paraphernalia lying open.

How in the world did he know this was here?

Returning the bells to their rightful place, Evelyn made her way back to the living room, only to witness Bug running past her again. Out he came with a different Christmas decoration. Dropping it in the same place as before, he sat and stared at her. Huffing and growing frustrated, Evelyn returned the ornament.

"Stop it, Bug," she whined when he repeated his breaking and entering of her Christmas stash.

Twenty minutes passed of them playing Bug's game. Eventually, Evelyn slumped to the floor in the middle of the growing pile of Christmas decorations. Bug was quite content ferrying the items one by one from her room.

The doorbell rang, which caused Evelyn to frown. Who the hell was at her door at...nine-thirty in the evening? Grumbling the entire way to her front door, Evelyn ripped it open with a scowl.

"Whoa, what's wrong with you?" a surprised-looking Alyssa asked.

"Alyssa?"

"That's me. You okay?"

"What…why are you here?" The tone of her voice was snippy, causing Alyssa to raise her eyebrows.

"I just wanted to stop by and say hi. Sorry, I'll go. See you tomorrow."

Evelyn could have screamed at herself. Taking her frustration out on Alyssa wasn't right. "No, Al, sorry wait. Come in."

"Are you sure?

"Perfectly. Sorry, I'm just having a bit of an issue with Bug."

"Bug? Is he okay?" Alyssa didn't hesitate, stepping past Evelyn and heading to the living room. "Um…"

"Yeah." Evelyn chuckled. Bug was sitting proudly in the middle of his Christmas decoration pile.

"I think I need some context." Alyssa grinned.

Evelyn momentarily forgot how to breathe. That grin was a lesbian slayer. It had the power to render mere mortals incapable of thought and movement.

"Evie?"

Snapping her eyes away from Alyssa's lips, Evelyn motioned them towards Bug. "He got all my decorations out. I tried to put them back, but he just kept going back to fetch them."

"He's a strange little guy." Alyssa grinned, and then her face sobered. "Is that why you looked so pissed when you answered the door?"

Rubbing her forehead, Evelyn sighed. "I haven't had any Christmas-related items on display in my house since my mum passed. I had a couple of glasses of red this evening and showed Bug my photo album. The next thing I know he's toddled off and found all this. We played a game of chase before I gave up and let him win."

"Ah, I see." Alyssa wandered over to the open photo album, looking at Evelyn, silently asking for permission. Evelyn nodded, taking a seat next to Bug. "You look like her, you know."

"Yeah, I take after her in nearly every way." Evelyn smiled.

"Would she want you to shut out Christmas, Evie?"

A lone tear breached, tracking down Evelyn's cheek. "No, she wouldn't."

"I can't imagine how you feel, sweetie. I have my parents. They're a little unusual, but they're still with me. I don't want you to think I'm interfering."

"I don't. It's just hard spending this time alone."

"But you're not alone."

Evelyn studied Alyssa's face. There was an emotion present that Evelyn didn't dare interpret. If she was wrong, she would blow up their friendship.

But what if I'm right?

Leaning in, Evelyn slipped her hand around Alyssa's neck, hesitating to allow Alyssa to back out. She didn't. Closing her eyes, Evelyn inhaled Alyssa's captivating scent. Her senses came alive, and the surrounding atmosphere sparked as their lips gently brushed without quite connecting. Alyssa's breath caressed her mouth. Their noses brushed gently, and their eyes searching each other.

"Kiss me," Alyssa whispered. Evelyn closed the last few millimetres of space.

From the moment Evelyn saw Alyssa, she knew those lips were going to be her undoing. Soft and plump, teasing yet forward.

Evelyn's hand held Alyssa closer, her fingers massaged the nape of Alyssa's neck, earning a whimper. Needing more, Evelyn softly stroked Alyssa's bottom lip with her tongue. Her reward was to be taken wholly by Alyssa's mouth.

Their lips clashed as the kiss heated. Tongues swirled, licked, and lavished. Alyssa brought her hands to Evelyn's face, cradling her jaw. This was more than a kiss. This was the beginning of something spectacular.

19

Panic, Pizza, and Pep Talks

ALYSSA

This was not what Alyssa expected to happen when she drove over to Evelyn's. Actually, she surprised herself by going there in the first place. Who seeks out someone else after a date? A successful date at that!

Josh was a lovely guy. He brought flowers after volunteering to drive over to Alyssa's place to pick her up, which would have definitely been out of the way for him. The restaurant was pleasant, and Josh was a proper gentleman. Not in the mansplaining, patronising way. He didn't order for her or anything. He was charming, but not slimy. Attentive, but not over the top. He listened and took an interest.

So why had Alyssa wanted to see Evelyn? Why hadn't she invited Josh back to her place? That was her usual behaviour. A one-night stand, or a casual hook-up arrangement. Something that Josh seemed okay with. Alyssa made sure he knew from the beginning that she didn't do serious.

Yet here she was. Sitting on Evelyn's expensive couch being kissed into oblivion. This was a head-swimming, stomach-flipping, world-tilting kiss. The heat between them built rapidly, and Alyssa knew she was dangerously close to taking Evelyn right here on the couch.

But that wasn't how this was supposed to happen.

Alyssa had fantasised about sleeping with Evelyn—she wasn't a nun, and Evelyn was completely gorgeous. But in all those fantasies, they'd take their time. They'd do exquisite things together in a bed. For hours. Having a frantic quickie on the couch with Bug snoring three feet away was not the way their first time should go.

Reluctantly, and with an impressive amount of willpower she didn't know she possessed, Alyssa pulled back. They were both breathing hard, lips swollen, a testament to how close they'd been to ripping each other's clothes off.

"Wow," Alyssa gasped. It wasn't the most eloquent response, but her brain had turned to mush.

"Yeah," Evelyn breathed, her voice rough.

Alyssa grinned at the dazed, goofy smile on Evelyn's face. God, she was beautiful. "As much as I would love to continue this, I think I should go."

"Oh." Evelyn's face fell, and Alyssa's heart clenched.

She grabbed Evelyn's hand, threading their fingers together. "I want to go on that date with you, Evie. I want to do this properly. You deserve that."

Understanding dawned in Evelyn's eyes, and her smile returned, softer this time. "I want that, too."

"So I'm going to go. For now." Alyssa stood, pulling Evelyn up with her. "But how about I come by in the morning for breakfast?"

Was that too forward? She had a mountain of things to do tomorrow, but the thought of waiting more than a few hours to see Evelyn again felt impossible.

"That would be perfect," Evelyn said, her smile widening. "I'll send you the door code. Just let yourself in."

With that, Alyssa made a hasty exit. Her willpower was crumbling with every second she spent in Evelyn's presence. The little devil that sat on her shoulder admonished her for passing up the opportunity to know Evelyn in a carnal way. But she wouldn't give into lust, not when this—whatever this was—felt monumental.

She was falling for Evelyn Crawford. Properly, terrifyingly falling. And that changed everything.

The other part of her also knew she needed to think about Josh. Nothing had happened between them physically. Well, a kiss on the cheek as they parted ways, but that was enough to set Alyssa's stomach rolling with guilt. Leading people on was not her thing—she detested it.

When Josh had finally bucked up the courage to ask her out, Alyssa had been on the verge of declining. Her feelings for Evelyn were already surpassing anything she'd felt before, consuming her thoughts in a way that should have thrilled her.

Instead, it terrified her.

So she'd said yes to Josh. Not because she wanted to, but because panic had seized her by the throat and wouldn't let go.

What if she let herself fall completely for Evelyn and lost herself in the process? What if she got so enamoured that Four Paws—her life's work, her purpose—fell by the wayside? She'd built the sanctuary from nothing, had poured every ounce of herself into it. What if loving Evelyn meant neglecting the dogs who depended on her?

And what if Evelyn didn't want anything substantial anyway? They were both busy women. Evelyn was constantly stressed, constantly tired, constantly carrying the weight of Crawford's on her shoulders. Wouldn't a relationship with Alyssa just add to that burden? What if Evelyn realized Alyssa was too much—too intense, too needy, too inexperienced at this whole "real feelings" thing?

Then there was Lil. Her best friend, her business partner, the person who'd been by her side through everything. What would Lil think if Alyssa suddenly started devoting time away from the shelter? Would she feel abandoned? Betrayed? Would their friendship survive Alyssa choosing someone else for once?

Basically, her mind had gone on a grand tour of Catastrophizing Central, population: one panicking pansexual. And in that spiral of terror and self-sabotage, she'd ended up sitting across from Josh in a restaurant, feeling absolutely nothing except the crushing certainty that she'd made a terrible mistake.

Because the only person she wanted to be having dinner with was Evelyn.

The shrill noise of Alyssa's phone filled her car as she travelled home.

"Hey, Lil."

"Where you at? Did you go home with Josh?"

"No, I didn't," Alyssa tutted. It's not like she just fell into bed with everyone. Well, mostly not. Okay, occasionally she did. Rolling her eyes, she returned her concentration to the road.

"Where are you then? Because I'm outside your house and you ain't in it!"

"I'll be five minutes, okay? Let yourself in and pop the kettle on. I could do with a chat."

"Oh, sounds juicy. I'll stick a pizza in, too."

"I already ate."

"Good for you. I haven't."

Laughing, Alyssa signed off the call. Maybe talking her dilemma out with Lil was the best thing. Her brain certainly wasn't capable of sorting itself out, that's for sure.

"Cuppa's on the side," Lil called from the bathroom.

Alyssa dumped her bag on the floor, kicked off her shoes, and slunk to the kitchen to retrieve her much needed tea.

"Hey there, lady." Lil parked herself on the chair next to Alyssa, appraising her look.

"Hey to you, too."

"Oh, that's not the voice of someone who just had a date with a hot guy." Lil's tone was pointed, and Alyssa caught the edge of disapproval in it.

Alyssa pressed the palms of her hands to her eyeballs. "I had a great time with Josh..."

"Did you, though?" Lil asked, her voice flat. "Because I still don't understand why you agreed to go out with him in the first place."

"Lil—"

"No, seriously, Alyssa. You've been spending every spare moment with Evelyn. You light up when you talk about her. You bake dog treats together, for God's sake. And then Josh asks you out and you just...say yes? What was that about?"

Alyssa groaned. "I panicked, okay?"

"You panicked," Lil repeated, her expression softening slightly. "So you went on a date with a perfectly nice guy you have zero interest in because you're terrified of your feelings for Evelyn?"

"When you say it like that, it sounds ridiculous."

"That's because it is ridiculous." Lil shook her head. "I know you, Lyss. I've watched you keep everyone at arm's length for years. But Evelyn? She's different. And you know it. You're also freaking out because you're not used to being in this situation. Evelyn isn't a fling or a casual hook-up. You want her to be your girlfriend."

Alyssa wanted to bop Lil on the nose because her mocking tone was unnecessary. Alyssa wouldn't have been surprised if Lil broke out in a chorus of *Alyssa and Evelyn sitting in a tree, K.I.S.S.I.N.G.*

"You're a child," Alyssa scoffed, rolling her eyes.

"Yes, but I'm right, aren't I?" There was that bloody smug grin again.

"Fine, yes, you're right."

"C'mon, tell aunty Lil all about it."

"Ew, don't speak like that. It's weird."

"Alyssa, spill."

So Alyssa did the mature thing and stuck out her tongue, blowing a raspberry. They both laughed.

But then the laughter faded, and Alyssa felt the weight of it all settle back on her shoulders. She picked at a loose thread on her jeans, not meeting Lil's eyes.

"It's stupid," she started. "I'm not someone who gets scared about commitment. I just...I've never wanted it before. It's never been for me."

"Because of Four Paws?"

"Yeah. Partly." Alyssa took a breath. "I've been happy with my life, Lil. I enjoy meeting people and having a bit of fun. The centre is my number one priority, and that's always been enough. More than enough."

Lil nodded, her expression patient. "But?"

"But Evelyn makes me want things I've never wanted before." The words came out in a rush. "And that terrifies me. What if I get so caught up in her that I lose focus on the sanctuary? What if I start prioritising her over the dogs, over everything I've built? Four Paws is my life's work. It's who I am. What if falling for someone means I stop being that person?"

"Lyss—"

"And what if it doesn't work out?" Alyssa continued, the floodgates open now. "What if I let myself fall completely and she realizes I'm too much? Or not enough? I've never done this before—the real relationship thing. I don't know how to need someone like that. What if I'm terrible at it? What if I mess it up and lose her, and then I'm left with nothing but regret and this gaping hole where she used to be?"

She finally looked up at Lil, and her voice dropped to almost a whisper. "I've spent my entire adult life being independent. Not needing anyone. And now suddenly I need her, and I don't know what to do with that. It feels like standing on the edge of a cliff, and I'm terrified of jumping."

Lil reached over and squeezed her hand. "So you went out with Josh."

"Yeah." Alyssa laughed, but it was hollow. "Because he's safe. He's a really nice guy, and I told him as soon as he asked me out I was only looking for casual, and that suited him fine. No expectations. No risk. No falling."

"No Evelyn," Lil added gently.

"No Evelyn," Alyssa agreed, her throat tight. "But the whole time I was sitting there with him, all I could think about was her. About how much I wanted to be with her instead. About how I'd rather be terrified with Evelyn than safe with anyone else."

"Does Evelyn know that's what you want with her?"

"I…" Why hadn't they ever discussed relationships? Hell, they'd talked about everything else, but thinking back, Alyssa couldn't remember a time when they'd spoken of their love lives in depth. What did that mean?

"Let's clear a few things up. I want you to have a life, Alyssa. You are the one that puts pressure on yourself to be the wonder woman of Four Paws. We have built a fantastic team, one we both trust. Nothing at all is going to go wrong if you take a tiny step back and focus on something else."

"But…"

"No buts. It's a fact. I want you to explore a relationship, Al. You've got so much to give, and I've seen the way Evelyn looks at you. She's just as smitten as you."

"Smitten? Really?"

"If the goo-goo eyes fit! Yes, smitten. I don't know her like you do, but that much is clear. If you gave it a chance, I think you could have something with that woman. Something great."

"I'm going round for breakfast in the morning."

"Okay. How did that come about?"

"I feel like an arsehole. Josh was the perfect date, but I just couldn't stop thinking about Evelyn. I remembered her face when I told her I had a date. She was upset, even though she tried to play it off. And to be honest, I felt horrible telling her I was going out with someone else."

"Okay, continue."

"Josh was funny, charming, all the things I look for, but with Evelyn...I feel a connection, something deeper. After I said good night to Josh, my entire body was craving to see Evelyn."

"Wow," Lil puffed. "That's new."

"Yeah, tell me about it. We've been getting close for some time. After I told her about my date, she asked me out to dinner. I thought she wanted a friendly working lunch, but she clarified she wanted it to be a proper date. I couldn't get her off my mind after that. So I drove over to her place."

"And how did that go?"

"Well, she gave me the best damn kiss of my life, Lil. I'm talking spine tingling, toe curling, clit throbbing good."

"Jesus. Why has it taken us this long to get to the juicy part of your night? Bloody hell, Alyssa."

Alyssa laughed. "You asked me to explain," she mock whined.

"So why are you here and not doing unspeakable things to that lovely lady?"

"Because I want to do it right."

"And how does that look to you? What's your way of doing it, right?"

"Dating. Exclusively." The clarity that washed over Alyssa was astounding. Why the bloody hell had she been so worried? Alyssa wanted Evelyn. Not just for a night or a few weeks.

"So go for it. Look, I'm not gonna get all psychoanalyse-y on you, but I think this should help. You're not scared of commitment, you just think you don't know how to do it right?"

Alyssa nodded in agreement. It's true she'd never been in a relationship.

"But here's the thing. You *do* know. You have loads of relationships!"

"With who?"

"The dogs."

Alyssa blinked slowly at Lil. Was she high?

"Don't look at me like I'm nuts. Just listen. With your parents moving you about so much, you didn't learn how to connect with people. Is that fair?"

"I suppose."

"But you learned how to connect with your pets. The thing is, Alyssa, forming a bond and a relationship is the same, whether it's an animal or human. Giving love, learning their traits and behaviours. Being compassionate, caring, and all that other gumpf."

Squinting in concentration, Alyssa tried to see where Lil was coming from. "Alright, I think I get what you're on about."

"You know how to maintain a healthy relationship, Alyssa. So far it's just been for your animals, but that can transfer to humans too. Hell, we're in a committed friendship, right?"

"Of course."

"So there you go. It will be the same with Evelyn except for all the hot sex."

Alyssa barked out a laugh. "Okay, I think that's enough from you. I get what you're saying though."

"Good. Go have breakfast and just see where it goes. Don't put a limit on it and don't, for the love of beans, worry about me, the team, or the dogs."

20

Breakfast in Bed
(Eventually)

ALYSSA

"Hello?" Alyssa slowly pushed open Evelyn's front door. She'd contemplated ringing the doorbell, but Evelyn did tell her to use the door code she'd sent through a text message last night. Still, it was a little weird letting herself into Evelyn's home. Especially when she couldn't hear the woman. What if Evelyn was still asleep?

The *tic tic tic* of Bug's paws was the first sign of life in the dark penthouse. Pushing forward, Alyssa closed the door, took off her coat and wandered into the living room. No sign of Evelyn.

Even though Alyssa had been in the penthouse before, she'd never had a tour, so blindly opening doors didn't seem like a good plan. Entering the kitchen, Alyssa threw caution to the wind and set the coffee machine going. Rooting through the fridge, she found some fruit and yoghurt. Would Evelyn like breakfast in bed? Was that too much?

Am I a creeper?

Bug tottered into the kitchen, lying down by the window. Ah, he found a sun patch.

"You had a good time, buddy?"

Bug yawned and collapsed in a dramatic heap. Ten minutes later, Alyssa was armed with a tray of coffee, tea, orange juice, toast, and fruit with honey yoghurt. Better to over prepare, right?

Wandering down the hall, Alyssa poked her head through the first open door. Not Evelyn's bedroom, but a guest room. Alyssa noted the bed covers, smiled, and made a note to talk to Evelyn about them. The next door along was ajar. The blinds were half drawn, allowing sunlight to filter in. Alyssa could see Evelyn asleep.

Creeping into the room slowly, Alyssa sat the tray on the bedside table closest to Evelyn and sat on the bed. It was now or never. Alyssa figured it was going to go one of two ways. Either Evelyn would love the surprise, or freak the hell out when she realised Alyssa had let herself in, used her kitchen, and entered her room without her knowing it. A pit of dread began filling in her stomach.

Suddenly this seemed like the worst idea in the world.

I need to leave!

Standing up, Alyssa went to tiptoe away but was stopped by a hand, grabbing her wrist gently.

"Where are you going?" Evelyn's sleepy voice whispered.

Alyssa's heart did a little flutter. Evelyn's sleepy voice was low and raspy. It was hot. Hell, Evelyn all mussed up from sleep was hot!

"I didn't want to scare you," Alyssa answered, settling back down on the edge of the bed.

"You didn't. I thought I was dreaming." Evelyn's smile was shy, which caused Alyssa to melt. God, could this woman get any more enticing?

"I made you breakfast. Maybe I should have waited, or come back later?"

"What time is it?"

Alyssa scooted away as Evelyn adjusted herself into an upright position. Evelyn's usually pristine blonde hair jutted out in different directions. Smiling even harder, Alyssa let her fingers reach out and tuck the blonde locks behind Evelyn's ear. Then she froze. Not only had she let herself into Evelyn's home, now she had touched her without permission.

What the bloody hell is wrong with me?

Snatching her hand back, Alyssa avoided looking at Evelyn. "Sorry about that. Um, it's...um...it's..."

"Alyssa, stop."

Chancing a look, Alyssa breathed out a sigh of relief. There wasn't a shred of annoyance or discomfort on Evelyn's beautiful face.

"Would you kiss me?"

Sucking in a sharp breath, Alyssa had to remind herself how to function like a regular human. What was it about Evelyn that stripped her of coherent thought and action?

Licking her lips, Alyssa's eyes drifted down to Evelyn's mouth. Pitching forward slowly, Alyssa gently sucked on

Evelyn's lower lip. The breathy moan Evelyn let out was almost too much to bear.

As the kiss deepened, Alyssa became very aware that Evelyn was in her nightwear. Specifically, a silk tank top that didn't really cover a whole lot. The rigid peaks of Evelyn's aroused nipples teased Alyssa. But she couldn't touch her, could she? Evelyn was definitely into the kiss. In fact, her hands were doing some roaming of their own.

"Take this off," Evelyn gasped between kisses, her hand tugging on Alyssa's jumper.

Not one to refuse a beautiful woman, Alyssa swept the top up and over her head.

"You're not wearing a bra!" It wasn't a question. Alyssa could get away without having to wear a bra. Her breasts were just small enough.

"Is that okay?" The kiss suddenly broke, and Alyssa wanted to cry. Had she just ruined the moment?

"You are sublime and I want to touch you everywhere," Evelyn stated.

Alright then, the moment was not ruined, at all!

"Go nuts," Alyssa chuckled, recapturing Evelyn's lips. They tugged, pushed, and pulled until Alyssa realised they were both nearly naked. So much for taking their time.

Evelyn's mouth was fire and velvet, devouring Alyssa's lips as if she'd been starved of affection for years and needed to make up for it immediately. Alyssa let herself be pressed back into the mattress, the softness of the duvet bunching up beneath her bare skin and the heat of Evelyn's thigh urgent between her own. Evelyn's silk top was already gone, tossed somewhere to the floor. Alyssa's own jumper had vanished in the fray, and now there was nothing but the delicious collision of their bodies and the frantic scramble of hands needing more.

Evelyn's mouth left a slick, fevered trail down Alyssa's neck, teeth nipping gently at the base of her throat before moving lower, pressing open-mouthed kisses along her collarbones. Alyssa arched, running her fingers through the perfectly chaotic mess of Evelyn's blonde hair, delighting in the way it tickled her own chest as Evelyn licked and tasted every inch she could reach.

"Is this okay?" Evelyn's voice was deep, a growl at the back of her throat.

"God, yes," Alyssa gasped, pulling Evelyn's head closer, arching her back, offering her chest. Evelyn wasted no time. Her mouth latched onto one nipple, swirling and sucking, while her hand found and kneaded the other. Alyssa gasped, her hips canting upward on instinct, desperate for more contact than the teasing friction of thigh on thigh.

Evelyn's other hand traced the line of Alyssa's ribcage, then her waist, and then lower, mapping every dip and curve as if learning them for a test later. Her fingers hooked into the waistband of Alyssa's joggers—the last barrier between them—and hesitated, just for a heartbeat.

Alyssa lifted her hips, pushing into Evelyn's hand. "Off. Please."

Evelyn grinned, sharp and hungry, and stripped the joggers down and off, taking Alyssa's knickers with them. "No half measures, I see," she murmured, settling between Alyssa's knees and simply staring for a moment, the look of awe on her face the most flattering thing Alyssa had ever seen.

Alyssa felt suddenly exposed, vulnerable in a way she hadn't expected, but Evelyn's eyes were reverent. She traced Alyssa's thigh with a trembling hand, then kissed the inside of her knee, working her way up with excruciating slowness.

"You're beautiful," Evelyn breathed, and Alyssa's cheeks flared with heat. She wanted to joke, to deflect, but then Evelyn's tongue was on her and all power of speech left her body.

Alyssa's hips bucked, pleasure ripping through her as Evelyn sucked and licked, tongue finding just the right pressure, the right angle. Evelyn was thorough and relentless, two fingers sliding inside and curling with practiced confidence, the heel of her palm grinding in time with her tongue. Alyssa came hard and sudden, a guttural cry escaping her lips as every muscle in her body locked tight, then melted into the mattress.

Evelyn didn't stop. Not even as Alyssa's thighs trembled and her hips shuddered. She licked her clean, gentle now, then pressed soft kisses up her belly, chest, throat, until she found Alyssa's lips again and kissed her slow and deep.

Alyssa could taste herself on Evelyn's tongue, salty and sweet and perfect.

"Okay?" Evelyn whispered, brushing hair back from Alyssa's damp forehead.

Alyssa laughed, breathless. "More than okay. Fucking spectacular."

"Good," Evelyn said, and kissed her again.

Alyssa pulled her close, rolling Evelyn to her side and then over, pinning her. "Now it's my turn."

Evelyn's eyes widened, just a little. Alyssa grinned and kissed her. She lingered at the hollow of Evelyn's throat, then down to the delicate slope of her breasts, and lower still. Evelyn's skin was warm and impossibly soft, and the way she shivered beneath Alyssa's mouth, the way her breath hitched when Alyssa grazed her belly with her teeth, made Alyssa's blood sing.

When Alyssa reached the waistband of Evelyn's black satin shorts, she hooked her fingers in and tugged gently. "Can I?"

Evelyn was already lifting her hips, baring herself without shame. Alyssa dragged the shorts down, tossing them to the far corner of the room, and took in the view. Evelyn was flushed, pupils blown wide, her chest rising and falling with quick, shallow breaths.

Alyssa kissed the inside of Evelyn's thigh, hands spreading her knees apart, and then, with a wicked look up, she dipped her head and tasted.

Evelyn's hand shot to Alyssa's hair, gripping tight as Alyssa swirled her tongue, savouring the sharp gasp and helpless moan that escaped the usually composed woman. Alyssa's hands held Evelyn's hips in place, her tongue and lips exploring with the kind of patience and care she'd reserved for only the most sensitive rescue dogs—until now. Here, now, every ounce of her attention was dedicated to making Evelyn fall apart.

It didn't take long. Evelyn tried to muffle her cries at first, biting her lip, but Alyssa was determined to undo her, to see her shatter. She flicked her tongue, slow and steady, then faster, harder, and when Evelyn's legs trembled and her thighs clamped tight around Alyssa's head, Alyssa slid two fingers inside, matching her mouth to the stuttering rhythm of Evelyn's breathing.

Evelyn came loud, shaking, her nails scraping Alyssa's shoulders as if she could anchor herself to reality through touch alone.

Alyssa didn't stop, not until Evelyn was begging, until every muscle had given out and she collapsed, boneless and panting. Only then did Alyssa crawl up the length of her body, resting her weight on top of Evelyn, and cradle her face, kissing her softly.

"Holy hell," Evelyn murmured, voice ragged.

Alyssa beamed, smug. "You okay?"

Evelyn laughed, the sound a little hysterical, a lot delighted. "Okay? I think I just left my body."

They lay tangled for a few minutes, letting their pulses slow. Alyssa stroked Evelyn's cheek, memorising the new glow on her face, the unguarded smile that was for Alyssa alone.

"Do you want breakfast?" Alyssa asked, nudging the tray on the bedside table. "I made you this whole...thing, but now I'm not sure if we should even bother with food. Unless, you know, you're still hungry."

Evelyn kissed her, a messy, open-mouthed thing that tasted like lust and laughter and relief. "I want you," she said, voice low. "But I suppose we should have some of that fruit, just so we don't pass out."

So they did. Naked, under the covers, feeding each other slices of orange and strawberries and taking turns licking honey off fingers, making a game of who could seduce the other into a second round first.

Unsurprisingly, Alyssa lost. Evelyn pinned her wrists above her head, her hair falling in a golden curtain as she kissed Alyssa until her lips were sore. The breakfast tray was abandoned as they pressed close, skin to skin. Evelyn was skilled, attentive, mapping Alyssa's body with hands and mouth and a kind of worshipful awe. Alyssa melted under her, gasping Evelyn's name again and again until her voice broke and her body followed.

Afterwards, they lay in a tangle of arms and legs, silent but for the sound of their breathing, the occasional giggle, and the gentle rhythm of Evelyn's hand stroking up and down Alyssa's back.

"So much for taking it slow," Alyssa whispered, pressing her face into the crook of Evelyn's neck.

"I think we made up for lost time," Evelyn replied.

Alyssa laughed. "I had this whole plan to do things properly. Take you on dates, be a gentlewoman..."

"We can still do that," Evelyn said.

"Maybe we can try restraint next time," Alyssa teased.

Evelyn snorted. "If you want restraint, you're barking up the wrong tree. I've wanted you for weeks."

Alyssa grinned. "You could have fooled me. You keep everything so controlled."

"Not anymore," Evelyn said simply, then yawned and tugged Alyssa even closer.

They drifted, lazy and sated, bodies slick and still tingling, the duvet twisted around them in a warm, contented cocoon. Alyssa listened to Evelyn's heart slow and smiled into her skin.

Before sleep claimed her, Alyssa nuzzled Evelyn's shoulder and whispered, "Don't make any plans for the rest of your life."

Evelyn hummed, drowsy, her fingers tracing lazy patterns on Alyssa's skin. "Okay."

21

Morning After, Interrupted

EVELYN

They'd fallen asleep tangled together, sated and warm, but sleep hadn't lasted long. Evelyn had woken to Alyssa's lips on her neck, her hands already wandering, and any thought of rest had evaporated.

Now, Evelyn rolled her hips slowly, her fingers digging into Alyssa's supple and muscular back. The heat radiating off of their bodies was immense. Beads of sweat rolled down her abdomen. The sweet pressure of Alyssa's centre pushing against her own was driving her insane. The rush to climax had slowed to a sensual crawl. Every movement was deliberate and calculated to give each other the maximum amount of pleasure.

The throbbing between Evelyn's thighs was almost painful. She desperately needed a release. Alyssa was teasing her, coaxing her body to heights she'd never experienced. Delayed gratification was torturous in its beauty. Alyssa held Evelyn on the precipice of climax for what felt like an eternity.

Needing more, Evelyn lowered her hands to Alyssa's backside. Grabbing firmly, she pulled Alyssa closer. The wetness of Alyssa's pleasure soaked Evelyn's thigh. Both women were wordless, their pants and moans echoing through the silent apartment. Evelyn's eyes rolled back in her head as Alyssa deepened her hip roll, biting at the pulse point on Evelyn's neck.

They moved in harmony, amping up their pleasure.

"Alyssa," Evelyn gasped as she edged ever closer to falling.

"Evie," Alyssa replied in equal want.

Evelyn squeezed Alyssa's arse harder, bringing up her thigh to allow Alyssa to grind deeper. They'd already explored each other with fingers earlier—multiple times, in fact—but this was different. This slow, deliberate friction, the weight of Alyssa's body against hers, the way their centres pressed together with nothing between them.

Normally, Evelyn's sexual encounters were a race to the finish. Touch, stroke, climax, done. Get to the end goal as fast as possible. That couldn't be further from the truth now, though. This experience, this revelation with Alyssa, was beyond her wildest dreams. They'd already made each other come apart with their hands, their mouths, but somehow this felt even more intimate. The unhurried rhythm, the eye contact, the way Alyssa was looking at her like she was something precious.

Evelyn was going to call out Alyssa's name in rapture any moment, and all they were doing was moving together, skin against skin.

"I'm...God, yes, Alyssa." There was nothing but that moment. The clarity of mind that came with such an explosive orgasm rocked Evelyn to her soul. There were no stars and bright lights behind her eyes as she came, there was only euphoria, only Alyssa staring down at her as she rode her climax all the way to sated bliss.

"Evelyn, oh, Jesus," Alyssa cried seconds after Evelyn had floated back down to earth. Holding Alyssa's body tighter, she helped steady the woman as she writhed and rocked. Time slowed as Alyssa's body sank into Evelyn, their slick skin cooling in the aftermath. Evelyn cradled Alyssa's head, which lay tucked into her neck. Their breaths were still ragged from exertion. Alyssa's weight felt heavenly on Evelyn's body.

Evelyn had found it difficult to sleep during the night. Her kiss with Alyssa made it nigh on impossible. The feelings coursing through her body after just one kiss were baffling. By three a.m. Evelyn finally drifted off, which is why she was still tucked up in bed when Alyssa arrived for their breakfast date.

Alyssa's nerves had been adorable. In other circumstances, Evelyn would have been shocked to see someone in her bedroom, but it was Alyssa's scent that had woken her, causing no alarm. Evelyn thought she was possibly dreaming until the bed dipped. Then Evelyn knew it was real. Alyssa, the woman who stole Evelyn's breath, was there, in her room.

How could she not touch her? Not kiss her again? Evelyn understood why Alyssa wanted to wait. She, too, wanted them to date and take their time, but in that moment, as Evelyn regarded Alyssa in all her ethereal glory, there was no way she could wait. It was inevitable that the kiss would lead to more and, wow, Alyssa hadn't disappointed in that department.

Alyssa shifted her head, kissing down Evelyn's neck. In an impressive move of strength and grace, Evelyn rolled them so Alyssa was on her back. Peering down into her lover's eyes, Evelyn was almost overwhelmed by the feeling that punched her in the chest.

Alyssa looked up at her with rosy skin. Her dark hair had got even bigger once pulled out of the ponytail Alyssa wore when she first walked in. She was a vision of creamy skin, delicate beauty spots, and rich wild hair. Had hair ever looked so perfect on a pillow? Not until now.

Licking the hollow of Alyssa's neck, Evelyn set off on her familiar journey downward. She already knew the taste of Alyssa's skin, the scent rising from her sex that made her mouth water. But somehow, the second time felt even better than the first. She took her time now, studying every inch of skin and muscle as she dipped lower, reacquainting herself with the landscape of Alyssa's body. Thick, tight, and soft. All that work at the rehoming centre had sculpted Alyssa into pure power.

A smile blossomed on her face when she felt Alyssa's hand gently push on her shoulder, clearly eager for Evelyn to reach her destination. When her tongue swept through Alyssa's pink folds again, it felt like coming home. The placement of Alyssa's hand on the back of her head heightened the sensation—a connection that propelled Alyssa's desire directly into Evelyn.

Reaching up with her hand, Evelyn gently kneaded Alyssa's breast, rolling and tugging her nipple until she heard the woman gasp and squirm. She'd learned what Alyssa liked earlier, and now she used that knowledge with confidence. It was difficult to decide which one of them was enjoying it more. Evelyn loved oral—giving and taking. Her own arousal usually grew as she pleasured her partner with her mouth. With Alyssa, her arousal surged so quickly, she was afraid she'd come before finishing what she'd started.

Sucking Alyssa's stiff bud into her mouth, Evelyn closed her eyes and savoured every taste, every brush of silk in her mouth.

"Evie, fuck! Don't stop." Alyssa's hips were rocking. Evelyn rode the rhythm of Alyssa's movements with practised ease. The gentle vibration of Alyssa's thighs and the rapid panting told Evelyn she would come soon. Needing to taste more, Evelyn thrust her tongue into Alyssa's opening, earning a shout to the heavens. The earthquake that was Alyssa's orgasm shook them both until Alyssa's legs collapsed, her hand dropping to her stomach.

"You taste magnificent," Evelyn murmured from Alyssa's apex.

"That...I..."

Evelyn was elated she'd rendered Alyssa almost speechless. Kissing her way back up, she settled on top of Alyssa.

"Evelyn." Alyssa gasped as Evelyn reached down and stroked her pulsing silk.

"Again," she whispered into Alyssa's mouth.

"You, too," Alyssa managed to reply. Evelyn felt fingers brush past her hip, then the soft stroke through her neat curls that revved up her excitement. Lifting slightly and shifting to the left, Evelyn positioned herself so they could both touch each other with abandon, no barriers between them.

A guttural groan burst from Evelyn's throat as Alyssa stroked her hard and fast with pure determination. Doubling her efforts, Evelyn entered Alyssa with two fingers, instantly curling them to rub along the ribbed flesh that would make Alyssa fall apart in her hand.

The smell of sweat and sex permeated the air as they picked up their pace. Neither one breaking eye contact as they climbed higher and higher until eventually they tipped, crying out in unison.

The toast was soggy and the coffee was cold, but Evelyn didn't care. After more orgasms than Evelyn could count, she needed sustenance. Alyssa lay sleeping soundly next to her. When was the last time Evelyn lay in bed at eleven a.m. on a weekend without her laptop on? Months ago, probably. Although even before she took over as CEO, Evelyn spent little time relaxing like this.

"Coffee!" Alyssa blurted, startling Evelyn. Holding her hand to her chest, Evelyn let out a nervous chuckle. Alyssa was sitting up, her huge hair shrouding her face.

"Al, are you okay?"

A very disoriented and supremely cute Alyssa struggled to swipe her hair away from her face. "Yes, sorry," she mumbled, still half asleep.

Evelyn passed her the cup of cold coffee. Without question, Alyssa downed the majority of it. It was quite comical how quickly Alyssa seemed to come to life.

"Wow, I had a really wonderful dream."

"Oh? Care to tell me?" Evelyn purred.

Alyssa turned her head and grinned slyly. "Actually, I don't think it was a dream, but a very, very decadent memory."

The sound of the front door slamming shut cut off any response Evelyn was about to give. Scrambling for her robe, Evelyn shot out of bed and headed for the door.

"Stay here," she hissed to Alyssa. Peeking her head around the door frame, Evelyn scanned the corridor. A noise was coming from her kitchen. Carefully, she made her way towards the disturbance.

What do I do if it's a burglar?

The familiar voice of Mindy put those worries to bed pretty sharpish—and replaced them with complete shock. She hadn't seen or heard from Mindy in over a month. Not since she'd made it crystal clear their relationship was over. What the hell was she doing here?

Her shock was quickly replaced with anger.

"What the bloody hell are you doing?" she shrieked, causing Mindy to jump.

"What are *you* doing here?" Mindy answered in kind. "It's my house!"

"But you're usually at work!" Mindy barked.

"Obviously not this morning. Why are you in my kitchen?"

"I came to set up a surprise for you, if you must know," Mindy huffed.

"Why?" Evelyn bellowed. "We haven't spoken in over a month!"

Both women were interrupted by Alyssa, who poked her head into the kitchen. "So, I'm gonna go…"

"No, Alyssa—" Evelyn began.

"It's cool, Evie. Speak later." And with that, Evelyn's morning got tanked. She rounded on Mindy with fury in her eyes.

"Mindy, what in the ever-loving fuck are you doing in my home? You don't live here, and we are not together!"

"Evelyn, don't you think it's time you forgave me? Come on, I made a mistake, but we're supposed to be together."

Shaking her head, hoping to dislodge the insanity of the conversation, Evelyn took a step towards Mindy. "Mindy, listen very carefully. We are over. I do not love you. I do not trust you."

"Well, that's charming. After all the shit I had to put up with?"

"Are you referring to my late nights at work?"

"You bet your arse I am. I waited around for you all those months and one minor mistake on my part and that's it. I'm kicked to the curb?"

"If by waiting around for me you mean partied it up several times a week—on my credit card—then yes, you're right. How very difficult for you. Let me take a wild stab in the dark. This new woman you were shagging isn't as well off as you thought? Hm? Can't provide the life you became accustomed to with me? About right?"

Evelyn knew damn well she was right. The blush on Mindy's face only confirmed it.

"So because you've found another body to warm your bed, I'm toast?"

"Alyssa, the body you are referring to, is so much more than a bed warmer. Although after this little stunt, I won't be surprised if she wants nothing to do with me."

A frustrated growl rumbled in her throat. Evelyn and Alyssa hadn't even had the chance to talk about their relationship, if that's what you could call it. Evelyn knew it was going to be a tricky discussion anyway with Alyssa's aversion to commitment. How the hell would they broach it now? Maybe seeing Mindy in Evelyn's kitchen would reaffirm to Alyssa that she was better off in casual set-ups. Christ, Evelyn wanted to scream.

"Evie, come on."

"Get out. Now!" Evelyn's tone left no room for argument. Her glare also squashed any protests Mindy was about to unload. Evelyn waited until she heard the door shut, before letting out a scream of frustration. Her perfect, *perfect* time with Alyssa had been utterly ruined.

Rushing back to her bedroom, Evelyn scooped up her phone and hit the call button. *Please pick up, please pick up.* Nothing. It rang until the voicemail kicked in. Great, Alyssa was ignoring her calls. And why wouldn't she? How was she supposed to act after witnessing Evelyn's ex-girlfriend making herself at home in the kitchen?

"Bug!" she exclaimed. Running from the kitchen to the living room, Evelyn's heart bottomed out. Alyssa had taken Bug with her. Dropping to her settee, Evelyn surveyed her empty home. "I'm always going to end up alone," she sobbed.

Lunch time was an acceptable time of the day to be drunk, right? Ah, balls to it. If Evelyn had to suffer through the stupid festive season all alone, then she was going to make sure she was well lubricated.

After the third unread text message to Alyssa, Evelyn gave up. She'd apologised and explained. What else could she do?

So, instead of trying to get hold of Alyssa, Evelyn cracked open a bottle of wine. Then another. Not a very good look for a CEO, but so what? Evelyn would go back to work tomorrow, then the next day, and so on until she died a lonely old woman.

Drinking two bottles of wine evidently wasn't good for her morale.

What would make her feel better? Well, Alyssa talking to her for one. Failing that, she needed to rant. The phone rang. Shockingly, for the first time since he'd left, Richard Crawford answered a bloody call.

"Hey, honey, how are you?"

Anger raged through Evelyn's body. "Where the hell have you been?" she barked. "I have been trying to get hold of you for fucking weeks!" Evelyn never swore at her dad. "How dare you just swan off and leave me in the shit? I have needed you and you just vanished with that trollop. How could you be so selfish?" she screamed.

Silence.

"Evie...I..."

"You what, Dad? What could you possibly say? You left me in charge of the business without consulting me. You left me at the mercy of a board that doesn't want me there. You neglected to tell me about a bloody working relationship with a goddamn pet rescue. You left me to organise the Christmas party. You. Left. Me!"

"I'm sorry, love, I just... I couldn't be around the business...I needed space."

"And what about what I needed? You think I want to be here? Alone, with no support? At least you have your floozy. I have no one."

"She's not a floozy, Evelyn."

"Sure, because your vast wealth holds no interest for a woman half your age and who has nothing in common with you. It must be love," Evelyn scoffed.

"Evelyn, have you been drinking?"

"You bet I fucking have. My life is in the toilet because of you. I never wanted to be CEO, Dad."

"I didn't know that lov—"

"Why would you? You never asked. You never talk to me now Mum's gone." A sob ripped through Evelyn. "You just forgot about her and then forgot about me." Tears streamed down her face.

"I could never forget about either of you," Richard's voice cracked. "Roslyn is one love of my life and you are the other. Milly knows the score."

"What does that mean?" she hiccuped.

"Milly will never replace your mother. No one will. I take her on holiday and spend money on her, but that's it, Evelyn. She's company for me, nothing more. I could never be with another woman that way. Never."

Evelyn wiped her nose on her jumper sleeve and then her eyes. All this time, she'd thought that her dad had simply found someone else, someone younger than her mum.

"You're not together?"

"No, we're not. Milly has no family. We bonded over our mutual grief. Neither of us want more than friendship. I should have told you, Evelyn. I should have done a lot of things for you, but I was—and still am—so lost without your mum by my side, honey. The thought of being home at this time of year is agony. But I should have thought of you, too. I could only see my pain. I didn't do a good job as your dad. Are things really that bad at the office?"

"I'm constantly stressed. I know I've put myself under a tremendous amount of pressure since you left. I can't do it anymore, Dad. I'm burning out."

"Alright, sweetheart. I'll sort it out. I'm sorry, Evie, truly."

"I miss Mum. I miss her every day, but it's worse this time of year. I know that, but Dad, everything is ten times harder when I feel alone. I need you, too."

"Oh, darling," he cried. Evelyn's dad hadn't cried in front of Evelyn since her mum's funeral. "I'm coming home."

A rush of emotion spilled out as Evelyn shattered. The years of hurt and loneliness coupled with Alyssa and Bug's departure came flowing out. Evelyn listened as her dad laid out his plan to get home. With a ringing in her ears and her heart palpitating, Evelyn disconnected the call.

22

Decorations, Declarations, and Dog Bedding

ALYSSA

Alyssa scrubbed her face. This morning had been perfect. Beyond perfect, actually. Then Mindy showed up, which put a spanner in the works, but it was okay. Alyssa knew she needed to leave Evelyn to deal with that hot mess, which was why she nipped out with Bug. Going home, taking a shower, and checking on the other dogs would waste a bit of time before she could return to Evelyn and her oh-so-comfy bed.

That had been the plan, anyway. However, as with all good intentions, it got mucked up. First by Alyssa losing her phone. The bloody thing couldn't have got far, but she couldn't find it for the life of her. Then there was a crisis at Four Paws. One of the puppies had taken a turn for the worse and needed emergency medical care.

When Alyssa finally got back, she found there was no power to her mobile home, so that took another hour to sort out. All in all, it was well into the afternoon before things settled and Alyssa could organise herself to head back over to Evelyn's.

It was on the journey back to the penthouse that inspiration struck. Hearing Evelyn describe her Christmas experiences since her mum died was heart wrenching. No one should feel alone, especially during the festive season, so she formed a brilliant plan to help Evelyn embrace a holiday she once loved.

Alyssa's newfound joy and optimism dissipated like a tissue in a puddle when she parked the car and stared at the mass of people filing into the shopping centre.

It was bursting at the seams with grumbling Christmas shoppers. Weary mothers dragging their screaming children from store to store. Lonesome husbands hanging around the food court, ladened down with bags their wives had dumped on them. Thank God Evelyn wasn't here. A sight like this would definitely reinforce her belief that Christmas wasn't worth celebrating. Although after talking to her, Alyssa knew it wasn't a genuine dislike of the season. Evelyn just felt lonely and sad. Time to turn that around.

Rolling her shoulders and neck, Alyssa psyched herself up like a boxer entering the ring. She had a vague idea of what she needed and an even vaguer plan of attack. Into the shopping centre she went, bobbing and weaving like a pro—dodging prams the size of small cars, sidestepping distracted phone-scrollers, and navigating around couples who'd decided the exact centre of the walkway was the perfect spot to have a full-blown argument about whose mother they were visiting for Boxing Day.

Forty-five minutes later, Alyssa emerged from the crowds hot and flustered but triumphant. Her arms were weighed down with bags. A total success. Now she just had to get Evelyn onboard. That was probably going to be the hardest part.

With a quick check of the time, Alyssa reasoned that taking an extra twenty minutes to grab Bug was a good idea. If anyone could soften Evelyn to the idea of Christmas, it was him.

Why was Evelyn's penthouse so dark? Crap, maybe she'd gone out. Alyssa stood inside the door, weighing up her options. First option was to leave and come back later. Messaging or phoning Evelyn was out of the question because she still couldn't find her bloody phone, and the one she'd grabbed from the sanctuary didn't have Evelyn's number listed as it was for work purposes only. Second option was to stay and surprise Evelyn with everything she'd bought.

Bug decided for her by wandering over to his pile of discarded Christmas decorations he'd hijacked from Evelyn's closet yesterday evening. Setting her bags on the floor, Alyssa shoved her nerves down. Evelyn could hate everything she was about to do and kick her out, never wanting to see her again. Shaking her head, Alyssa got to work as Bug lay watching in a supervisory role.

An unknown amount of time later and Alyssa had to concede there was a distinct possibility that she'd gone a tad overboard.

Evelyn's penthouse looked like Christmas had upchucked all over the place.

The only thing missing was a Christmas tree, and that was only because Alyssa couldn't get the guy to deliver within the hour. Checking the time again, she ran downstairs to wait for the tree. Darrel—the tree man—had messaged her work number to say he'd had a cancellation and was on his way over now. Hurrah, another victory!

"Perfect," she whispered to herself and Bug. It had taken an hour to place the tree and get it decorated. Looking around, Alyssa smiled, and then it wavered. She'd taken a huge risk sprucing up Evelyn's place. The woman could detest it and feel like her space had been violated.

"Shit," she hissed.

What had she been thinking? Well, she hadn't, had she? No, Alyssa had floated along in a post-sex love haze, only thinking about how romantic it would be to do this for Evelyn.

In truth, this could be an utter disaster!

The squeak of a door almost gave Alyssa a heart attack. There was someone in the penthouse. Oh shit, what if it was Mindy? Alyssa hadn't even considered that possibility. She'd just presumed Evelyn would deal with her ex and ask her to leave. What if it was a burglar?

Picking up a Nutcracker statue that was positioned by the open fireplace, Alyssa creeped towards the hall that led to the bedrooms. Counting silently in her head to three, she shrieked like a banshee, raising her weapon ready to strike down the intruder. Evelyn's scream pierced the house with such force, Alyssa instinctively flung the Nutcracker behind her and ducked.

"What the *fuck*?" Evelyn screamed again, clutching her chest.

"Evelyn," Alyssa panted, her heart rate that of a jackhammer. "I didn't know you were here."

"Why does everyone think me being in my own home is surprising?"

Alyssa didn't know what to say. She was too struck by how tired and sad Evelyn looked. "Are you okay?" she asked, staggering to her feet. Evelyn had dark circles under her eyes, and her hair was a mess. Had she been sleeping all day? "Did something bad happen with Mindy?"

Evelyn laughed. "You tell me. You left, ignored my calls and messages, and took Bug. But it's okay, I know you don't do relationships or anything. I shouldn't have presumed."

Alyssa's eyebrows reached her hairline. "I left to give you time to sort out things with Mindy. I didn't want anything to escalate because I was there. Then I lost my phone, had a puppy emergency, and lost power in my house. As soon as I could, I came back here. That was a few hours ago. I didn't realise you were home."

"You weren't upset?"

"No, of course not," Alyssa replied with a hint of desperation. "Evie, we all have exes. You met mine, kind of. I just wanted to give you some privacy, but I certainly didn't mean to be gone for so long."

"Oh," Evelyn whispered, her eyes straying from Alyssa's.

"I did something," Alyssa blurted. The only reason Evelyn hadn't seen the grotto that was now her home was because they were still in the hallway.

"Okay," Evely replied, elongating the word.

"I think I did something bad. I thought it was a good idea at the time, but now I think you're going to be mad and wish I'd stayed away." Alyssa was panicking.

"Alyssa, it can't be that bad."

"Well, let's find out." Alyssa chuckled nervously. Taking Evelyn's hand, she pulled her around the corner.

"Holy shit," Evelyn gasped. "Alyssa."

Alyssa winced. "I know, shit, I'm sorry. I was feeling all warm and fuzzy on the way over here, and then I thought about how sad you were because it was Christmas, and I got this stupid idea in my head that if I decorated your house, and spent the evening with you watching Christmas films and eating gingerbread, you would feel better. Now I know I messed up big time. I'm so sorry, Evelyn. It was completely insensitive and rude of me to force this on you, knowing why you don't enjoy the season. I was being selfish. I'll just go."

Alyssa was already making her way to the door before Evelyn caught up and pulled her back to the living room. "Will you slow down? I didn't say it was a bad thing. Just a shock. It's..."

Alyssa perused the room. Reds, golds and greens sparkled and shone from every corner. "Tacky? Over the top?"

"Beautiful," Evelyn sighed. "I called my dad."

Interesting change of topic, but okay. "Oh, right, how is Richard?"

"I shouted at him."

Alyssa wasn't entirely sure what was happening. Evelyn seemed lost.

"Let's sit down."

"I thought you'd left me, and I sort of lost the plot. I drank way too much and then called my dad."

"Sweetie, I'm so sorry you thought I'd left. I would never do that, not because your crazy ex showed up. I just wanted to give you some space to work it all out."

Alyssa drew in a breath. The time had come to put her cards on the table—which was beautifully decorated, by the way.

"It's true that I didn't do relationships. I always said it was because the rescue centre was my sole priority. I couldn't give a woman my attention, so I didn't bother. After talking to Lil, I think I understand myself a little better. She pointed out that with all the moving around I did as a kid, I never really learned how to connect with people. Especially not romantically."

Alyssa would have to delve into that a little deeper, but not right now.

"I always had a bond with animals, especially dogs, so instead of learning how to connect with women, I used Four Paws as an excuse. I don't know why, but I did. Then you came along. From the second I saw you, something in me changed. You must think I'm nuts, but I swear it's true. I wanted to get to know you. Hell, I just wanted to be around you."

"Even if I was a bit of a bitch when we first met?" Evelyn's eyes shone with vulnerability and doubt.

Alyssa chuckled. "Yes, even then. Anyway, I can be hard-headed. Lil says it's because I'm an Aries."

"You are fiery," Evelyn smiled.

"I am, and that gets me into trouble sometimes. So, after talking to you and hanging out in your office, I knew you were different."

"But you went out with Josh?"

"I did, and I feel bad about it. Don't get me wrong, he's a great guy, but I only agreed to dinner because the feelings I had for you freaked me out a little bit."

"But not now?"

Alyssa scooted closer to Evelyn on the couch. "They still scare me, but in a good way. The moment my dinner with Josh finished, all I wanted to do was see you. And then you kissed me and my world turned upside down. I wanted you so badly last night."

"Me, too."

"And then this morning..."

"Yeah." Evelyn smiled, her cheeks tinted red.

"It was perfect, Evelyn. So much more than sex. I lost myself in you and that has never happened. But I was happy that it happened, happy I got lost in you."

"I feel the same. It's fast...we've only known each other a few weeks, but I am *so* drawn to you. Not just your body, which is ridiculously sexy, but to your charm and kind nature. I'm so turned on by your passion it's unreal. I think that's why I overreacted this morning. Our bubble was burst. It's been a struggle these past few years. There was no happy ending for me in sight. Nothing will ever make my mum's passing easier. I don't want you to think I'm trying to fill a void by being with you."

"I don't think that, Evie."

"Good. I also don't want you to think I'm latching on to you because I'm lonely. I don't put the responsibility of my happiness on you, Al."

"I know that too, Evelyn. But I want to make you happy."

"Our time together has made me very happy. For a long time, I've felt out of sorts. Nothing in my life seemed to line up. I've felt a disconnect. Then you waltzed into my office and boom!"

"Boom?"

"Yes, boom! Actually, I need to amend that."

"Okay," Alyssa chuckled.

"Bug broke into my office and boom! That little guy was the beginning. It's because of him that you had to see me. It's his wisdom," Evelyn stated.

Alyssa grinned. "His wisdom?"

"Yes, he's a special dog. He has this...God, I don't even know how to describe it. That dog knows things."

"And you think he knew we had to meet?" Alyssa asked with amusement.

"I mean, yeah. Think about it. He made a beeline for my office and refused to quit stalking me," she laughed. "He knew I needed someone to show me how to relax. I lost count of how many times you came up to fetch him, only to find us looking out the window or sitting on the floor playing."

"He's very persistent," Alyssa laughed.

"Exactly. He is wise. Bug gave me what I needed. He also made sure I kept seeing you. He knew what you needed, too."

"And what is it *you* need, Evelyn?" Alyssa's tone was husky. Her eyes had grown dark.

"I need you, Al."

Alyssa might not be an expert in relationships, but she knew how she felt. It didn't matter that they'd only known each other for less than two months, or that they still had a lot to learn. Wasn't that a part of a relationship? Delving deeper, asking the hard questions, learning, exploring? That quest never stopped, no matter how long a couple had been together. So why should their limited time knowing one another be an issue? Alyssa wanted to stick around, take her time unravelling Evelyn. Coaxing out her secrets, gaining Evelyn's trust. Being the one Evelyn relied on. Just like Four Paws, Alyssa felt that undeniable need to give Evelyn her all, and she had a little black and white dog to thank for it.

"Can we do everything you wanted to do? Watch the movies and eat gingerbread?" Evelyn asked.

"I'd love nothing more," Alyssa whispered, gently caressing Evelyn's cheek.

"Maybe I could show you some pictures? Like I did Bug."

Alyssa loved that Evelyn wanted to open up and share something so precious with her. "Yes, completely yes. Why don't we get comfy? I'll go make us some hot chocolate, because let's face it: nothing compares to hot chocolate with marshmallows in it whilst snuggled down in front of a film."

The smile that beamed from Evelyn's face was blinding. Alyssa's heart swelled. She'd brought that smile to Evelyn's face, and she wanted to keep on doing it.

"Is that really your favourite Christmas film?" Evelyn asked.

"God yes, it's like the best film ever. *A Muppets Christmas Carol* is Christmas for me. Didn't you like it?"

"I love it. It's my favourite, too. I've never met anyone else who felt the same way."

"It's Bug's favourite, too!"

"It is not. Don't play daft."

Alyssa shot up in her seat. "I swear it. Last year Bug spent Christmas Eve with me and we sat and watched it.

That dog's face never looked away from the screen. I think he felt a connection to Michael Caine's character."

Evelyn's laugh rang through the room. "You silly sod."

"I swear it. Cross my heart. Bug recognised a kindred spirit." Alyssa nodded with finality. "Speaking of Bug..." The bedsheets in the spare room Alyssa had glanced that morning popped into her head.

"What about him?" Evelyn asked, her hand stroking Alyssa's thigh absentmindedly.

"Evelyn, did you buy a new duvet set for Bug?"

Bingo! Evelyn's hand stilled, and a red flush washed across her face. "Well...I mean, he needed somewhere to sleep, and I have a spare room."

"So you bought him a dog bone bed set?" Alyssa asked, trying to keep the grin from her face.

"I...I wanted him to feel welcome."

She was just too fucking adorable for Alyssa to handle. "Come here," she whispered, claiming Evelyn's face with her hands. Their lips met softly, but there was an intensity that drove the kiss deeper. Alyssa wanted to consume this adorable, sweet woman.

Alyssa rolled over, expecting to find the warm, naked body of Evelyn next to her. What she found was an empty space, chilled by the night air.

They'd spent hours talking, watching movies, eating and drinking. Then they spent hours exploring each other. First on the rug in front of the fire, then on the dining room table, and finally in Evelyn's king-sized bed. Bug had taken himself to his room by nine. It still tickled Alyssa that Evelyn had set up an entire bedroom for her four-legged friend.

Now, with only the soft moonlight spilling in through the blinds, Alyssa lay sated, yet a little worried. What if Evelyn was regretting everything they'd divulged to each other? Why wasn't she in bed, tucked into Alyssa? These were the things that Alyssa wasn't used to worrying about.

Stretching out her limbs, she crawled out of bed, threw on her t-shirt and set off in search of Evelyn. The twinkling of the Christmas tree lights cast a magical glow around the living room. Alyssa leaned against the wall, taking in Evelyn, who sat on the floor cross-legged, staring up at the tree. She looked so peaceful. Alyssa didn't want to disturb her, but she also wanted to make sure she was okay.

"Hey," she said softly. Evelyn turned her head, smiling.

"Sorry, did I wake you?"

"No...well, your absence did. Everything good?"

"Everything is wonderful. Come, sit down with me."

Alyssa strolled over and lowered herself to the floor. "It's so pretty."

"Yeah. My favourite thing as a kid was to sit and stare at the lights. I loved to look at all the different decorations. I also loved stealing the little chocolates off the branches when mum and dad weren't looking," she said with a cute giggle. "I woke up and felt this urge to sit here."

"Is there something on your mind?"

"Just how much lighter I feel. I know I had a bit of a wobble yesterday, but I think I needed it. I needed you and Bug. Everything seems clearer to me now."

"Tell me," Alyssa said, linking her fingers with Evelyn's.

"I'm going to tell my dad that I want to step down as CEO. I love the company but not the job. Ever since Mum died, I've thrown myself into work, trying to prove my loyalty to the thing she loved and built. I can't keep on doing that, and I know she wouldn't want me to. She also wouldn't want me shutting myself away, especially at Christmas. I'm doing her a disservice ignoring it. You helped me see that by doing all this," Evelyn waved around her room. "I also wanted to talk to you about Bug. I know you're not letting the dogs get adopted until January, but I want to put my hat in the ring for when it's time."

"He's yours, Evelyn. Bug chose you from the start."

"Then I need to get some more things in for him. Another bed cover."

Alyssa chuckled. "Are you seriously giving him an entire bedroom?"

"Of course I am." Evelyn stated. "The other thing that became strikingly clear is that I want you, Alyssa. I want you to be with me. At Christmas but also for all other Christmases. I know it's fast and you might need time to adjust. I'll be waiting for you when you're ready. I just need you to know that I'm all in."

Alyssa felt her eyes water. "Evelyn, I'm all in too. I don't know what I'm doing, and I might completely suck at being your girlfriend, but I will try my utmost to give you everything you need. The sanctuary has been my everything for so long, but now I know I can share that space. Is that okay?"

"You wouldn't be the woman I fell for if you didn't put your everything into the things you love. I will never ask you for more than you can give. And maybe, in time, I can help more with Four Paws?"

"So we're doing this?"

"Honey, we did this a long time ago. We just had to let our heads catch up to our hearts."

23

Seventy-Two Hours and Counting

ALYSSA

There were exactly seventy-two hours left in the Four Paws and Crawford's partnership, and Alyssa was determined not to think about what came after.

Not that there was much time for existential dread. Evelyn—her actual girlfriend, a phrase that still felt strange and wonderful in equal measure—was currently in the main conference room, negotiating with a senior sales manager about appropriate festive attire for the final day celebration.

"I'm not wearing the hat," the sales manager said firmly.

"The hat is optional," Evelyn replied, her tone suggesting it absolutely wasn't. "The jumper, however, is not."

Alyssa watched through the glass wall, nursing a cup of tea that had gone cold twenty minutes ago. The sales manager, a man who could convince a vegan to buy pork scratchings, looked genuinely rattled. There was something deeply satisfying about watching Evelyn in full CEO mode, even if it was over something as ridiculous as Christmas jumpers.

The last day of the partnership wasn't meant to be a production. Alyssa had suggested cake in the break room and maybe a group photo. Evelyn had other ideas.

The top floor of Crawford's headquarters had been transformed overnight. Tasteful garlands hung from doorways, fairy lights were strung along the windows, and someone—probably Maggie—had arranged small potted poinsettias on each desk. Every workstation had a plate of biscuits and a thank-you card from the Four Paws team.

The main event was meant to be low-key: employees who'd been fostering or adopting through the partnership could bring their dogs in for the afternoon. A sort of informal meet-and-greet in the break room. Nothing too elaborate.

Except Evelyn had also arranged for catering. And a photographer. And apparently sent a company-wide email mandating "festive jumpers or face my wrath."

Alyssa's phone buzzed. A text from Lil, who'd arrived an hour earlier to help wrangle the incoming dogs.

Lil

Please tell me you're wearing the jumper.

Alyssa glanced down at the Fair Isle monstrosity she'd pulled on that morning. It was aggressively festive, the kind of thing that should come with a migraine warning. Bug had a matching bandana, which he'd already tried to eat twice.

She sent back a photo. Bug looked deeply unimpressed.

By half ten, the break room was packed. Fifteen dogs and their humans, plus what seemed like half the office staff who'd found excuses to wander up from other floors. Bug had positioned himself near the biscuit table, playing host with the gravitas of a bouncer at an exclusive club.

Alyssa had made it clear to everyone involved: these weren't full adoptions yet. She'd extended home visits through the holidays, but final paperwork wouldn't be signed until January. She wanted to see how the dogs settled, how the families coped with the reality of pet ownership beyond the honeymoon phase.

Evelyn had backed her up with the kind of authority that made grown men nervous. "If you're not serious about this," she'd told the group during the initial meeting, "don't waste Alyssa's time. Or the dog's."

No one had argued.

Now, watching a marketing assistant crouch down to let a nervous terrier sniff her hand, Alyssa felt something settle in her chest. This was working. Actually working.

"Alyssa!" One of the IT guys—James, she thought—waved her over. He was holding a lead attached to a small, scruffy thing that looked like a mop with anxiety issues. "Just wanted to say thanks. Properly. Biscuit here has been...well, she's been brilliant."

"Biscuit?" Alyssa tried not to smile.

"My daughter named her. She's eight. Obsessed." James looked slightly embarrassed. "Anyway. We're doing the paperwork in January, yeah? Making it official?"

"Absolutely."

"Good. Because my wife says if I even think about bringing her back, she'll divorce me."

Alyssa laughed. "I'll make a note in the file."

The afternoon unfolded with the pleasant chaos of any gathering involving dogs and humans in close quarters. There was barking, some minor squabbling over treats, and one incident involving a Labrador and someone's abandoned handbag. Bug supervised it all with the air of a disappointed headmaster.

Evelyn appeared at Alyssa's elbow, sliding an arm around her waist. "How's it going?"

"Good. Really good, actually." Alyssa leaned into her. "You've done an amazing job with this."

"We've done an amazing job," Evelyn corrected. "Though I'll admit, I may have gone slightly overboard with the catering."

"Slightly?"

There were three tables of food. Sandwiches, sausage rolls, mince pies, and what appeared to be an entire cheese board.

"I wanted it to feel special," Evelyn said quietly. "This partnership...it's meant something. To the staff. To me."

Alyssa squeezed her hand. "To me too."

They stood there for a moment, watching the organised chaos. Bug had somehow acquired a small following of admirers and was accepting tribute in the form of sausage rolls.

"Speech time," Maggie announced, appearing with a microphone that Alyssa was certain hadn't been there five minutes ago.

"Oh, I don't think—" Alyssa started.

"Non-negotiable," Evelyn said, gently pushing her forward. "You're the expert. They want to hear from you."

Alyssa took the microphone with the enthusiasm of someone being handed a live grenade. Public speaking had never been her forte. She preferred dogs to people for a reason.

"Right. Well. Thanks for coming, everyone." She cleared her throat. "I know this partnership was a bit unconventional. Bringing dogs into an office isn't exactly standard practice, but you've all been brilliant. Patient, kind, and genuinely committed to making it work."

A few people clapped. Bug barked, which Alyssa chose to interpret as encouragement.

"These dogs—" She gestured to the room. "—they've had rough starts. Some of them were abandoned, some neglected, some just unlucky. But they're here now, and they're thriving, because of you. So thank you. Really."

More applause. Alyssa handed the microphone back to Maggie like it was contaminated.

Evelyn stepped up, taking the microphone with considerably more confidence. "I'll keep this brief. This partnership has been one of the best decisions Crawford's has made in years. Not just for morale, though that's been a lovely side effect, but because it's reminded us what we're actually here for. Connection. Community. Purpose beyond profit margins."

She paused, scanning the room. "As a thank you, everyone here today gets an extra day of leave in the new year. Because if we can manage this level of chaos and still hit our targets, we've earned it."

The room erupted in cheers. Someone started a chant of "More dogs! More dogs!" which Evelyn shut down with a single raised eyebrow.

"Now, if you'll excuse us," Evelyn said, handing the microphone back to Maggie. "Alyssa and I have some matters to discuss."

She took Alyssa's hand and led her out of the break room, through the office, and into her private suite. The door closed behind them with a soft click.

"Matters to discuss?" Alyssa asked, amused.

"Very important matters," Evelyn said seriously. Then she smiled, and it was the kind of smile that made Alyssa's stomach flip. "Like how we're going to survive the next three days without completely losing our minds."

"I thought we were doing quite well, actually."

"We are. But there's still the final paperwork. The handover meetings. And—" Evelyn's voice softened. "—saying goodbye to all of this."

Alyssa pulled her close. "It doesn't have to be goodbye."

"Doesn't it?" Evelyn's expression was unreadable. "The contract ends in seventy-two hours."

"Contracts can be renegotiated."

"Can they?"

"Evelyn." Alyssa tilted her head. "Are you asking me if I want to continue working together?"

"I'm asking if you'd consider it." Evelyn's voice was careful, measured. "Not like this, obviously. Having dogs in the office full-time isn't practical. But the staff have been enthusiastic. There's been talk of continuing the partnership in some capacity. Quarterly adoption events, perhaps. Volunteer days at the sanctuary. Ongoing fundraising support."

Alyssa felt something warm unfurl in her chest. "That sounds...actually quite sensible."

"I know. Terrifying, isn't it?" Evelyn's smile was genuine now, unguarded. "I've already drafted a proposal for the board. Pending your approval, of course."

"Of course." Alyssa grinned. "I'd need to see the details, but yes. I'd consider it. More than consider it, actually."

"Good." Evelyn's relief was visible. "Because I wasn't quite ready to stop seeing you every day. Professionally speaking."

"Professionally speaking?"

"Well, I suppose we've moved slightly beyond professional."

"Slightly," Alyssa agreed, her smile widening.

They stood there, close enough that Alyssa could count the freckles on Evelyn's nose, could see the flecks of gold in her eyes.

"I should get back," Alyssa said, not moving.

"You should," Evelyn agreed, also not moving.

"People will talk."

"Let them."

Evelyn kissed her then, soft and unhurried, and for a moment the rest of the world fell away. No partnership deadlines, no contracts, no expectations. Just this. Just them.

When they finally pulled apart, Alyssa was grinning like an idiot. "You're very distracting, you know that?"

"I've been told."

They returned to the party hand in hand. The afternoon had mellowed into early evening, and someone had dimmed the lights and turned on the fairy lights. It gave the whole space a warm, golden glow.

Bug had fallen asleep in the corner, surrounded by a small pile of dogs who'd apparently decided he was the safest bet. Alyssa took a photo, knowing Lil would want evidence.

Sarah from HR approached, looking slightly nervous. She glanced at Evelyn, then back at Alyssa. "Can I tell you something?"

"Of course."

Sarah hesitated. "This partnership—it saved me, actually. I was going to quit. Burnout, depression, the usual. Then I got paired with Maisie." She gestured to a small terrier curled up nearby. "And suddenly I had a reason to come in. Something to look forward to."

Alyssa felt her throat tighten. "I'm glad."

"I just wanted you to know. What you're doing—it matters. More than you probably realize."

After Sarah left, Evelyn squeezed Alyssa's hand. "See? You're changing lives."

"We're changing lives," Alyssa corrected.

"Fine. We're changing lives. Together."

"I like the sound of that."

As the party wound down and people began to leave, Alyssa found herself standing by the window, looking out over the city. The lights were coming on, Christmas decorations twinkling in shop windows.

Evelyn joined her, slipping an arm around her waist. "What are you thinking?"

"That this is nice. That I could get used to this."

"The partnership or the girlfriend?"

"Both."

Evelyn laughed, the sound warm and genuine. "Good, because I'm not planning on letting you go anytime soon."

"Promises, promises."

Below them, the city hummed with life. People heading home, heading out, heading somewhere. And up here, in this quiet moment, Alyssa felt something she hadn't felt in a long time.

Settled.

Bug wandered over, leaning against her leg with a heavy sigh. She reached down to scratch his ears.

"What do you think, Bug? Should we stick around?"

Bug's response was to flop onto his side, apparently exhausted from his hosting duties.

"I'll take that as a yes," Alyssa said.

Evelyn smiled. "Then it's settled. I'll present the proposal to the board next week. Once you've had a chance to review it properly."

"Sounds like a plan," Alyssa agreed. "But for now, let's just enjoy this."

And they did. Standing by the window, watching the city lights, with Bug snoring softly at their feet and the last remnants of the party humming in the background.

Epilogue

FIVE A.M. AND FURRY EXTORTION

"Alyssa," Evelyn whisper-hissed. "Al!"

"What?" came a mumbled reply.

"He's doing it again."

"Just ignore him."

"I can't. His eyes are boring into me."

The bed dipped as Alyssa rolled over to face Evelyn, who was staring wide-eyed at Bug. This was the scene that had greeted Alyssa every morning for the past three weeks—the time Evelyn had been living in the mobile home with her and Bug.

Bug, the master of manipulation and puppy eyes, had wrapped Evelyn further round his little paw in record time. Anything the pooch wanted, he got from Evelyn, much to Alyssa's annoyance.

Annoyance because this, here and now, was the result of Evelyn pandering to Bug. A five a.m. wake-up call by the furry menace. He didn't scratch or whine, oh no. He silently crept into the room, jumped on the bed like a ninja, and sat by Evelyn's head, staring down at her until she woke up.

Alyssa knew from experience now that Evelyn was a light sleeper, especially when it came to Bug. The woman refused to close the door in case he needed something. Evelyn likened it to a mother hearing her baby cry. Alyssa had rolled her eyes until she strained them when that conversation took place. So, the result was a daily conversation at the arse crack of dawn about Bug creeping Evelyn out. Good job Alyssa was an early riser.

"Babe, if you don't want him being your creepy alarm clock, close the bedroom door."

"But what if he needs us?"

"Evelyn, honey, c'mon. If it was an emergency, we would know. The door doesn't need to be open. Plus, think of how much sexy time we could have without interruption!"

"That's a good point." Evelyn mumbled and then smiled against Alyssa's neck, her hand instinctively reaching for Alyssa's boob. Another thing Alyssa had learned about her girlfriend—she was a breast woman for sure. Not that Alyssa was complaining, she just wished Evelyn could feel up her boobs without Bug interrupting for food.

"Alright, we'll close the door."

Alyssa laughed. "Is that decision based on the fact you're turned on now you've had a good feel of my ladies?"

"One hundred percent, yes! I'm going to feed Bug quickly and I'll be right back. Don't move or start without me."

Alyssa smiled and stretched out her limbs, listening to the birds begin to wake, and Evelyn's soft crooning as she whispered to Bug how much of a good boy he was. Honestly, Alyssa couldn't have asked for a better owner for that little fella. Bug understood Evelyn, sometimes better than Alyssa.

Even though Evelyn was much happier now she'd stepped down as CEO of Crawford's Pet Supplies, there were still times she withdrew, or stressed herself out with work. Alyssa knew how to help, but it was Bug who really settled Evelyn. They just had a bond that was inexplicable, and Alyssa loved it.

She also loved that since stepping away from her family's company in the spring, Evelyn had joined Alyssa at Four Paws as director of events. It had been Lil's idea, actually. "You need someone who can wrangle corporate types and make spreadsheets look sexy," she'd said over drinks one night. "And Evelyn needs something that's hers. Seems obvious to me."

It had been obvious once Lil pointed it out. Evelyn had been floundering a bit those first few months after stepping down, trying to figure out who she was without the CEO title. Working at Four Paws had given her purpose without the crushing pressure of legacy and expectation.

In the time Evelyn had worked at Four Paws—which was coming up to eight months—she'd already organised a summer fundraiser that topped anything in the sanctuary's history. An adoption drive, backed by Richard Crawford, the new—old—CEO. Her father had returned to the role after they'd finally had the conversations they should have had years ago. It wasn't perfect, but it was progress. They had dinner once a month now, just the two of them. Sometimes they talked about Roslyn. Sometimes they didn't. But they talked, which was more than they'd managed in years.

And last but not least, the Christmas party that was being shared with Crawford's HQ.

As for Alyssa, well, she'd learned that sharing her passion with the woman she was hopelessly in love with was a gift. It didn't matter how hectic the sanctuary got, or how involved Alyssa needed to be, she always had Evelyn there, supporting her and often helping her with the workload. They'd fallen into an easy rhythm—Alyssa handling the animals and day-to-day operations, Evelyn managing the fundraising and corporate partnerships. Lil handled the volunteers and kept them both sane.

It worked better than Alyssa had ever imagined it could.

"I'm back," Evelyn panted.

"Did you run a marathon?" Alyssa laughed.

Evelyn closed the door and ripped off her t-shirt. "Yes, I did. I was in a hurry to get back to bed," she grinned.

Alyssa's pulse responded with a quick uptick in rhythm. The sight of Evelyn crawling towards her, naked, was an exquisite and underwear-wrecking sight. Even close to a year later, that hadn't changed. If anything, it had gotten better. Knowing someone's body, knowing exactly what made them gasp or moan or beg, that was its own kind of magic.

"Have we got time?" Alyssa asked with a pant. Today was the first of November. An entire year since Alyssa and Evelyn met. And of course, all the dogs at Four Paws were off on an adventure to Crawford's HQ for the day—a quarterly tradition now, one that the staff looked forward to almost as much as the dogs did.

"We always have time for sex, Al."

It's not like Alyssa needed any convincing. The year they'd been together had been phenomenal, especially in the bedroom. Learning about each other's wants and desires had been fantastic. Alyssa had never felt so comfortable with another human being. All the worries of being in a relationship fell by the wayside after the first few months.

Why she ever thought she wouldn't be able to connect properly with a woman was ridiculous in hindsight. Maybe it was just with Evelyn, though. They got each other. They knew each other's quirks and odd characteristics. They also understood each other's moods and emotions. Like, for instance, right now. There was no mistaking Evelyn's mood. Which read: I'm about to devour you entirely until you can't walk straight.

And honestly? Alyssa was absolutely fine with that.

Evelyn was practically salivating as she made her way up the bed. Alyssa was a dream come true. She was sexy, smart, and Evelyn's. It was hard to believe they'd been in each other's lives for an entire year. A year that had flown by with a lot of changes.

Leaving Crawford's was the right choice. Evelyn was free to pursue a career she felt she really earned—even though her dad and Alyssa argued she'd already earned her career at Crawford's. The point was, Evelyn had done it her way, and she couldn't be happier.

The transition hadn't been seamless. There'd been moments of doubt, nights where she'd woken up in a panic thinking she'd made a terrible mistake. But Alyssa had been there, steady and sure, reminding her that growth was supposed to be uncomfortable. That choosing yourself wasn't selfish, it was necessary.

And she'd been right. Of course she'd been right.

Evelyn was over the moon when her dad turned up just three days before Christmas to officially take back the reins. He'd timed it deliberately—wanting to give Evelyn the gift of freedom for the holidays, he'd said. No more board meetings, no more quarterly reports. Just time to breathe and be with the people she loved.

The handover had been surprisingly emotional. Standing in the office that had been hers, watching her father settle back into the chair he'd vacated so quickly, Evelyn had felt something shift. Relief, yes, but also pride. She'd kept the company afloat during one of its most difficult periods. She'd honoured her mother's legacy. And now she was free to build her own.

Alyssa had invited Evelyn and Richard to spend the holiday with her parents. Alyssa laughed repeatedly when Evelyn and her dad realised they would spend Christmas Day eating turkey out the back of a campervan. It turned out to be one of the best Christmases Evelyn had ever had, and she knew her mother would be smiling down on her.

Her dad had fit in surprisingly well with Alyssa's parents. He and Alyssa's father had bonded over a shared love of terrible puns and single malt whisky. Her mum had fussed over everyone, making sure no one's plate was ever empty, and Bug had held court in the middle of it all, accepting tribute from everyone.

It had been chaotic and warm and nothing like the formal Christmases Evelyn had grown up with, and it had been perfect.

Evelyn would always be grateful to Alyssa and Bug for giving her back the magic of Christmas. In fact, she would always be grateful, full stop. Her life was everything she wanted it to be. Challenging, yes. Sometimes messy. But hers. Authentically, completely hers.

Alyssa wiggling beneath her brought Evelyn back to the task at hand. "Babe, we need to hurry. I have to help get the dog—"

"Alyssa, I'm about to eat you out. Zip the lip, put your head back, and enjoy this, love."

"Well, alright then," Alyssa grinned.

Yup, Evelyn would always be grateful for the wisdom of Bug. That grumpy little dog had brought her everything she'd been missing. Purpose. Joy. Love.

And really excellent morning sex.

Thank you!

Thank you for reading The Wisdom of Bug.
Spill the Tea (in a Review)!
If this book gave you butterflies, made you swoon, or kept you up way past your bedtime, I'd love to hear about it! Reviews help indie authors like me reach more readers who are searching for their next sapphic romance obsession. Drop a review on Amazon, Goodreads, or wherever you love to share your bookish thoughts. Even a quick "loved it!" makes a huge difference.
You're the best!

Stay Connected

Don't Miss Out!

Love steamy sapphic romance? Join my newsletter for new release alerts, promotions, book recommendations, and special reader-only perks. Sign up now: https://alysonroot.com/

<u>Become a VIP Member</u>

Want the ultimate insider experience? My VIP membership gives you early access to new books, exclusive bonus content, behind-the-scenes insights, member discounts, and a front-row seat to my creative process. Plus, you'll be part of a community of readers who love these stories as much as I love writing them. Join the VIP club:

VIP MEMBERSHIP

Let's Talk About Pleasure

I write characters who own their desires, communicate openly, and prioritise their pleasure—because that's how it should be in real life, too.

As a sex-positive author, I'm all about breaking down stigma and celebrating what feels good. That's why I'm thrilled to partner with *Wet For Her*, a queer-run online adult toy store that's as inclusive and empowering as the stories I write.

I use their products myself, and I can vouch for their quality, care, and commitment to the community. Ready to explore and get 10% off your purchase? Visit them through my affiliate link:

Web link: Toys

or

Checkout Code: ALYSONROOT

Your pleasure matters!

Transparency Corner: Yep, this is an affiliate link. If you make a purchase, I get a little kickback. Think of it as buying me a metaphorical coffee while exploring some fun products. Win-win!

Other Titles By Alyson Root

A Dance Towards Forever

Diving Into Her

Always Emilie

Broken Parts Included

Love & Other Wild Things

Finding Molly Parsons

Keeping Carmen Ruiz

The Wisdom of Bug

Sleigh Bells Ring

Risking Immortality

Waiting for Eternity

Fighting for Infinity

Mob's Seduction

Playing Her Heart

Welcome to Ero-TEA-Ca: We're Open!

Once Upon a Time in December

About the author

Alyson was born and raised in the heart of England. She moved to Paris in 2015 when she met her wife. Together they moved to the west of France, where they now live with their two dogs. Alyson spends her time reading sapphic fiction books, writing and Scuba Diving.

Alyson discovered her love of writing in her mid-thirties. Her debut book, *A Dance Towards Forever,* was inspired by her wife and their very own love story. Alyson wrote *Diving Into Her* and award-winning *Always Emilie,* which added with her first book, created The French Connection series.

www.alysonroot.com

a.rootauthor@alysonroot.com

www.ingramcontent.com/pod-product-compliance
Lightning Source LLC
Chambersburg PA
CBHW050611170726
48283CB00001B/198